MUSE

Book Three

By

A.L. Crouch

Dedicated to the silent cries, the invisible scars, and the brave faces. To the housed homeless, the parented orphans, and the hunted derelicts.

Wake up, sleepers. Step out from the shadows.
The light calls.

Unfurl your wings and fly.

For you were once darkness, but now you are light in the Lord.

Live as children of light.

Ephesians 5:8 (NIV)

One

You were wrong about me.

That's why I'm writing to you after all these years. You have to know that you were wrong. It's all gone now, everything I tried to build upon your false hope. You had me believe that there was more for me, for my future.

I blame you.

You, who would have me see the light, brought me nothing but darkness. Now, as I'm enveloped in this inescapable black, I can see who you really are. They say that the devil disguises himself as an angel of light. That's true enough, at least. Even before the accident, you had me blinded to the truth. Now I realize that nothing you ever promised could be mine. All you did was cast your own reflection on me like sunlight from a mirror.

I know the truth now.

The light doesn't wait for me. That bitter reality is so obvious to me now. I know it's pathetic for a man to share his childhood fears, but I want you to know exactly what you've done, what you've made of me.

I can't remember a time when I wasn't afraid of the dark. As a child I ran from it. I'd hide from the shadows as they hunted me, jowls wetted, drawn by the scent of my fear. The way HE always hunted me. The darkness has always been there, waiting for me just on the other side of dawn. Now it's found me for the last time. There is no hiding from it anymore.

The black is cold.

It seeps into my skin and chills my bones. I've learned that warmth, like light, is fleeting. Only the bitter darkness ever remains. It's coolest in the shadows, and it's in the shadows that I'm trapped.

You put me here.

To think that I believed I could start over, that the darkness could somehow be vanquished by your words of hope and light. I started painting again. You knew that. What you didn't know was that I was painting better than ever before. You made me think I could use my art to start a new life. Instead, my newfound inspiration led me to do something I swore I would never do. Ratting on my street brothers wasn't easy, but I had to do it. It was the only way I could get out of that godforsaken prison before my dreams of a brighter future left with you. I sold them all out for my freedom. With a single testimony, I destroyed the lives of men who thought I was a friend, a brother.

And my own fate was sealed with theirs.

I came here, to downtown Wilmington. Everyone said this was the place for aspiring artists to be. The downtown art scene was booming. After so many years behind the walls of Central, to live on the coast with the sunlight and warmth was a dream. I was dreaming big.

It took all the money I had left from my past . . . exploits, but I was able to finish art school and secure a mortgage for my tired, little studio. It's not much more than a collection of antique bricks and wood paneling, but it's right off the water, something that was important to me once. Yes, I bought my dreams with dirty money, drug money, but I thought the pureness of my aspiration could somehow wipe it clean.

Instead, it cursed me and this place.

Even with the help of a small-town dealer, I sold few paintings. My art flowed from my fingers like a rushing wind, but no one was buying. The summer after I opened the studio had been the busiest. My impressionist portraits were the first to go, so I focused on perfecting that technique. I painted the faces of strangers, of people long gone, and of women who caught my eye. I once painted a portrait of you. It still hangs on the back wall with all the other paintings I couldn't sell.

Penniless for the first time since childhood, I moved into the loft above the studio. It didn't bother me. I still carried hope, the hope you gave me that my dream would light a path to a new life. I painted day and night, keeping that hope alive. This past winter it all withered away.

My life and dreams were hurled into eternal darkness.

I remember the day it happened vividly. It's seared into my mind like the last seconds of a nightmare. That evening was unusually cold, the kind of cold that sends your breath swirling about your head in a ghostly haze. Walking back to the studio from the small pool hall around the block, I was enjoying a fresh beer buzz and a cheap cigar. As I walked the old brick street toward the Riverwalk, my mind was occupied with the timeless face of the woman who sat beside me at the bar. I planned to paint her perfect features, all angles and softness.

Leaning against the wooden rails, I huddled further into my coat and looked out at the water of the Cape Fear River, admiring the way the moonlight reflected off its glass surface.

I didn't hear them surround me.

"Well, well, well. Look who it is, boys. The big man himself." A familiar voice snickered from behind me, filling my heart with instant dread. "You got time for some old friends?"

Sighing, I took a slow drag from my cigar before turning to face my brothers from another lifetime. Their lips were upturned into crude smiles, but the way they clenched their fists by their sides assured me they weren't here to exchange pleasantries. One of them held a baseball bat.

"I should have known you'd come for me," I said, releasing smoke from my lips to waft in the air between us. "What took you so long?"

The man to my left stepped forward and flashed a wide smile. The streetlight twinkled off his golden dental work. As he stepped closer, the others closed in.

"I wanted the privilege of doing this myself," he said. "You left me to rot in that prison. I waited a long time for this. I'm going to make sure it was worth the wait."

Nodding, I looked down as I tapped the ash off the end of my cigar and used my peripheral to scan for an escape. They had me boxed in. The Riverwalk was blocked both left and right. I gazed up at the studio across the street, just on the other side of the tall railing. There was a chance I could run for it.

"I won't ask how you found me, Smiley." I looked him in the eye. "You always were smarter than I gave you credit for."

"Smarter than you, huh? Did you really think you could narc on us and not pay? We're here to collect. We're going to make an example out of you. This is what happens when you betray your own," Smiley said, his grin twisting into a gruesome scowl. "I have my own reasons for what I'm bout to do to you, though. You was supposed to have my back, but you left me to rot in max security when they took you back to Central. I've been looking forward to this for a long time."

"But I DID have your back at Central for years," I said, stepping closer.

"You think that matters now? You think that's gonna buy you any favors from me?" Smiley growled, closing the gap between us. I held up my hand to him.

"I'd say I've earned at least one," I stalled, taking another drag. "Let me finish my cigar. You owe me that much."

If knew if I could get them to stand down for even a second, there was a chance I could make a break for the railing. If I made it to the studio, I could barricade myself within its high brick walls. Smiley only came closer, getting in my face.

"I don't owe you nothing!" he shouted, rearing his fist back to take the first swing.

Before his knuckles could connect with my jaw, I ducked and shoved him back. My cigar fell to the wooden planks. The air rushed from Smiley's lungs in a shocked wheeze as I threw him into the railing as hard as I could. Without taking even a second to look to the others, I threw my right leg over the top rung as Smiley stumbled beside me. My other leg was almost over when someone grabbed it and yanked me to the ground. My back hit the planks with a sickening thud. White-hot pain shot up my spine.

I tried to recover, but they were on me. One kicked me in the ribs while the other landed punch after punch to the side of my face. In a daze of agony and fury, I fought back, kicking one man squarely in the chest. He tumbled backwards into Smiley who still staggered to get to his feet. With a violent cry, I leapt up and threw myself into the other and wrapped my fingers tightly around his throat. The victory was short lived.

I was yanked backwards by my hair, tufts of ebony scattering in the bitter wind. Punch after punch came from every direction, bouncing my head against the wooden planks like a gothic door knocker. Crushing pain threatened to devour me, and I cried out despite myself as my wits raced for a means of escape. In the back of my mind, I knew how this would end. Years ago, I was the one to exact this kind of street justice.

There was only one escape from this brutality.

As your words of light and my aspirations for a better life splattered the planks around me in warm crimson, I clung to the only hope I had left. I prayed that death would come quickly.

When the beating came to an abrupt halt, I struggled to roll over, coughing out the blood that pooled in my throat. Through swelled eyes that vibrated in new agony with every rapid heartbeat, I looked up into the familiar faces of my attackers. The youngest held the baseball bat high above his head. He smiled as though he had been chosen to pinch hit in the tenth inning, and his eyes let me know he was determined to end this game with one swing. He started to bring the bat down on my head with unyielding fierceness.

"No!" Smiley screamed from behind him, and the man stopped with a start and lowered the bat.

In that moment, a new kind of hope crept into my semi-consciousness. I reached a battered hand out to the man that had once been my ally. He squatted beside me and looked me from head to toe before meeting my pleading eyes.

"How does it feel?" he asked, his voice hushed against my ear. "How does it feel to be the man on the bottom while I'm the one calling the shots? Who's got the power now? I could end your life with one word."

Smiley stood and brushed my hand away, letting it hit the planks beside him. I could only gurgle a response as I watched him yank the baseball bat away from the other man.

"Gotta give you credit, though," Smiley continued. "Being your stooge taught me one very important thing."

Smiley's knuckles whitened as he tightened his grip on the bat. He turned back to where I lay, writhing, and raised it above his head.

"Always do your dirty work yourself."

Much of what happened after that remains a blur. The first blow to the head sent my thoughts spinning back to another time. The pain that seemed like a lifetime ago rushed back into my memory.

As my hands came up in a feeble attempt to shield myself from the next blow, it was my father who stood over me as he had almost every night. A belt replaced the baseball bat, the silver buckle cutting into my young flesh with the same sickening precision. My brother's screams filled the small house. Just like then, I cried out for the beating to stop. And just like then, I knew it wouldn't.

I also thought of you.

I prayed to the God you believe so passionately in for an end to this pain and misery. Then the beating ceased, leaving my body twitching and shattered while I battled to remain conscious. Fighting back the darkness that clutched at me, I opened my eyes.

At first all I saw was a haze of thick red. I blinked back the moisture as my mind, drifting on a sea of anguish, struggled to assess my injuries. There was blood everywhere, draining from my wounds to drip and mingle with the channel below. My broken body refused to move though my survival instinct screamed for me to flee.

Smiley withdrew the baseball bat, now dripping red. He handed it to one of the men staring down at me with vacant eyes.

Wiping his hands on his pants, Smiley bent down to pick up my cigar, which by now had burned almost to the head. Taking a slow drag from it, he squatted beside me and let the smoke escape in a steady stream through his grinning lips.

"I gotta hand it to you. You really know how to take a beating. You should be dead by now," he whispered to me. I could scarcely hear him over the slowing of my heartbeat in my ears.

"You are gonna die, though," he said, blowing on the end of the cigar until it glowed orange. "You're gonna bleed out right here on the walk. Maybe they'll make a plaque for you here, at this spot where you died. The tourists can pay their respects while you burn in hell. Won't that be nice? Just remember this while you're roasting for what you did. Remember who did this to you."

The last thing I saw before Smiley seared my eyes forever closed with the glowing end of the cigar was the look of pure evil and hatred on his face.

It was the last thing I would ever see.

It was how I was sure that there was a hell and that I was on my way there. I saw the demons of earth in the blacks of his eyes. It was a look I'd seen before and spent a lifetime trying to forget. It was the same look my father gave me right before I killed him. The same screams that came from his mouth those last seconds before I pulled the trigger rang out into the night again. Only this time they were ripped from my own throat as the scorching heat of the cigar scalded my eyes and the darkness claimed me for good.

I'm not sure how long I lay there. Minutes, maybe hours. Unable to cope with the horrors of this lurid new reality, my mind drifted between cognizance and delusion. The pain was acute, as was the black that was now inescapable. Somewhere in the distance the sounds of sirens wailed. Soon after, the sound of footsteps mingled with the fuzzy static that filled my ears. Consciousness faded until I was lifted onto the stretcher. The pain of the movement roused me, and then I faded again.

I woke to the sounds of hurried footsteps, frenzied movement, and anxious voices. I saw nothing. The physical pain subsided, but the blackness remained. The room was crowded. I could feel people all around me, doctors and patients. The numerous, steady beeps of the heart rate machines sounded in the background like ticking clocks. I was in a crowded trauma room. That much was clear.

"We won't be able to save his eyes," a voice above me proclaimed.

More was said, but my soul was trapped in those words. The more I tried to accept them as my new reality, the more enraged I became. I would never see again. I would never again gaze upon the wonders of the setting sun as it cast an array of colors across the ocean. Never again would I see a smiling face or take in the features of a beautiful woman.

I would never paint again.

Somewhere in the distance, the steady rhythm of a heart monitor changed to a single, constant tone. Voices turned frantic. The movement around me rushed away, quickening to someone else's aid. I lay trapped and alone in the darkness that was my new home, enraged. I knew then I would live, and that thought filled me with bitter hatred. Why couldn't I be the one to die? Why did someone else get to escape into death while I faced a lifetime of blackness? I would have rather faced the fires of hell.

It is a choice I would still make, a choice I still contemplate though I've adjusted to my new life as a disabled wretch.

Thoughts of you drive me on.

The need for you to know that you did this to me. You need to know that there is no new life for me.

There is no light.

In those moments, as I lay broken on the Riverwalk teetering between life and death, I learned the truth behind your false hope. There is no warm glow waiting to welcome me. For me there is only darkness.

That's all there's ever been.

You were wrong about me, Logan.

You were wrong.

Sincerely,
Blake Roberts
. . . Or as you once knew me, Boss

Two

"*Are you ready to send your email to Logan Foster?*" my phone prompted when my dictation came to an end. I hesitated as retrospection dissolved into reality.

"Cancel," I said with a sigh, leaning back in my chair.

"*Would you like to save this email as a draft?*" the digital assistant asked.

Running my hand over the table, I located my sunglasses and slipped them on.

"Yes," I said, standing.

"*You have one hundred and twenty saved drafts,*" my phone informed me as I grabbed my hoodie off the back of the chair and slipped it over my shoulders.

"Yeah, yeah," I mumbled, pressing my phone's home button again and waiting for the series of beeps before I spoke. "What's today's weather?"

"*Today will be mostly cloudy with a low of 47 degrees and a high of 56 degrees,*" came the answer.

Slipping the phone into my pocket, I walked the eight steps to my bed and bent down to feel for my shoes. My hand was met by a cold, wet nose.

"What do you say, Mutt? Want to go for a ride?"

The wind from his tail brushed my face as he wagged it with sudden excitement. Lacing up my sneakers, I heard the jingle of his collar as he bounded across the room. His thick tail thumped the hardwoods as he waited for me by the loft door.

"No licking any strangers today, you got me?" I asked, giving his muscular head a pat.

He responded with a wet snort and pawed the loft door. Walking the eleven steps to the door, I opened it and waited for Mutt to stagger down the stairs before I followed. I heard him run to the front door and plop patiently onto his haunches while I paused on the gallery floor as I always did. Conjuring the memory of what the space looked like a lifetime ago, I ran my hand across the paintings that hung on the walls like lynched corpses. Reminders of a dead dream.

Pulling my hood over my head, I was careful to cloak the scars that formed a raised patchwork across my scalp. Then I found my blacked-out shades in my pocket and covered my eyes. When I opened the door to the outside, I was met with a chilling breeze and the subtle sound of a car passing over the brick street in the distance. A seagull's wings beat overhead. There was no need to lock the door behind me. No one would come to call, and with the windows of the studio boarded up, there would be no off-season customers.

Mutt took the lead. I followed the patter of his steps down Dock Street toward the bus stop. I could perceive his excitement. It radiated from him in warm waves that cut through the brisk morning air. For a moment, a tinge of guilt nagged at me. This was the first ride we'd taken in months, and now the air had grown cold with the arrival of winter.

Then I felt the stares. They came from the restaurant to our right, from the balconies across the street. Eyes were on me. They burned into my flesh as ferociously as the glowing end of that cigar. The condemnation in their accusing glances was rivaled only by my own resentment. I didn't need to see them to feel their judgement. The freak had come out.

Hunkering further into my hood, I adjusted my shades. With a grunt, Mutt surged forward, no doubt sensing my hesitation. I focused on his excited breaths, on the tapping of his feet against the sidewalk. Within minutes we were at the bus stop.

Mutt, pleased with himself, licked my hand before again plopping onto his haunches to await the bus.

"Good job, boy," I said and gave his head another pat.

Digging my phone from my pocket, I pressed the home button and waited for the beeps before I spoke.

"Time," I said into the receiver.

"*It is 7:28 a.m.*," it answered.

"Perfect timing, Mutt. We only have to wait a couple of minutes," I said.

It was rare that I felt gratitude for anything in this new life, but I knew that if it weren't for my smart phone and Mutt, I would be lost. So I was thankful that I'd left my phone on the table the night I went to the pool hall. It was something I never did but turned out to be a welcomed mistake.

Mutt wandered into my life shortly after I returned from the hospital. I often wondered if he, in his child-like doggy brain, ever regretted his choice to share these dejected years with me. When he let out his merry bark and leapt to his paws as the bus trilled around the corner, the answer was clear. He was happy as he scurried up the steps to greet the driver with a sloppy kiss.

"Hey there, fella," the bus driver said with a laugh. "Haven't seen you for a while."

I gripped the railing and pulled myself up, scooting Mutt along toward the back. My nose was assaulted with the familiar musk of public transit, a pairing of scratched aluminum and worn vinyl seats, which had absorbed the essence of its many passengers.

"You going to your usual stop today?"

"Yes, thank you," I said, ducking my head to avoid the driver's eyes as I passed.

Mutt barked, and the metal doors squeaked closed. I followed Mutt's pants to the back row where he leapt up into his usual seat. Squeezing past him to the window seat in the corner, I gave him a nudge with my elbow.

"What'd I say about licking people today?"

He answered by whipping his tongue across my nose. It smelled of Kibble and a hint of the driver's aftershave.

"You're impossible," I grumbled, wiping the moisture from my face with the back of my sleeve.

The bus sounded empty, devoid of the usual coughs and steady breaths. We only delayed a second at each stop across town. No one got on. For that I was also grateful. The off-season had arrived on the cold prelude of the holidays, keeping the tourists at bay and the locals tucked into home and hearth with gathering loved ones. I hated the Christmas season but relished the seclusion. As the hearts of men warmed with merriment and united cheer, winter would grow colder. The streets that didn't contain shops and venues for celebrating would be empty. The stares would cease, at least for a short while.

The hour drive was shortened by the lack of oncoming passengers. I passed the time listening to Mutt's steady pants and allowing my mind to wander to past holidays. Growing up, our small house was always filled with the usual aesthetic décor, but good cheer was lost on its inhabitants. The tree dazzled from where it sat in the front window. Lights of green and red twinkled into the snow-sprinkled night. Passersby would see its majesty and the flashing lights hung around the windows and warm at the sight. They were unaware that inside lurked a monster, fueled by regret and profound disappointment and made all the more fierce in this season of goodwill. Our home held a surrogate Christmas spirit, a malevolent master, which kept us captive in false merriment the entire season.

Mutt barked and jumped to the floor. His rod-like tail whipped through the air between us, jarring me from my reverie. The bus came to a whining stop. I rose to follow, my body already weary from the morning excursion.

"Wrightsville Beach," the driver called and then laughed as Mutt laid another smooch on his cheek.

"How much do I owe you?" I asked the driver. I heard him pat Mutt's side.

"I'll put it on your tab," he said with a laugh, his usual answer. "See you on the way back."

I gripped the metal rail and descended the steps shakily, following Mutt's clumsy footfalls. With a chuckle, the driver closed the doors and pulled away. I strained to take in the environment. Mutt waited patiently at my heels, his pants blending with the sound of a seagull's cry. The streets were quiet, barren. In the distance, waves crashed along a placid shore.

"Okay, boy," I said, taking a deep breath. "Let's go."

The walk from the bus stop to the beach was a short one. Mutt knew to stop at the bench nearest the shore and wait while I removed my shoes and socks and rolled up my pant bottoms. The sand was cool and soft around my toes. Mutt stayed close so I could feel by his proximity which way to go.

As we walked toward the water, the ebb and flow of the waves soothed me with their unmistakable song. When the sand turned firm and moist, I paused and waited for the rush of icy water to flow over my feet. I heard the crash of the next wave and felt the stinging cold fluidity of it as it crept up the shore to greet me. Mutt snorted beside me, his patience weakening with angst. His paws shifted with restrained agitation.

"Is it all clear?" I asked, already knowing the answer. "You're not going to go licking any strangers?"

He barked, hopping up and down with an excited whine.

"Okay, but we're not staying long," I said, an automatic lie. "Go ahead."

Wisps of sand exploded onto my legs as Mutt took off, full charge, down the beach. His paws punished the tide as he dipped into the water and ran back out before charging in the other direction. I felt a surge of envy at his vehement joy. When the water crept back up the shore to embrace my feet again, I walked into it, making myself one with the chilled sea.

When the water was to my knees, I paused and let my mind's eye look out into the ocean. I remembered what it looked like, how the turquoise water spread out for miles and miles. I remembered the way its foamy fingers painted the buff sand a dark, liquid brown. In my mind, I saw the brilliance of the sun's reflection upon its glassy surface and scoffed at how I would shield my eyes from its luster. Now I would give anything to see it just once more.

Warmth spread across my face and traveled down my shoulders. I knew that the sun had broken through the clouds, could feel its attempts to penetrate my soul with its life-bringing fire, but it was no use. Though I could see it in visions of memory, the sun, like the sea, was drowned in darkness. The warmth of it was as fleeting upon my head and shoulders as a flame snuffed out by a gust of frigid air. Defeated once again, I stumbled backwards until my feet hit dry sand. Then I sat, staring out at nothing but a memory.

The anger that I often fed upon crept up from my soul, and I struggled to force it back. But like an inescapable addiction, it consumed me, filling me with untethered rage. I removed my glasses and touched my trembling fingers to the scaly skin that covered my now useless eyes. The place where I'd once proudly displayed two tattooed teardrops was now raised and plastic smooth.

"When will I have suffered enough?" I yelled to the heavens, to a God I scarcely believed was there. "Could you not have just let me die? You took everything from me. My art, the one thing that brought me peace. You took it from me. Why not my life too? How much more misery do you have in store for me?"

I knew the answers would not come. They never did. Exhausted and weary, I lay back on the beach and let my mind fester. Visions of brushing paint onto canvas, of late nights watching the moonlight dance upon the waters from the Riverwalk, the sense of freedom and optimism that glowed within my breast, were all overshadowed by a cloud of self-pity, bitterness, and black. What remained clear were the memories that haunted me day and night.

In contrast to the black I'd grown accustomed to, they bombarded me with their crispness. The childhood that I fought my whole life to scorch from my mind was brought wheeling back by the glowing end of a burning cigar to forever haunt me. I chuckled at the irony of it as I lay in the cool, damp sand while the darkness showed me what I did not want to see.

My brother, younger than me but wiser in spirit, looked up at me from his make-shift bed of sheets and blankets on my bedroom floor. The green and red Christmas lights flashed in the window, turning his auburn hair unnatural colors. His grey-flecked eyes widened as I recounted what happened the night before. Carefully raising my shirt, I showed him the bruises hidden beneath my pajama top. Raised blue and black welts speckled my rib cage like a hideous wrapping.

I was the one who needed my brother there that night, more than he wanted to be there. Hoping that his presence would act as a shield of innocence and somehow battle the inevitable, I made him think sleeping in my room was his idea. It was all my fault.

"Don't tell Mom," I pleaded in whispers as I watched the lights blaze in the small window. "He'll hurt her if you tell."

Before he could protest, we heard the back door open and then slam shut. We heard the staggering boot steps make their way into the kitchen, to the fridge. As the night overtook the day, we heard him pull back the tab on his newest beer. In the dark, we lay down in our beds and breathed silent prayers that tonight would be different.

"Don't tell Mom," I whispered into the silence.

"I won't," my brother whispered back as the boot steps came into the hallway and silenced us both.

We listened, in hopeful terror, to the jingling of the keys on his belt as he came down the hall towards our room.

The daydream vanished from my consciousness when a wet mass landed on my lap. The light of the memory faded, and I was once again thrust into blackness. Mutt panted beside me, shifting on his paws with anticipation. I picked up the soggy stick of driftwood and tossed it aside.

"I don't want to play right now," I said.

Again he plopped the stick onto my lap, this time with a pleading moan. His eager paw swiped at my leg, his snout nudged my shoulder. With a sigh, I picked up the stick and felt a shift in the sand as Mutt took his ready stance, his tail sending grains into the air.

"Fine," I grumbled, throwing it down the beach. "But we're only staying for a few more minutes."

Minutes turned to hours as I sat on the beach listening to the crashing of the waves and to Mutt's contented breaths. When the sun ducked to meet the tide, I felt the breeze grow cooler, felt the dissention of daylight as it fought against the impending night. Mutt chewed his stick beside me as I imagined what the sunset looked like as it cast its hues upon the water. We always lingered until dusk. My thirst to see the vivid oranges and reds streaking across the sky and mimicked by the waves held me there with despondent expectancy, as if I might someday sneak a glimpse of it.

"Time to go, Mutt," I said, standing to stretch the weariness from my muscles. Mutt snorted and shook the sand from his body. Following his lead, I found the bench at the top of the beach and laced up my shoes.

The bus ride home was quiet except for the hushed voices at the front of the bus. A young couple, headed for the downtown Wilmington bar scene no doubt, giggled and chatted about the unusual passengers in the back. I could feel their curious glances, their stares, but I was too tired to care. Mutt's tail twitched in his seat whenever they turned to sneak a peek.

"You're not licking them," I said, hunkering further into my hoodie, further into the shadows. Mutt lay down in his seat with a disappointed whine and plopped his head onto my lap. The chatter and stares subsided until we arrived downtown when, with one final glance and giggle, the couple exited just before our stop.

"God, I hate people," I mumbled as Mutt jumped up when our stop neared. I got off the bus and waited for Mutt to receive his customary ear scratch from the driver.

"You have a good night now." The driver's voice held a warm grin.

"Thank you," I responded, turning away.

"Until next time." He closed the doors with a metallic squeal, and the bus pulled away.

"Let's go home," I said to Mutt, weary from our trip.

The streets were quiet. Bar goers were driven from the porch tables by the winter chill to seek the warmth inside. The water of the Riverwalk spattered the planks with each heavy December gust as we neared. Mutt led me to the stoop where my foot hit something solid. The paper crinkled as I picked up the bag of delivered groceries and went inside. I hefted the bag upstairs and set it on the table before collapsing into a chair. Mutt sat patiently at my heels.

"Here you go," I said rummaging through the bag to withdraw his weekly rawhide. "I guess you deserve it."

Mutt jumped to snatch it from my hands. I heard him drag it to his bed in the corner of the room as I pulled out bread and peanut butter for a sandwich. Full and exhausted, I walked the six steps to the closet and changed out of my damp, sandy clothes. I retrieved my phone from my pocket and pressed the home button until the series of beeps broke through the silence.

"Play podcast," I said into the speaker.

"Would you like to start where you left off?"

"Yes," I said, feeling along the wall by the bed for the charger.

Climbing under the covers, I let the familiar voices drown out the chaos in my mind. I focused on the ongoing conversation and news from the art world as Mutt chewed contentedly in the corner. My consciousness drifted further into the black, and I fought to cast my thoughts to a time not so long ago when I was part of that other world. No matter how hard I fought off the dreams though, I felt them ride in each night, a procession of grim raiders eager to invade as sleep claimed me and my defenses fell away. My dreams were vivid, as if my subconscious were trying to make up for the lack of sight by day with overwhelming visions at night.

They always started with the flashing of green and red and the jingling of the keys on my father's belt. They rang out like a warning siren as he staggered down the hall. Next came the boot steps sounding on the floor outside the room. My brother's whispered prayers as he grabbed my hand cut through the sound of our shaky breaths. In my slumber, I tossed with the anticipation. I knew what came next. Pain, screams, and pleading did nothing to penetrate the murky void of my father's eyes. I saw the fiery heat of his anger, the black of the shadows contrasting the festive flash of color in the room. With each punch he landed on my torso, bright white flares of pain filled my eyes and faded in a sickening swirl.

I never should have talked my brother into being there. The assault of guilt that followed as my father's anger turned from me to my brother was even more excruciating than his blows. It was always at this point in my dreams that I realized I was every bit as cruel as my father.

"Don't tell Mom," I pleaded in my dream. "Don't tell Mom."

Somewhere amidst the horror in my sleep, a strange noise mingled with our despairing cries.

A child's song broke through the dark and roused me to consciousness. I heard it from where I lingered between dream and wakefulness.

"This little light of mine," it sang out, *"I'm going to let it shine."*

Foreign and soft, the words lingered in the air like a strange perfume. I sat up with a start and wiped my brow with the back of my shaking hand as the black overtook me again. Dream mingled with reality as I listened for the source of the voice I wasn't certain

I had heard. The room was silent save for the sound of Mutt's tail thumping excitedly on the hardwood in front of the door. I pushed the home button on my phone.

"Time," I said after the beeps.

"*The time is 1:42 a.m.,*" it answered. Too late for a visitor.

Mutt whimpered, eager to be let downstairs to greet whoever was down there. Emerging from the bed, I felt along the table and retrieved my shades. When I was assured that my eyes were covered, I followed the sounds of Mutt scratching at the door frame. With harsh whispers, I shooed him away and bade him to sit before I pulled the door open.

The stairway was silent as was the floor beneath. I waited, my own heartbeat bouncing off my eardrums. My sweaty palms gripped the railing as I closed the door and took a few steps down. I searched the darkness again for the sounds of an intruder. The dread which was awakened by my dreams caused my breath to quicken. My instincts screamed at me to flee from the shadows.

"Is someone down there?" I asked, my voice cracking.

When the silence remained unbroken, I was convinced that my imagination had gotten the better of me. Walking back up the steps, I opened the door and was almost trampled by Mutt. He raced past me and down the stairs. His ecstatic whine and the clumping of his feet as they danced upon the floor gave me pause. The dread returned, mingled with annoyance.

"Mutt, get up here," I commanded. "It's late."

With a sigh, I waited to hear his paws traverse the stairs below. What I heard in their stead made my breath catch in my throat and my blood run cold. A child's laugh floated up to where I stood with my arms folded across my chest.

Staggering, my mind raced to rationalize what I'd just heard. My brother's angelic face flashed before my dead eyes. I thought perhaps I was still asleep, that I was hearing his voice from a lifetime ago. But I had never been blind in my dreams. In my dreams I could see clearly the past I could never forget. This was no dream.

When I heard the laugh again, my anger flared. I took a step toward the sound of the intruder.

"You're not supposed to be in here!" I shouted. "This is a private residence."

Waiting, I searched the silence for a reply. When no answer came and I heard Mutt begin to climb the stairs, I convinced myself that whoever it was had gone. Mutt passed me on the steps, licking my hand before making his way back inside the loft. I lingered a moment before slipping down the remaining steps to check the door. The deadbolt was locked . . . from the inside.

"Don't tell Mom," a child's voice whispered from the studio.

With a cry, I staggered up the steps, stumbling and slipping on each one. I slammed the door to my room behind me and turned the deadbolt. Mutt whined at me when I stumbled into the table on my way back to my bed.

"Shhh," I whispered, wanting desperately to dismiss the voice downstairs.

It's my mind playing tricks on me, that's all, I told myself over and over as I commanded my phone to play the next podcast in the series. I'd once heard that the loss of sight sometimes brought about imagined noises, and so I rationalized the whisper away until my heartbeat returned to normal and my hands steadied. *It was only my imagination, just a manifestation of a nightmare.*

But Mutt had heard it too. He'd rushed to meet the owner of the voice. He still whined in his bed in the corner as if he wanted to go back to whoever or whatever was down there. Fear gripped me even though my mind grew weary. Perhaps I was being haunted by the past in more than just my memories.

Recoiling from the thought, I followed the podcast voice back into reminiscence. I focused on my life before the accident and the fleeting happiness I'd found through my art. My nerves were momentarily soothed, but I could not escape the dreams. No amount of rationalization could hold them at bay. In the throes of agitated sleep, my twelve-year-old voice echoed again the whisper I'd heard in the dark.

"Don't tell Mom."

Three

I awoke to the raucous chatter of herring gulls squawking in the distance and to Mutt's cold nose nudging my arm. He whined his usual morning plea when I stirred. The events of the previous night came back to me as I sat up and stretched my weary limbs. The new day's resentment replaced the dread of the night before. Bad enough that I was robbed of my sight, now I was starting to hear things that weren't there.

Scoffing at my cowardice, I grabbed my shades from the table and walked to the loft door. Mutt bustled down the stairs, but I paused on each step, my ears searching for a child's voice. Hearing nothing, I let Mutt out the front door to do his business. A gust of winter air, scented with salt water and chimney smoke, caressed my torso and made my skin prick beneath my shirt. Mutt trotted back in, and I quickly pushed the door shut. Turning, I ran my hands along the walls, along the dusty paintings that hung there, to see if any were missing. All were accounted for and only one, the portrait of my little brother, was askew. Satisfied that the voice I'd heard had indeed been my imagination, I straightened it, and I went up to get dressed.

Mutt was elated as he led me again to the bus stop. This time I was going for my own benefit. I needed the sound of the waves crashing along the shore to soothe my now frazzled nerves. The bus was empty again. I thanked the early hour and colder than average temperatures for a swift and heedless ride. This time Mutt lingered with the driver as he received his customary scratch. I thought I heard the flash of a camera phone along with the driver's giggles. Finally Mutt scampered down the steps to meet me. The driver laughed as he pulled the door to and drove off.

The beach was deserted again. The sand felt frigid between my bare toes. Hunkering down into my hoodie, I let Mutt go in a whirl of sand and barks. This time I didn't sit. Instead, I stood facing the ocean I longed to see. Visions of my brother danced into my mind's eye, and with them came the guilt. Dark thoughts overtook me. *You're just like your father*, my mind repeated over and over again in whispers. They mingled with the sounds of laughter from a small voice hidden in the darkness of my studio. As much as I tried to throw the sound back down the abyss of my imagination, there was something familiar in the joy of that laugh. It was the innocent laugh of a child whose world was still a landscape of hope and light. I couldn't remember what that felt like. I wondered if I had ever known.

As a stinging breeze blew across my face, I lifted the glass from my eyes and faced the brunt. The wind whipped past my ears in a frantic shriek and lifted my arms from my sides as my hood whipped against me. I let my mouth drop open. My screams hovered above the wind in a release of sorrow and rage, but they were lost against the crashing of the angry tide.

Then within the thrash and the fury of the wind, a voice other than my own was lifted to my ears. A song birthed from the lips of a child formed on the wind.

This little light of mine . . .

With a gasp, I turned from it as my heart raced in time with the flapping wings of a pelican overhead. The voice was everywhere and nowhere all at once. I called to Mutt, who came running with oblivious abandon.

"Do you hear that, boy?" I asked. He barked in response, running off to find something for me to throw.

With a shrug, I sat down at last into the cold sand and replaced my shades. The song was lost amidst the breaking waters. When Mutt plopped a soggy stick in my lap, I threw it and awaited the coming of dusk. This time I didn't imagine the colors of the sunset streaking across the sky. Instead, my thoughts were hijacked by the memories of a child just as lost as the voice in the wind.

The bus ride home was as blissfully silent as before. I fought sleep as I listened to the whining of the tired engine as we trundled along the familiar highway. By the time we made it back to the apartment, the temperature had dropped to an ungodly degree. Mutt scratched at the door while I fumbled with my keys. He was just as eager to seek refuge from the night air as I. But when I opened the door, Mutt caught a scent that made him stiffen and bristle at my side. Then with a bark, he bounded into the empty studio before I could grab him.

I hesitated a moment and then stepped inside, driven in by the bitter cold. Shutting the door, I shivered as Mutt sniffed at the floorboards in the corner.

"What is it?" I asked him. "Is someone here?"

Mutt snorted, and his excitement abated. He took the steps with a dejected whine, ready for his supper. My curiosity got the best of me. I ran my hands across the paintings once again. My brother's portrait hung askew just as before. Straightening it, I paused to listen for movement. Hearing nothing, I followed Mutt up to the loft.

I filled Mutt's bowl and settled down with a sandwich at the table. Taking off my hoodie, I dug my phone from my pocket and sat back in my chair.

"Email," I said into the receiver after the beeps.

"*You have one new message.*"

"Read it," I commanded.

"*From Scott Bramble. Sent at 7:52 a.m.*" The digital voice read:

"*Dear Mr. Roberts,*

Thank you for contacting me about the status of your artwork. I was saddened to hear about your accident and send you my well wishes and prayers. Unfortunately, I am unable to continue representing your work at this time. I'm sorry. I know it's a difficult

time for you, but your paintings just aren't selling. Should you have any new portraits for me to consider in the future, please do not hesitate to contact me. I'm sorry, Blake. I really am.
   Sincerely, Scott Bramble"

"Ahh!" I screamed, throwing the phone onto the bed. "How exactly am I supposed to paint anything new? Don't you think I would if I could? Stupid son of a . . ."

Mutt barked and pawed at his food bowl. I hadn't filled it to his liking. Still enraged, I filled it again and stormed down the stairs to the studio. I felt my way to the small closet at the far end of the gallery. It opened with a scornful groan, and the air that met me on the other side was stale and musty.

Feeling the contents, I searched for my easel, throwing half-finished portraits and frames aside. When my fingers found its smooth, wooden edges, I yanked it free of the mess and set it down in the open space of the gallery. Driven by a helpless rage, I went back into the closet and grabbed haphazardly for a blank canvas, my palette, and some paint tubes and brushes.

When I'd collected my materials, I sat in front of the easel and took a deep breath.

"There are blind painters who do this," I mumbled to myself as I squirted random paints onto the palette. There was no way for me to know what colors I was using, no image in my mind to paint, but I willed myself to try. Mutt's paws sounded on the stairs, and he walked to me, his steps cautious. When he licked my hand, I patted his head. Then an idea struck me.

I ran my fingers along Mutt's muscular jawline, along his high forehead, and followed the lines of him up to his ears, which flopped over at their corners. I scratched behind one of the folds, and he made himself comfortable on the floor at my side.

With a picture of Mutt in my mind's eye, I set the palette down and pressed the paintbrush to the canvas. I used my other hand to feel ahead of the stroke. When I felt the tip of the brush run dry and start to give a slight resistance, I held my fingertip where the brush stroke ended and attempted to dip the brush in more paint with my other hand.

It was no use. Without both hands, I couldn't reach the palette. With a growl, I lifted my finger from the painting and moved the palette to my lap. Tracing my finger over the fresh paint on the canvas, I found where I'd left off. The paint smeared beneath my fingertips, but I continued anyway, trying to conjure the image of Mutt as I had before.

Keeping one hand on the portrait at all times, I dipped my brush and followed the soft lines until I had a complete outline. Then I sat back and tried to imagine how it looked, using my fingertips to trace my work.

"What do you think, Mutt?" I asked. His tail thumped the floor at the sound of his name. "Does it look like you?"

Mutt only moaned. I heard him roll onto his side with an indifferent flop.

"That good, huh?"

With a sigh, I dipped my brush into a different paint on the palette and raised it to the canvas, but hesitated, not knowing which colors I was blending. Frustration began to rise, tightening my shoulders and making my heart sink, but I pushed it back and pressed on. I had to be able to do this. I had to.

I passed the evening hours trying to keep track of each stroke on the canvas, but the more paint I added the more impossible it became. As the seagulls' cries died away and silence of deep night took hold, I lost focus. The palette's colors ran together in my mind and beneath my fingers making me lose track of the lines. No matter how hard I tried, I couldn't keep Mutt's image sharp in my mind and on the canvas at the same time.

My hands shook, my arms were exhausted by the effort. Standing, I seethed as the palette slid from my lap to the floor. I grabbed the canvas with a cry and broke the binding over my knee before throwing it across the room. Then I kicked at the paint tubes and brushes that littered the floor around me, rage and desolation taking hold of me again.

Sinking into my seat, I cradled my scarred and battered head in my useless hands. Mutt staggered over and nudged me with his wet nose, but I only sat and let the darkness consume me. One word echoed in my mind: *hopeless*.

"I didn't like it either. Why did you paint that purple rhino anyway?" a tiny voice asked from the corner of the room. Mutt jumped to his feet with an excited yelp.

"Rhinos are grey," the voice said.

Adjusting my shades back over my eyes, I whirled around in the direction of the voice and to where Mutt ran, all tongue and slurps, to greet our guest. I heard the child in the corner laugh and giggle at the slobbery attack. My heart sped with apprehension even as my anger flourished.

"What are you doing in here?" I yelled, wishing I had my hood to cover my head. "This is private property. We aren't open for business. You shouldn't be here."

"Some rhinos are brown," the boy said between giggles, ignoring my question, "but they still look grey to me."

I stood and stomped toward the voice, kicking tubes of paint out of my way.

"It wasn't a rhino! Mutt, come here," I shouted, and the licking stopped. I heard his reluctant paws step closer, but his whine pleaded for permission to go back.

"I like your dog," the boy said.

"I told you, this is private property," I said behind clenched teeth. "How did you get in here?"

"I don't know," he answered, his voice softer.

"What do you mean, you don't know?" I asked. "Get out of here!"

There was silence for a moment, and I thought that perhaps the boy had snuck out the way he came. The way Mutt's tail thumped the ground beside me told me otherwise.

"You want me to leave?" the boy asked, almost a whisper. "But it's so dark."

"Get out!" I yelled again and waited. When I heard his light footsteps walk to the front door, I followed behind cautiously.

He opened the door and then paused. "Are you angry with me?"

"Yes, I am. You shouldn't be here!" I spat, slamming the door behind him and waiting to hear his footsteps walk away down the old brick street. Instead, I heard his small, dismayed voice on the other side of the door.

"Don't tell Mom," he pleaded, turning my blood to ice in my veins.

I opened the door, staying behind it in the safety of the shadows.

"It was you last night," I said, my tone firm though my hands shook. "I want you to stay the hell out of here, or I am calling the police. Do you hear me?"

Only the cold night wind answered and the sway of the water beneath the Riverwalk across the street.

"Do you understand me?" I hollered into the night, but the only response was my own voice, carried back to me by the frigid night wind. There were no footsteps on the old brick street. Only silence.

Shutting the door again, I locked both the door knob and the deadbolt. I leaned against it, trying to catch my breath. *Was he rea, or just my imagination?* As I questioned my sanity, Mutt leaned against me. He sat by the door and whined, saddened that our guest was now gone. Patting his head, more to calm myself than him, I took a deep breath. *It was just a kid*, I told myself. *Wandered in from one of the hotels up the street, that's all.*

"Let's go," I said, steadying myself.

Feeling for the stair railing, Mutt followed me up the steps. I tried to push my failed attempt at painting and the strange encounter from my mind. I checked the locks again and made a mental note to order new deadbolts for the front door. When my nerves were assuaged and Mutt was satisfied and snoozing in his bed, I dug my phone out from my pocket and sat back in my chair at the table. Thoughts of children's pleas and broken dreams awakened the rage that was at constant war inside. Only one thing ever made me feel better.

"Send an email," I instructed after the beeps.

"To whom should I send it?"

"Address it to Logan Foster," I said and waited for the prompting to start my one hundred and twenty- first draft.

"You were wrong about me . . ."

Four

The dream was the same. I marveled as my conscious mind gave way to sleep at how helpless I was to my own ghosts, at how even in dreams the outcome would remain the same. I couldn't change what happened in my nightmares any more than I could change the past. She would still leave us, and they would still die. It would still be my fault.

"Daddy, stop!" my brother cried, scrambling to escape my father's fury. "What did I do? What did I do?"

No one could explain to us then that my father's anger burned against himself. He raged at his loss of control over his addiction while he punished us for it with his fists. I kicked and clawed at him, praying desperately for the black void in his eyes and the twisted snarl of his lips to fade, praying that somewhere inside of him my brother's cries could rouse the loving father we scarcely saw.

"Leave him alone!" I screamed.

Grabbing at his muscular arms, I used all the might in my twelve-year-old body to pry him away from my little brother. My father let him go, and his little body hit the wall, knocking the lights from their plug. The room went dark.

When my father's anger flared back to me, I watched through tear-filled eyes as my brother ran from the room. He looked back in time to see my father shove me into the wall with a furious cry.

"You think you can tell me what to do?" he sneered, the booze on his warm breath stinging my nose. "I'll teach you some respect. I don't work two jobs so you can have a roof over your head and still disrespect me!"

Before his fist came down on me again, I looked to my brother who stared at me, his panicked eyes questioning me. *What do I do?*

"Don't tell Mom," I mouthed before the blow blurred my vision with shadow and mingled light. Through the haze I watched my brother run out the front door towards the diner down the street.

My restless sleep was interrupted by a distant cry. It jarred me from where I dozed at the table. I wiped my mouth with the back of my sleeve, still more asleep than conscious. Muffled sobs sounded from downstairs. My heart sped when the cries registered as reality.

"Mutt," I called, a hushed whisper, but he did not respond.

I waited for the tinkering of his footsteps on the floorboards, but they were silent. In the distance, his soft whine signaled distress. My hands flailed across the table's surface until they found my shades, and shoving them onto my eyes, I grabbed my hoodie and made for the door. Counting the steps, I reached for the knob, but found the door ajar.

With a creak, I swung it open and stuck my head out, searching the darkness for Mutt's whimper. The crying grew louder as did Mutt's whine, forcing me to ignore the fear that rose like bile into my throat.

"Mutt?" I called. "Where are you, boy? Who's there?"

Taking the stairs two at a time, I kept the sound of his whine in my ears and let it draw me to him.

"Don't be mad," a small voice pleaded, stopping me cold.

"What are you doing here? I told you to never come back here!" I yelled, anger mixing with fear. "Where's Mutt? Is he hurt?"

As I stepped closer, my hand was met by Mutt's cold, wet nose as his tail beat against my left calf. Bending down, I ran my hands across his torso as he licked my hands, assuring me he was fine.

"He doesn't like it when I cry," the small boy said, his voice quivering as Mutt left my side and flumped over near the child in the corner.

With a relieved sigh, I pulled the hood further over my head as anger overtook all fear.

"I told you to never come back here, you little vulture," I said. "You have until the count of three to leave before I call the cops."

"Please don't make me leave again," he said with a sniffle. Mutt whined beside him.

"One," I said, pacing away toward the stairs.

"Please!"

"Two," I growled as I started up, my temper flaring.

"I don't want to go back," the boy forced out between sobs. "He'll be so mad at me if I go back."

"Three," I said, whirling at the top of the steps.

"No!" he cried as I reached my hand back for the door, but something stopped me, freezing me cold where I stood.

Beyond the cool plastic of my shades, a warmth radiated, permeating the darkness behind my scarred-over eyes. Light, soft and static, glowed around the rims. My mind's eye stared at it, trying to distinguish it from the false light of memory.

When I removed my shades, the light grew brighter, more clearly defined. Trembling, I ran my fingertips along the scaly skin covering my useless eyes. The light remained.

My breath caught in my throat as my mind reeled. I descended the stairs. The light grew more acute with each shaky step. When I turned to the corner of the room, I raised a hand to shield my eyes from the brightness, but I realized with paralyzing awe that I wasn't seeing this light through my eyes at all.

Lowering my hand, I focused on the center of the glow where a figure began to take shape. Huddled in the corner of the room, tears staining his sullen cheeks, sat a small boy. He looked up at me, his doe-like auburn eyes haunted.

"Please don't make me leave," he whispered.

"What is this?" My mind reeling, I staggered backwards, tripping over strewn paint tubes and broken frames. "Who are you?"

The boy raised his hand and moved it in a slow motion from side to side. I realized he was petting Mutt, who still lay by his side whining. I could see only the child, surrounded by a warm glow. Everything else was still drenched in darkness.

"What's the matter with your eyes?" the boy asked, peering over his knees, which he hugged to his chest.

"They were burned shut," I stammered. "I'm . . . I'm blind."

"You can see me, though," the boy said matter-of-factly, standing to wipe his hands on his grey sweatpants. His red shirt was smudged with soot as was his face. He couldn't have been more than five years old.

"I can see you," I whispered, unable to take a breath and unable to look away. "Why can I see you?"

"I don't know," he said with a shrug. "I can see you."

"That . . . that's different. Where are you parents?" I asked, staggering backwards. "Where's your mother?"

"I don't know," he repeated.

"Do you know anything?" I snapped, backing into the railing. "Why are you here? You shouldn't be here."

The boy looked down as he shuffled his size two sneakers. "I don't want to be with him anymore, and I need to find Red."

"Him who? Your dad?" I asked, trying to make some sense. "Where is he? What's red?"

"Daddy's in the room. I don't know where Red is," he said, tears coming back to his eyes.

"The room . . . you have a room. So you ARE staying at one of the hotels up the street," I said, my blood pressure lowering slightly. "I think we should go talk to your dad. Maybe he can explain what's going on..."

"No!" the boy shouted, cowering back into the corner. He flung his arms around a black mass in the darkness, and I heard Mutt lick his face in response. "I don't want to go back. Please don't make me go back."

"Well, you can't stay here!" My temper flared again as I turned on him, but then I looked into the child's eyes and saw an all too familiar terror in their watery depths. The fear of the hunted kept them wide and searching. In his giant pupils I saw the reflection of a monster, face darkened under a black hood, who towered over his small frame as he shivered in the corner. When I realized I was looking at my own reflection in the blacks of his eyes, my breath left me in a rush. The light the boy emanated began to spin with my sudden dizziness. Turning away from him, I stumbled to the stairs.

"What the hell is happening to me?" I questioned, tripping on the steps. "You shouldn't be here."

When my hands found the door, I flung it open. Throwing myself inside, I yelled for Mutt. His defiant whine traveled up the stairs.

"Please don't go," the boy cried. "Don't leave me."

When I called for Mutt again, I waited to be sure he would not come before I slammed the door and locked the light away.

Five

You were wrong about me, Logan. Everything I had I lost because of you, because of your hope, and because of your lies. I've grown too weary to explain what you've taken from me. I'm too tired to count the losses. Sleep is fleeting these days, as is my sanity. I'm haunted by my nightmares not only when I sleep, but also when I wake. Yet another perk of being unable to open your eyes to the light of a new day. The night is eternal for me. Dreams no longer creep in with just the coming of the dawn.

I think that's why I see him.

The child wanders in and out of my life as fleetingly as my dreams, here one moment and vapor the next. Something dawned on me last night as I trembled with confusion. For a moment I thought about your stories, about the woman who visited you in a vision. I thought that maybe the child was like her. It was a comforting thought, and I almost believed it.

Then the dreams came and with them the all too familiar screams, and pain, and loss. I awoke again to the truth. There is no light for me, no matter how bright the vision. The child I see serves only as a reminder of all I've lost. He wanders in here to torment me. I think God sent him. He allows me to see him so that I can look into that child's eyes and remember that I'm a monster.

As if I needed the reminder.

I blame you for this suffering, Logan. I blame you for giving me the courage to aspire to things I was never meant for. Painting brought me peace, but darkness and pain are all this life has ever had to offer me. I look forward only to the end . . .

The loud scratching at my loft door stopped my dictation before I could finish the thought. Rising, my bones stiff and feeble, I put on my shades and walked to the door.

"*Are you ready to send your email to Logan Foster?*" my phone prompted from the table.

"Cancel. Save as draft," I said, cracking the door to listen.

Mutt whined from the other side and scratched at the door again. When I opened it wide, his paws danced an agitated circle in front of me.

"What? Your new best friend didn't let you out this morning?" I asked, taking a deep breath and motioning him to go first back down the stairs.

I listened to the tinkering of his nails as they traversed the antique oak in front of me. Lowering my shades, I searched for the boy's light in the gallery below. When I reached the bottom step, I whirled toward the corner, half expecting to see his huddled body asleep on the floor. I was met by only darkness. The boy was nowhere to be found.

I stayed a minute. My ears searched the room for his breath in case my strange, unexplainable vision had failed. The room was quiet with the exception of Mutt's impatient yip at the door. Impervious and numb, I adjusted my shades and opened it to the chirping of the sea-going fowl as they announced the new morning. I scoffed at them and turned to go inside.

A fluttering sound caught my attention as paper flapped about against the cold morning wind. My hand searched the door until it found the notice taped to the outside. I didn't need my eyes to know that it was a foreclosure notice. The mortgage payments stopped when the last of my sales money ran out. I'd blocked the bank's calls months ago. I knew all too well from my childhood that I had weeks, maybe months, to make a payment or Mutt and I were on the streets. Without my eyes, without my art, there was no way I could make one.

In that moment the sleepless nights, the helplessness, and the rage all accumulated in the marrow of my bones. It radiated with a numbing ache throughout my body. Without even thinking, I tore up the notice and dropped my shades to the ground. Then I stepped out, barefooted and hoodless, into the frigid morning air. My feet stumbled and scraped upon the old brick street as I crossed to the Riverwalk, hands outstretched and searching. In the distant recesses of my mind, the whipping wind mingled with the swishing of the water beneath the wooden planks. Their whispers ushered me forward.

When my hand met the railing, I climbed over and pitched forward until I fell into the railing on the other side. Breathless and broken, I clung to it, my head downcast toward the water. I imagined the sight of it. Memories of a golden grin and crushing baseball bat mingled with what I remembered of the grey waters. Its glassy-smooth surface reflected the winter sky in my mind.

I imagined a cloudless morning and let the ripples of the water match the splashing sway of the current beneath me. I imagined the retired battleship across the river looming like a sentinel of antique steel and gunpowder. The ghosts within stood ready to guide me to my soul's end.

I climbed onto the top railing and balanced on the beam. Raising my arms, I lifted my chin to face the spray coming off the river as I contemplated the fall. I could just let go right now. Let go of the struggle and the pain. Let it all sink with me to the bottom of the icy waters. My own voice echoed inside my head to do it, to just sink and fade away.

I took in a deep breath and held it as I leaned forward, waiting for the wind to take my body with it into the spray. My thoughts became clear and focused. What a simple thing, to just cease breathing. Slipping away to death would be as easy as that. Just stop breathing. So much simpler than the struggles I faced in my future and more inviting than continuing to confront the wars of my past. I let go.

Then a thought entered my mind that made me second guess my decision, though it was too late to stop the momentum of my body as it plunged to meet the water. What if my nightmares played out in death like my own private hell of rekindled memory? What if my father was there to greet me in the fires? In the second before I hit the water, I could only laugh at the irony of it.

The tip of my nose had just skimmed the icy river when I was jerked backwards by a sharp tug on my pants waist. My arms flailed as I was tugged backwards again and again with violent thrusts. My waistband was caught in a vice of muscle and growling determination. When Mutt succeeded in jerking me back to the railing, I grabbed hold of it. He licked my face, panting in a fever of excursion and excitement from where he leaned over the top rung.

"Just let me do it," I breathed. "I just want it to be over, Mutt."

Mutt only licked my face and barked. His tail thumped the metal of the railing between us. It was then that I heard the song, soft and distant, float to me on the wind.

"*This little light of mine, I'm going to let it shine*," it sang.

Mutt gave another excited bark and latched back onto my shirt, tugging. Our guest was back.

I laughed, a joyless wheeze, and struggled to climb back over the railing. Mutt pulled me to the planks, and I landed, a lifeless thud. Lying there, I tried to muster the strength and will to get up as Mutt nudged my cheek with his cold nose. As angry as I was that an end to suffering would not come, I was also grateful that Mutt stopped me and brought me back to my senses. As much as I longed for death, I feared hell more than even my worst nightmares.

"I hate you," I said, and he licked my face. He knew from the inflection in my voice that the opposite was true.

The song came again on the breeze, and I listened to the melody of it as I clung to Mutt and pulled myself to my feet.

Together we walked toward it as Mutt led me back to the front door of the studio. I bent down and grabbed my shades but lowered them when I saw that the light was back. It glowed just inside the door. When I stepped in, the boy was huddled in the corner rocking back and forth while he hugged his knees to him.

"*All around the neighborhood,*" he sang into his lap, "*I'm going to let it shine.*"

When he saw me enter, he looked up. My mind's eye looked into his. Again I saw his fear and was reminded of the look on my brother's face as he ran from my room that night so long ago. He'd been about the same age. I also saw myself in their glossy amber and knew that our souls were somehow linked by our pasts. Whether for prosperity or for torment, I couldn't know.

"Who are you?" I asked, closing the door behind me.

The boy lowered his knees and crossed his legs in front of him nervously as he peered at me from behind thick lashes.

"My name is Julian," he said. "What's yours?"

"Boss . . . I mean, Blake," I said. "My name is Blake."

"Are you still mad at me?" he asked, barely a whisper.

With a sigh, I sat at the bottom of the stairs and rubbed my bare face with my hands before answering.

"No, I'm not mad at you," I said. "I mean, yes, I am. Hell, I don't know what I am right now."

Though I couldn't see it, I heard Mutt walk to the child and plop down on the floor beside him. Julian reached a hand up and stroked what looked to me like thin, black air.

"How old are you, Julian?"

"I'm five and a half," he answered, looking at Mutt and not me. Hoodless and without my shades, I knew I was a hideous sight. It was easy to understand why I made him nervous.

"You're awfully young to be trespassing on private property," I said, and he looked at me, his eyes wide.

"Don't tell Mom," he pleaded.

"You keep saying that. What is it you're afraid of?" I asked. "Where is your mom?"

"I don't know where my mom is," he said, his eyes filling with tears. "Dad said she'll be upset with me if she knew I was causing trouble."

"You said your dad was at the room. Where is he? Doesn't he care that you're here?"

"He doesn't know I'm here," he whispered. "Please don't tell him. He won't understand. He'll just get mad at me."

I stood and walked toward him. As I did, I noticed that he was wearing the same clothes as the night before, only now they were matted and wrinkled.

"I don't understand either," I said, struggling to keep the frustration from my voice. "And I'm trying not to be mad, but I need to know why you're here. Why do you keep coming here?"

Julian shrugged and went back to petting Mutt. "Because, this is where I go."

I let out a loud breath and threw my hands up. "Well, don't get used to it, kid. This place is going to be the bank's property soon."

"What does that mean?" he asked.

"Nothing. Look, I don't care where you came from. I just want to know one very important thing from you, okay?" I took a deep breath as Julian nodded. "Why can I see you?"

"I don't know." Julian only shrugged again and went on petting Mutt. "I can see you too."

"The fact that you can see me is not nearly as significant here," I said, pacing away toward the stairs. It was clear that I would get no answers from the child. My exhaustion was mounting as was my frustration.

"Why do you walk like that?" he asked. "Like you're carrying something heavy?"

I turned to look at him, finding it impossible not to. He was the first thing I'd seen in over a year. It also made him the most glorious. Even if he was sent here to torment and annoy, I found myself feeling grateful for the chance to see something . . . someone again. Julian studied me, his head cocked to the side as he watched me with a child's fascination. His innocence stifled any remaining anger and left only mild irritation in its place.

"Half the bones in my body were broken not too long ago, not that it's any of your business," I answered. "It takes a lot more effort to move around than it used to. Plus, I'm old."

He giggled. "You're silly."

"And you're annoying," I said, walking to the stairs.

Taking a few steps, I leaned over the rail to look at him again. "You're not going to leave here, are you?"

Julian looked down at his shoes and shrugged. I was beginning to pick up on his body language. Shrugs were obviously his way of giving an answer that he knew would be met with disapproval. It was as if he were waiting to be punished at any hint of a misstep.

"Just tell me one thing," I said, and Julian raised his head to look at me. I studied his red-brown eyes again, eyes too big for his small face. "Are you like . . . a demon or something?"

"I don't think so," Julian said. "What's a demon?"

"You know, like in that Edgar Allan Poe poem." I searched my memory for the name of the one piece of literature I had ever truly understood in school. "*The Raven*! That was it. Were you sent here to haunt me all the rest of my days? Because my memories do a fine enough job of that."

"What memories?" he asked, obviously lost.

I looked him over from head to toe again, taking in his matted and dirty clothes and his unruly hair.

"No, you're not a raven," I said with a sigh. "You're more like a vulture. That's what you are."

"Birds are my favorite animal," Julian said, perking up and getting to his feet. "Ravens are cool, but I don't like vultures. They're nasty. Can I be a cardinal instead? They're my favorite."

"No," I snapped. "Cardinals are resilient and beautiful and bring only joy. Vultures, on the other hand, feed off the flesh of the dead. They're persistent, and they hover overhead waiting for you to die. That's why you're a vulture, understand?"

Julian looked up at me with puppy-dog eyes. "Vultures poop on their own legs."

I paused, contemplating that useless tidbit of information.

"What you do with your poop is your own business," I finally said, waving him off. I made my way up the rest of the stairs but called down to him. "You might as well go back to wherever you came from. You can't haunt a ghost."

"I don't want to go," he said. I could hear the tears he held back.

"Well, little vulture, if you're determined to hang around here picking at my sanity, you might as well make yourself useful. Why don't you clean up this mess?" I said, motioning over the railing to where I knew paint tubes and canvas still littered the floor. When I reached the door, I peeked over to see Julian investigating the clutter around him.

"And if the cops come looking for you, I'm telling them you're a trespasser," I said before closing the door. "I'm not going back to jail over some kid, imagined or otherwise."

I left the door cracked in case Mutt wanted his breakfast. Counting the steps to the closet, I grabbed clean clothes and a fresh hoodie before locking myself in the bathroom. The hot spray of the shower eased the tension in my muscles. The air grew thick as steam filled the cool spaces around me. As the water ran down the numerous scars of my body, I thought of that poem, *The Raven*, and its famous refrain: *Nevermore*. If Julian was sent from some tempest to torment me, the joke was on him. I'd already accepted that I would be free from anguish, *nevermore*.

Resting my head against the tiles, my mind wandered to that night all those years ago. Too tired to fight the memories anymore, I let them come. Rubbing my hands together in the spray, I remembered how the blood ran from them to swirl and mix in the drain. I remembered looking into the mirror once I washed it from my skin, knowing it would stain my soul forever. My own amber eyes reflected the all-consuming fear within them. If it were possible, tears would flow from my eyes now as they had then.

Shaking myself from the reverie, I turned off the shower. When I did, I heard Julian's song from outside the bathroom door.

"This little light of mine . . ."

With sudden rage, I wiped the moisture from my limbs and pulled on my clothes. Throwing the hood over my head, I stormed out of the bathroom. It took a minute to see through the brightness that now emanated into the small loft apartment from where Julian sat at the table. As he sang, he dipped his fingers into nothingness and spread them across the black surface in front of him.

"What are you doing in here?" I snapped. "This is my room. I don't let anyone up here!"

Julian flinched and turned to look at me. "Finger painting," he said with another shrug. "I made you a picture."

"You got into my paints?" I asked, stomping over to him. I looked down instinctively but saw nothing but darkness beside him. "Those are mine. You have no right to . . ."

"You don't like it?" he asked, lowering his head in shame.

I took a deep breath, choking back the anger that threatened to boil over. Exhaling slowly, I balled my fists at my sides.

"I can't see it. I've explained this to you," I said, my forced calm sounding more impatient than I'd hoped. "Look, I get that you like being here for whatever reason, but upstairs is off limits, you got me?"

"I thought you would want to paint with me," he said, dejected, still staring at his feet.

"I can't paint," I said.

"Yes, you can. I saw your pictures. You paint real good," he protested. "Well, except for the purple rhino. That one was bad."

"Yeah, well, that's the best I can do now. I told you, I can't paint," I said with a sigh, pulling out the chair beside him to rest my tired legs. "And it wasn't a rhino."

"What was it?" he asked.

"I was trying to paint my dog," I answered, leaning back in my chair and crossing my arms over my chest.

Julian laughed, and a part of me relished the joyous sound of his innocent abandon. It disarmed me, soothing me like the crashing of the surf.

"Mitchell isn't purple, silly," he said, a high-pitched squeal.

I sat forward, unamused by whatever joke I was missing. "Who?"

"Your dog," he said between giggles. "He's not purple."

"My dog's name is Mutt," I corrected. I heard Mutt's paws approach at the mention of his name. He licked my hand, and I felt the swish of his tail as he turned to Julian.

"That's not what his tag says," Julian said, his laughter stopping as he bent down to grasp Mutt's collar. "It says his name is Mitchell. M-I-C-H-A-E-L. That spells Mitchell."

"No, that spells Michael. It says . . . Michael," I mumbled.

Dumbfounded, I sat back and thought of the day that Mutt showed up on my stoop. Shivering from the cold and emaciated, he had barked at my front door until I opened it. Then he'd made himself comfortable beside the furnace. It was only weeks after my accident, and there was more pain than fight in my body to protest.

He was dirty and smelled of dust and salt water. He also sported a collar; the tag jingled from it like a sleigh bell. I knew then that he belonged to someone else, but when I searched his frame with my fingers and felt clearly every rib bone and indentation, I decided that it didn't matter. I fed him, and he'd remained at my side ever since.

"That's what I meant," Julian said, setting his chin. "Michael."

"Yeah, well," I said, indifferent, "his name is Mutt now."

"Okay." Julian turned back to his painting. "I'll give Mutt a new collar."

"What are you doing?" I asked, my patience running out. "I told you to stay downstairs."

"You don't want me to finish my painting? I'm almost done," he said, looking up at me with a smile. "You can hang it on your refrigerator!"

"I don't want to hang it on my refrigerator," I said. "I want you to go down . . ."

Before I could finish my sentence, Mutt plopped his head on my lap with a subtle whine. It was obvious that he enjoyed having our guest in such close proximity. The way he acted when Julian was around made me wonder if there was a child somewhere that he missed.

"You're painting Mutt?" I asked Julian, who turned eagerly back to his masterpiece.

"Uh, huh," he answered.

"Can you tell me . . ." I stammered as I petted Mutt's head. "What does he look like?"

Julian took a second to put the finishing touch on his paper, and then he held it up for me to see. I saw only him, the paper fading into the darkness around him.

"This grey is darker than he is, but I painted the white patches on his back and tummy. I gave him a red collar, just like in real life." Julian beamed, and I smiled despite myself.

"Grey, really? I always imagined him brown," I said, "like a short-haired Beethoven. From those movies."

"That's silly," Julian said, shifting papers around on the table. "Beethoven is a St. Bernard. Michael . . . oops. I mean, Mutt, is a pit bull."

"Pit bull . . ." I repeated as a new image of Mutt formed in my mind, grey and white and strong. "Makes sense, actually. You sure know a lot about animals for your age."

"I know the most about birds," he said. "They're . . ."

"Your favorite," I finished for him. "I know."

"Yep!"

I watched as Julian adjusted something in front of him, and then taking a deep breath, he dipped his fingers again before wiping them across the surface.

"What are you doing?" I asked, patting Mutt's head before standing. "It's time for you to go back downstairs."

Julian looked up at me, devastated.

"Please, just one more," he pleaded. "I have all this red left over. I can make a big cardinal with it. They're my favorite."

"Yeah, so you've told me. Look," I said, the warm fuzzies vanishing. "It's bad enough that you just show up whenever you want to. You're not going to invade my room too. So beat it."

"Awww," he said, slumping his shoulders and sticking out his bottom lip.

"Don't give me that face either." I walked to the door and opened it for him. "Life is full of disappointments, kid. Get used to it."

"Just let me finish this one part," he said, dejected. "I have to get the red off my fingers. It's the slimiest color."

"Hurry it up," I said.

Then a thought struck me as his last words sank in. I walked to him and watched as he wiped his fingers across the surface, one after the other, trying to rid them of a color I could not see.

"Wait a minute," I said, and he turned to look at me. "What did you say?"

"I have to get the red off my fingers?"

"After that," I prompted, impatient. "About the way it feels?"

"Red is slimy," Julian said with a shrug. "Not like white or grey. They're thick like mud."

Sitting at the table, my heart thumped in my ears. I felt around until my fingers found a blank piece of paper. Situating it in front of me, I turned to Julian.

"Show me," I said, raising my fingers.

Julian looked at me and squinted, contemplating. His eyes darted from my face to the hand that I extended into the space between us. Cautiously, he took my hand in his. Heat vibrated up my arm at his touch. I drew back with a gasp. He looked up at me, his eyes wide as coasters, and I knew he felt it too.

"What was that?" he asked, his voice hushed.

"I'm not sure," I said, but my mind flashed to Logan's many stories about his woman in white. Warm static. That was how he described her touch. The touch of an angel . . .

"Let's try that again," I said extending my hand once more.

When Julian grabbed it and brought it forward, his warmth penetrated the skin of my hand and seemed to warm it from the inside. With a smile, he guided my fingers to the paint on the palette. When my index finger touched the cool liquid, he let me go, and his warmth vanished from my hand.

"This is red," he said, watching me smear it between my fingers. "It's slimy, see?"

"It is," I said with a laugh. "It really is."

When my fingers were thoroughly doused in the slickness of it, I used my other hand to find my paper. With long strokes, I smeared the paint across the blank parchment, taking in the feel of the color beneath my fingers.

"Show me a different one?" I asked when my fingers ran dry.

Again his warmth enveloped my hand as he giggled and brought my fingers to the palette again. This time the liquid was thick and sticky, like the mud that clings to the bottom of your shoes on a rainy day.

"This is grey," Julian said as I smeared it across the paper in a different spot, relishing the feel of the color against the smooth surface. "I like that one."

"Show me more," I said, unable to keep the excitement from my voice.

With a laugh, Julian guided my fingers to the array of colors on the palette, marking the differences in each one. I learned that black was smooth like petroleum, white thick as toothpaste. Blue, what Julian described as the color of the sky, was almost gritty in texture, and it felt like spreading peanut butter across the page.

When he finished showing me the colors he'd selected, I was eager to try to put it all together.

We each painted our own interpretations of Julian's favorite bird. He pointed to where I should paint the beak, and I did my best to form it amongst the drying colors. As the hours passed, I found it easier and easier to distinguish one color from another on the page.

For the first time since the accident, I felt the beginnings of joy. Discovering this new way of painting opened a door into the dark basement of my life and let a little light inside. I clung to it, to this feeling I could scarcely describe. I was too afraid to call it hope.

When I was satisfied that I had painted something that could at least be distinguished as a bird, I sat back. Though I was exhausted and hungry, I felt more satiated than I'd felt in years. With a chuckle, I rubbed my hands on my pants and held up my paper.

"This may be the ugliest cardinal in history," I said, turning to Julian. "What do you think?"

When there was no answer, I lowered the paper. The room around me was cloaked in black. I'd been too wrapped up in my newfound ability to notice that the light had vanished. The room was silent except for the quiet whine that Mutt sent into the room from his bed in the corner.

Julian was gone.

For a minute I just sat there absorbing the darkness where the child had just been. Then I stood and felt along the table for Julian's painting. I hung both his and mine on the refrigerator, then opened it to make myself a sandwich. Mutt hovered beside the table and whined for scraps. I threw him a piece of turkey.

"Where'd he go, Mutt?" I asked, futilely. "I know you saw him leave."

Mutt only gulped down the lunch meat and licked his chops, then whined for more. When I finished my meal, I let my hands wander across the table to the paint drying on the palette. The colors were tacky now, but as I ran my fingers over them I could still tell which was blue, which was grey, and what colors had mingled together into different shades of each. In my mind I could see their vibrancy. I could imagine the drying paintings that now hung on my fridge in what must be a comic display of the state's bird.

With a laugh, I grabbed the palette and made my way downstairs. Gliding my feet across the floor, I expected to meet a mess of paint and littered canvas with my toes. To my surprise, the mess was gone. Feeling my way to the closet, I opened it and investigated the inside. The paint tubes were put away in their tub, the broken canvas in the trash.

"Well, I'll be . . . ," I mumbled. "The kid actually cleaned."

My easel was folded neatly in the corner. I grabbed it and a tub of paint and set up in the corner of the room where Julian always seemed to appear. Then I went back for a new canvas. It took a long time to go through the paints to find colors that I now recognized by touch, squirting each one onto a piece of scrap paper until I was confident enough in its identity to put it on the palette. When I was set up and ready, I took a deep breath and picked up my brush. I used the tips of my fingers to identify the different colors, my brush to spread them across the canvas.

With a fresh image in mind, I painted for hours with fevered precision. Using one hand to paint and the other to keep track of the colors, I focused my will, coalescing the canvas image and the image in my head. It took longer than I was used to, but that didn't matter. Consumed with rekindled passion, I passed the day with joy and energy.

I paused only to let Mutt outside, and when I let him back in, noted that the day was giving way to night. The air grew colder with the waning sun. I worked into the evening hours, polishing and perfecting the painting until exhaustion and contentment took hold. Sitting back in my chair, I rested my head and laughed into the darkness of the studio. I had done it. It wasn't perfect. Of that I was sure, but it was the beginning of a second chance. That thought filled me with the closest thing to hope I'd felt since losing my eyes.

I let the brush and palette fall to the floor. Mutt wandered to me and laid his head in my lap. I petted him until my weak muscles relaxed and my mind slipped into unconsciousness.

Six

"No!" I screamed. "Don't!"

I watched through tear-filled eyes as my brother ran off into the distance. I knew he was going to the diner, just as I knew I could do nothing to stop him. My father grabbed me by my pajama collar and raised me above him, slamming my shaking limbs into the wall.

"Who do you think you are?" he hissed, clasping me around the neck. I looked into the pits of his eyes as he squeezed my throat closed. They were foreign to me, lost to the darkness that possessed him and kept him in its grasp.

"Please, Dad," I choked out. "Please, don't hurt me anymore. I'm your son, Dad. I'm your son."

For a moment there was a flicker in the darkness of his eyes as they glared up at me. A flash of recognition and remorse fought through the black. My head started to spin as I fought his grip. My lungs screamed for air.

"Please . . ." I croaked out again. It was all I could say beneath his crushing hand.

His eyes widened with what looked like sudden sobriety and regret. He began to lower me. My toes kicked and sought the solid ground beneath them.

"That's enough!" a wavering voice screamed from the doorway. "Leave him alone!"

My father released me and turned. I fell to the floor, gasping for air. When I looked up, my mother stood in the doorway.

Her smudged apron vibrated around her shaking body. My baby brother stood at her side as she raised her arm. The pistol in her hand was aimed at my father.

"Is that me?" an excited voice asked.

I shot up in my chair with a startled cry, ripped from my dream by the proximity of the voice. Julian, in all his luminous glory, stood beside me with a smile. He pointed at the painting on the easel.

"What the hell, kid?" I spat, struggling to sit up. "You can't just show up like that."

Julian's smile fell, his shoulders drooping. "Did I scare you?"

"No, you didn't scare me," I said, wiping my brow with the back of my hand. "I just wasn't expecting you."

"Did you have a bad dream?"

"Something like that," I said, turning to him. He was dressed in the same sweatpants and shirt, still wrinkled and smudged with dirt.

Julian shrugged. "I used to have bad dreams, but I have only good dreams now."

"How nice for you." I stood to stretch. My muscles were stiff and tight.

"So, is that me?" he asked, pointing to the painting again.

"Yeah, that's you," I said, picking up my brush and palette to rinse them in the sink. "How does it look? Does it look like you? You're the first face I've seen in over a year. Made it easier."

"My hair's sticking up," he said with a giggle.

"That's because it IS sticking up." I pointed to the sloppy tangle atop his head.

Julian reached up, and, finding his hair at odd angles, began to pat it down. It was no use. His hair sprang back up, a jumble of cinnamon waves.

"So I take it, it does look like you then?" I asked, turning to dry my brush.

"Uh, huh," he confirmed. "It's almost as good as that one."

"Which one?" I asked, turning to see him pointing into the blackness.

"The one under the stairs," he said. "That one."

A lump formed in my throat, and I choked it down, turning my back to rinse the palette.

"Who is it?" he asked. "In that painting? That little boy has dark skin like yours. I like that one."

"That's my little brother," I said, straining to keep my voice matter-of-fact.

After I dried the palette, I felt my way to the closet and grabbed a stool and a new canvas. When I turned back to Julian, he was still staring at the painting I could no longer see, only remember. I set the stool beside the easel and switched canvases, setting my latest painting against the wall to dry.

"Where is he?" Julian asked.

I cleared my throat and lowered myself into my chair.

"He's gone," I said. "Listen, while you're here, I want you to do me a favor."

"What?" Julian asked. His face glowed with excitement.

"I want you to sit here on this stool while I paint you," I said, motioning to the stool. "I think I can do a better portrait if I can see you while I work. You have to be still. Can you do that?"

"Sure," he said as he skipped to the stool. "I can do that!"

"Good." I reached for new paints.

"That one's green," he said when I picked one up.

"Don't tell me," I said, picking the colors I thought I needed. "I have to be able to do this by myself."

"Why?" he asked with a smile. "I can help you."

I squirted some paint onto my scrap paper and identified the ones I wanted. Then I filled my palette and looked at Julian. He sat watching me, his legs swinging back and forth beneath him.

"Yes, well," I said, positioning my hand on the canvas. "You're not always around, though. Are you?"

Julian shrugged and lowered his head, "No."

"Head up," I instructed. "And I'm not so sure you're even real."

Julian cracked up, a joyous laugh, as he grabbed his sides and doubled over. The sound of his giggles caused me to chuckle with him. I lowered the brush and watched him compose himself with a deep breath

"Of course I'm real, silly," he said with a squeak. "I'm sitting right here!"

"Sure," I said, turning my attention back to my work. "But next thing I know, I'll be sitting here in the dark all by myself, and Mutt will be whining for you. Just like you disappeared on me this afternoon. The least you could do is warn me before you take off like that."

"What if I can't?" he asked, doe-eyed.

"Just a suggestion." I studied the features of his face.

"Okay," he conceded and then began to squirm in his seat.

"Be still," I reminded him. "Where do you go, anyway?"

Julian straightened on the stool and did his best to keep his torso still, though his feet still swung beneath him.

"I have to go back," he answered.

"Back where? Back home?" I asked, starting my outline.

"No, it's not home," he answered. I peeked at him as he looked off into the room. "Home is where your family is."

"So where's your family then?" I asked. "You said you were with your dad."

"My dad says that he's the only family I need now that my mom is gone," he said, his voice hushed.

My heart sank at the familiar story of abandonment. Julian said before that he didn't know where his mother was, not that she had died. It was obvious that she had left him. I just didn't know how obvious it was to him yet.

"Well, at least you have someone, kid. At least your dad's there for you," I said, running my fingers over the paints on my palette. "That's more than some people ever get."

"Yeah, but I miss my mom," he said. "I miss Red."

"Is Red your Mom's name?" I asked, watching him blink back the tears that filled his eyes.

"No," he said, trying to hide a sniffle. "He's my friend."

"Well," I said with a sigh. "I know what it's like to miss people. You get used to it."

"I guess," he said.

"Promise," I assured.

Julian looked away and wiped at his eyes with the heels of his hands. I was impressed that he had such control over his emotions. At five years old, he was more of a man than some I'd known in prison. It was a sign that his life hadn't been an easy one, but I knew from experience the strength of a child's resilience.

"Where's your home?" he asked, turning back to me, his eyes now dry.

"You're looking at it," I said with a snort, motioning to the room around us.

Julian looked around at the dark studio, at the paintings that hung like motionless memories on the walls. His gaze landed on the one below the stairs.

"Where's your family?" he asked.

I lowered my brush with a sigh. "Again, you're looking at it."

"Don't you have any people that you care about?" Julian asked, turning to face me. His brow furrowed as he bent his head, gauging my reaction.

"That's the difference between me and you, kid," I said, turning back to my palette. "I don't need anyone else."

I located the edge of the peanut butter and mixed in some smooth slimy to make what I thought would be a deep shade of amethyst. Julian's eyes were far off as he contemplated what I'd said. I studied the indentions of his cheekbones and the purplish crescents beneath his eyes, committing him to memory before I turned back to the portrait.

"You don't have any friends?" he asked, meekly.

"I've had many comrades throughout the years," I said, concentrating on my brush strokes. "But I only ever got close to one of them. I guess you could say he was my friend."

"What's his name?" Julian asked, and I peeked at him as I dipped my brush again. His wide eyes watched me intently.

"His name is Logan." I turned back to where my hand held my place. "His portrait is next to my brother's."

"The blonde guy?" Julian asked, turning to look. "He looks nice. Where is he?"

"Up in the mountains somewhere," I said with a shrug. "Living a charmed life with his new wife."

"You're not friends anymore?" he asked, beginning to wiggle again.

"You ask a lot of questions, you know." I lowered the brush and rested my weary arms. "How about we try not talking for a little bit?"

"Okay," Julian said with a sigh.

"And sit still," I commanded, and he sat up straight, watching me as I filled my brush again.

I painted for a few minutes in blessed silence, letting my mind picture the canvas in front of me. Blending red, yellow and white into what I hoped was a flesh tone, I began to fill in my outline and bring Julian's image to life. I was distracted by his soft, honeyed voice as he began to sing from where he perched on the stool.

"*This little light of mine*," he sang. "*I'm going to let it shine*."

"Why do you do that?" I asked, stopping him mid-melody.

"Do what?" he asked.

"Sing that song," I said. "You sing it all the time."

"I learned it in Sunday school," he said with a smile. "We sang it every Sunday. My mom used to say that it's good to sing. It makes you feel happy even when you're scared. My dad says it's annoying."

I laughed, finishing the last details of my work. "I guess it's a little bit of both."

Setting the palette on the floor, I sat back in my chair and stretched my stiff limbs. I motioned to the painting, and Julian got up and came to where I sat.

"How does it look?" I asked.

Julian stared at it, taking in each brush stroke.

"Wow," he said. "It looks even better than the last one. I like the colors."

"I still have to add some detail when the paint dries," I said, my heart warming with the compliment. "I did the outline with a thick base so I can find the lines later."

"My hair's still sticking up," he said with a pout.

"Yes, it is," I said, raising a hand to pat his wildly crowned head. When I touched him, the warmth that spread through my hand and up my arm startled me again. We looked at each other a moment and then laughed at the weirdness of it. Mutt stumbled over from the corner to join the party. I scratched him behind the ear and then dug my phone out from my pocket.

"Take a picture," I said into my phone after pressing the home button. I handed the phone to Julian. "Do you know how to take a photo? Just aim and press the red button on the screen."

"What do you want me to take a picture of?" he asked, taking the phone from my hand.

"Take one of this painting," I instructed. "And of the one I did earlier. If they're as good as you say, I'll need proof."

"Okay," he said, and I heard the camera go off. "Can I take a picture of me and Mutt?"

"I don't know . . ." I said. "If your dad comes looking for you, I'm not sure I want your picture on my phone. That's called hard evidence."

"Please?" he begged, and Mutt whined in unison.

"Fine," I conceded. "But only when you're done taking my pics. Just one, you hear me?"

The camera went off twice more.

"Okay, I'll just take one. I'll take it in front of my painting. Then people can see that my hair really does stick up," he said, calling Mutt into the shot with him.

"Five years old and already knows how to take a selfie," I mumbled, shaking my head.

"Say cheese, Mutt," he said, and the camera went off one more time as I placed the palette and brush in the sink.

"There!" Julian exclaimed proudly. "It looks good. My shirt even matches the . . ."

When Julian stopped mid-sentence, I turned to see him staring far off into the blackness. He looked startled, as if he were hearing something off in the distance that sent him into a panic.

"What's wrong?" I asked.

"I have to go now," he said. "But I don't want to go."

"What do you mean, you have to go?" I asked, stepping closer. "What's going on?"

"Can I stay here with you?" he asked, his lip quivering. "Please?"

"I . . . I don't know how to answer that," I stammered. "Where do you have to go?"

There was no response. The light faded, and with it, Julian's image. Then the world around me returned to black as my phone fell to the floor with a metallic thud.

"Julian!" I called out, but only Mutt's disappointed whine answered back.

"Damn it," I said, walking to where he was just standing. I felt along the floor until I found my phone.

Plopping down into my chair, I sat for a while, my mind full of questions. Mutt wandered over and nudged my hand with his snout. He whined as I petted him.

"I know, boy," I said. "I wish I knew what was going on too."

I reached out to Julian's portrait and ran my fingers gently across its surface. The paints were drying nicely, and I could still feel the thickness of the outline amongst the colors.

"Send email," I said into my phone after the beeps.

"*To whom shall I send it?*" the digital assistant asked.

"Scott Bramble," I answered.

"*What's the subject of your email?*"

With a grin, I leaned back in my chair and let my confusion melt away as my newfound hope filled me with a warm contentment.

"*Mr. Bramble, I've got something new for you.*"

Seven

By the time the art dealer got there, I had dusted, swept and polished the studio as best I could. In my mind the studio shined as in those first months long ago with the exception of the boards that still covered the windows. The door was unlocked when Mr. Bramble entered at noon. I could hear the clicking of his leather Oxfords across the floor below as I listened at the loft door.

My instructions were clear: Come by and look at the paintings. If you like what you see, leave me an email with your offer. I would not meet him face to face, would not subject myself to his shock and stares. My newfound dignity was fragile at best. If he was to reject these newest paintings, let it be because of their unsightliness, not my own.

Mutt grumbled in the corner, disappointed by my refusal to allow him access to our guest. I held my breath, listening as Bramble walked to where my paintings of Julian were displayed in the center of the gallery. His footsteps paused there. I could imagine him studying each brushstroke. After what seemed like an interminable breath, his footsteps retreated. The front door opened and closed, my soul trapped in the finality of that simple act.

Taking a shaky breath, I opened the loft door and stuck my head out far enough to listen for movement below. When I heard nothing, I opened the door. Mutt scrambled out ahead of me. His snout caught Bramble's scent and followed it diligently across the floor. I felt my way to the center of the room and let my mind's eye gaze upon the paintings as Bramble had. Dark fingers of doubt curled around my throat and began to squeeze.

Digging my phone from my pocket, I held it in front of me and willed it to notify me of his incoming email. Minutes passed as I waited for it to ring, my heart quickening in my chest with each passing second.

"What are you doing?" Julian asked from where he sat in the corner of the room, causing me to jump and almost drop my phone.

"Jesus!" I screamed as Mutt scampered over to him. "You have to stop doing that. Did he see you?"

"Did who see me?" he asked with a shrug. "And you shouldn't say that."

"Say what?" I asked, turning my attention from Julian's brightness to pace to the front door. I put my ear to the entrance to see if I could hear Bramble on the other side.

"Use the Lord's name in vain," he said. "It's a sin."

"You learn that in church too?" I asked. In the distance, I heard the sound of an engine turning over.

"Uh, huh," he said, getting to his feet.

I turned to face him. He had on the same clothes. His hair was still a mess.

"Yeah, well, I've committed worse sins than that, kid," I said with a sigh. "What's one more?"

"That's why you should believe," he said, skipping over to me. "Believing gets rid of people's sins."

"Well, aren't we preachy this afternoon?" I spat, my nerves more on edge with every minute that passed without an email. "If there is one thing you learn from me, Julian, let it be that some people are just too far gone to be saved. Don't waste your time trying."

Julian looked up at me, his amber eyes holding me captive as he grabbed onto my free hand. This time neither of us flinched at the electric heat of his touch.

"No one is ever too far gone," he said, almost a whisper. "Some people just get so lost in the dark that they can't see the truth."

"The truth?" I asked.

"That there's always someone with you in the dark, handing you the light of the world," he said. "All you have to do is take it."

I could only stare at Julian, this young child who clasped my hand in the midst of my darkness. Something stirred inside me at his words, words too wise for his years. I thought back to Logan's testimony of forgiveness and grace. I thought about the way he described his angel as a lifeline out of the darkness of his past mistakes.

For a moment my heart warmed as it had then, with a hope of a different future. Maybe Julian wasn't sent to torment me. Perhaps he was my lifeline. Then I remembered the terror that had filled his eyes before he vanished last. My legs ached as I struggled to kneel down beside him and look into his innocent eyes.

"Julian," I said, calmly. "Where did you go last night? Why were you scared to leave?"

"I had to go back." Julian's eyes grew dark as he shrugged. "I don't want to go there anymore. I like it here with you."

"Where is back? Back home? Back to your room?" I asked, trying to keep my voice calm.

"I told you," he said, his eyes filling with tears. "It's not home. Home is where your family is."

"Then where . . . ?" I began to ask when I was interrupted by a chime from my phone. Then all other thoughts vanished. I had a new email.

Letting go of Julian's hand, I clutched my phone in front of me. My heart raced in my chest.

"This is it," I said.

"This is what?" Julian asked, clueless to the magnitude of the moment.

"I'm about to find out if those paintings are my new beginning." I breathed.

"What are you waiting for, then?" he asked with sudden excitement. "Check your phone!"

I took a deep breath and pressed down the home button.

"Check new email," I said into the receiver after the beeps.

"You have one new email," the digital voice complied.

"Read it," I commanded.

"From Scott Bramble. Sent at 12:27 p.m..," it read:

"Dear Mr. Roberts,

I came by to see your newest portraits, and I must say that they are quite good. They may be your best work to date. You say you painted these recently? In your condition? From what you described about the accident . . . that is quite extraordinary.

I would like to set up a show in your gallery six months from now. Have more new pieces ready to sell. If I'm right about this, and I usually am, you're going to be a sensation. Everyone is going to want a painting from the mysterious, blind impressionist. Your work is simply brilliant. I'll have a carrier come by for those first two. I have a buyer in mind. And Blake, whoever that boy is that's been a muse for you, keep him around.

Sincerely, Scott"

My hand shook as I pressed the home button again. I was afraid to breathe, afraid to move, lest this new joy come crashing down, too. As Julian leaned over, his brightness jarred me from my disbelief.

"You did it," he said with a smile.

I looked at him, at his smiling cherub face, and laughed. Bramble had called Julian my muse, but I suddenly realized he was much more than that. Julian was my angel.

With a cry, I grabbed him up into my arms, his heat filling my heart and making it beat anew. He laughed and hugged me around the neck as I twirled him around. Mutt barked and jumped at my heels, joining in our excitement.

"I have to paint more!" I exclaimed when my breath was spent and my limbs weakened.

"I'll get the stool!" Julian exclaimed as I set him down. He ran for the closet, and I stood watching, catching my breath as he disappeared behind its door.

"I'll need a new canvas and that box of paints in the corner," I instructed. "I know what colors those are."

When Julian didn't answer, I went to help. Feeling for the closet door, I expected to see Julian's light on the other side, but the closet was just as dark as the rest of my world. I searched the room for his luminance, but the light was gone. My toe hit something hard that scraped across the floor with a wooden screech. When I bent down, my fingers found the stool tipped over on its side.

I righted it and closed the closet door with a sigh. Mutt licked my hand and rubbed his head against my side, joining my disappointment.

"He's gone again, boy," I said. Mutt already knew.

Dejected, I set my chair in the corner and sat, suddenly weary. As much as I wanted to paint, as happy as I was to be given a second chance, none of it made sense without Julian. So I awaited his return, believing that he would. He always did.

The warmth in my heart grew each time his light appeared and we were together again. Julian had become the only part of my existence that I looked forward to, the only thing that mattered. Our time together gave me hope and purpose . . . something I thought the darkness had stolen from me.

Julian did return, as often as he disappeared. Our time together was spent laughing and discovering the feel of new colors. For months I painted Julian's likeness while he giggled on the stool before me. Each time he appeared to me, his clothes were a little dirtier, his hair more unkempt. There were times when he left me with a look of fear in his eyes, and I would pace the studio until he returned.

He spoke little about where he went when he left me though I asked him about it many times. He seemed to want to forget the other side of his reality, and who was I to argue with that? So I made it a point to forget, too.

When he was with me all, was right in the world until the next time he vanished, never with any warning at all. Each time a piece of my heart vanished with him.

Winter passed, and the earth warmed with the appearance of spring. Mr. Bramble came by on occasion to sell a painting or two from the new collection. My work had caused a stir in the art community. Collectors from across the globe were requesting my paintings of Julian. They sold as quickly as I could paint them. As they did, Bramble would send out my mortgage payment as instructed and leave the rest of the money in an envelope outside my loft door. I let it accumulate in a box beneath my bed.

The nightmares subsided. I felt alive again. Outside of the studio, life buzzed anew as tourists made their pilgrimages to downtown Wilmington's Riverwalk and shops. The boats from the river cruises, filled with laughter and loud conversations, passed by every hour. The wail of a trumpet sounded in the distance as a street performer serenaded a growing crowd. Inside the studio, I painted Julian for the hundredth time. The sunlight, which streamed in through the cracks in the boards, warmed my back.

"When are you going to take down the boards?" Julian asked as he wiggled on the stool.

"Not for a couple of more months," I said, finishing the detail of Julian's dirty cheek with a velvety chocolate brown.

"But it's so dark in here and so sunny out there," he said, pointing to the windows. "Mutt likes the sun. He's lying in a ray of it right now."

"Yeah, well, the show is not until June," I said. "And there's nothing wrong with the dark. I'm used to it. You should be used to it too by now after all the time you've spent here."

"You know, eventually you're going to have to let the light in," Julian said with a shrug. "You'd be happy then."

"What makes you think I'm not happy?" I asked.

"Are you?" he asked.

"Are YOU?" I threw back.

"When I'm with you and Mutt, I'm happy . . . or with Mom and Red." Julian's eyes looked off past where I sat with my palette. The longing in them struck a nerve too familiar. He missed his mother.

"You're not happy with your dad?" I asked, trying for the millionth time to pry for answers.

Julian only shrugged and looked at his worn-out sneakers. I let out a breath and went back to painting.

"What's the point of letting the light in anyway?" I asked, adding a smudge of dirt-colored paint below the cheek line. "I can't see it."

"But you can see me," Julian said, looking up at me with a smile.

"Yes, I can see you," I answered automatically.

Those words had become our mantra. *I can see you.* Though the mystery of why I could see him was never answered, it no longer seemed to matter to either of us. We both understood that it was a gift somehow, and we didn't dare to question it.

"Maybe you can just take down some of the boards," Julian persisted.

"It's not time yet," I said, finishing my detailing. "The studio will be open all summer long. Until then, you'll just have to. . ."

"Wait . . ." Julian said, panic in his eyes. "It's almost summertime?"

"Almost. Memorial Day is a little over a month away," I said, lowering my brush. "Why?"

Julian hopped down from the stool and paced away to his corner.

"My dad says that we are leaving in the summertime," he said, wringing his hands.

"What do you mean, leaving? Where?" I asked, my mind refusing to register the information. "You can't leave now."

"I don't want to go," he said, turning to look at me. His bottom lip quivered, and his eyes filled with tears.

"I don't understand, kid," I said, setting the palette on the floor. "I still don't know where you come and go from. There's so much about you I don't understand. How can you be leaving?"

"My dad says that summertime is when it's time to go home. He says we'll be together forever in our new home. He says things will be better, but I don't want to go. Don't make me go, Blake." As a tear escaped onto his cheek, he ran into my arms.

Wearily, I held him close as his warmth engulfed us both. His little body shook against me as my heart fractured. I hadn't thought about our time together coming to an end. Until then, it hadn't entered my mind as a possibility. I'd accepted the gift of his friendship without knowing the conditions. As Julian sobbed into my shoulder, anger sizzled from beneath the shattered pieces of my heart. How cruel to not know my time with him was borrowed.

"I don't know what I can do," I whispered. "What can I do? Why didn't you tell me you were leaving? Why didn't you tell me?"

Before he could answer, his light dimmed like the last rays of the afternoon sun. The warmth in my arms faded, and Julian was gone again.

With a cry, I stood and raged against the darkness around me. With one swipe, I toppled my latest painting to the floor. Mutt was at my side instantly. He licked my hand, but I shoved him away. With a squeal, he retreated into the corner and whimpered. I didn't care. My mind was frantic as my body trembled with anger. *I should have known*, I thought. *I should have known. Hope would always be lost on me.*

Stumbling toward the stairs, I stomped up to my loft and plopped down at the table. I dug my phone from my pocket and did the only thing I could think to do. It had been months since I had written an email like this, but it was the only thing that helped. The only thing that eased the sting of misery and squashed the pain of lost hope. Logan's hope.

You were wrong about me, Logan. Whatever hope is out there for me is fleeting. You and your words haunt me more than the child that was sent to me. A lifeline, that's what you called your visiting spirit, your Guardian, and that's what Julian has become. What a sick joke to take him from me just as my life is starting over. He will leave me, just like she left me. Just like you left me.

The hope in me will die again.

Damn you and your words for sparking it in me again and again. There is no real hope for me . . .

Rage overwhelmed me. I threw the phone across the room and buried my face in my hands. If my eyes weren't covered with the scars of my past, I would have wept. Instead, I let the storm of emotion rage over me as I questioned everything. Why send me a lifeline to give me this new start, only to yank him away from me before it even really began?

Sure, I'd had enough practice now to paint almost anything without the use of my eyes, but Julian was my muse. I needed him. He was my inspiration. Painting had forged our relationship, whatever it was. Without him, it felt pointless. It was losing the joy of my art, the one thing that held my past at bay, a second time. Suddenly, I realized it was more than that, more than losing my muse. Losing Julian would be like losing my family all over again.

With that thought, I wandered over to my bed and rested my weakened muscles atop its downy surface. The anguish and familiar pain closed in around me. I barely noticed Mutt jump up onto the bed and cuddle at my side. His warmth couldn't penetrate the darkness that engulfed me, but I clung to it anyway. When what seemed like hours had passed, I let the darkness take me to that all too familiar place of fitful sleep. For the first time in months, the dreams came riding in on a wave of exhaustion and anguish. I let them come, let myself see for the billionth time where my life had gone so terribly wrong.

"Lower the gun," my father said in my dream, taking a step toward my mother, his hands raised in surrender. Sweat beaded his brow with crystalline drops.

"You're not going to hurt us anymore," she proclaimed, her voice wavering as he stepped even closer.

Her eyes glistened, unable to hold back the tears that gathered. I lay on the floor panting for breath, watching in frozen horror as my father eased his way closer to where my mother stood. He held his hand out to her, the jagged edges of his face softening in false warmth.

My mother shook like a weakened branch in an autumn breeze as he continued to close the distance between them. I waited, holding my breath, to see if she would back down, praying that she wouldn't. My brother clung to her apron. He tore his eyes away from my father's advance long enough to see the fear in mine. Then he tightened his grip with a squeal, his knuckles as white as the fabric he clutched.

"You don't want to do this, Louise," my father said, his voice gentle and deceiving. "Give me the gun."

Tears streamed down my mother's face, leaving streaks of black mascara in their wake. My father stepped closer, and she readjusted her aim, causing him to freeze mid-step. The duration of a death sentence passed as they stood glaring at one another.

I watched with sickening dread as my father finally took another step closer. I watched my mother's face tighten and then contort into a mask of horrid resignation. She let the gun fall to the floor in front of her. My father watched it drop and then looked back up at her, a snarl curving his upper lip. A sob ripped from my mother's throat as she gave in to bitter hopelessness.

"Momma!" my brother cried as my father leapt at her, snatching her copper hair in his fingers.

She pushed my brother aside as my father's eyes turned black as pitch and the rage enveloped him again. With a growl, he thrust her into their bedroom. My brother ran to me. I tucked his small frame beneath my arm.

For the rest of the night, we lay huddled under my bed, listening to the sounds of my mother's head as it hit the dividing wall over and over again. When all was quiet, we dared not move for fear of drawing attention to ourselves. We sat and waited, only our shaky breaths breaking the silence.

It wasn't until the first light of morning fought its way between the slats of the blinds that we heard my father's snore and knew that he was asleep. Unfolding ourselves from each other's arms, we crawled out from under the bed.

I crept down the hall first, my brother clasping my hand behind. We tip-toed toward our parents' room to see if our mother was still alive. Before we got a foot from my room, their bedroom door opened. We retreated soundlessly to the corner. My mother staggered out, her face bruised and raw.

At first we were elated. She was alive. Now she finally understood why we had to leave. Surely she would take us away from our father's rage.

Then we saw the suitcase in her hand and the regret on her swollen face. She turned to where we huddled together in the hall.

"I'm sorry" was all she said before she turned and grabbed the car keys from the table.

Then she walked out the front door.

"Do you wish to send all one hundred and twenty-two drafts to Logan Foster?"

The digital voice roused me with a start. I swept my hand across the bed in search of my phone as my brain scrambled back to reality.

"*Messages sent,*" the voice said, causing me to shoot up in the bed as the words' significance struck me.

I looked across the room, my heart racing in my chest. Julian sat on the floor by the loft door looking at something in his hands. Though I couldn't see it, I knew he had my phone.

"What did you do?" I screamed, stumbling to my feet. "What did you do?"

Julian flinched and looked up at me with his huge, innocent eyes.

"You're going to need a friend when I'm gone," he said, his voice quivering. "You said Logan was your friend."

White hot rage engrossed me. *Logan couldn't see those emails. He couldn't see!* I lunged for my phone, knocking Julian into the wall behind him as I snatched it from his hands. When he recovered, he hugged his knees to his chest and sobbed. Tears flowed from his eyes as my shaking fingers sought out the home button.

"Drafts," I yelled into the receiver, frantic.

"*You have zero drafts. Would you like to start a new email?*" my phone answered.

With a cry, I turned back to Julian who cowered in the corner.

"I told you to never come up here!" I yelled. "You had no right to send those emails!"

"I . . . I'm sorry," he cried.

"You're sorry?" I continued, towering over his shaking body. "Do you know what you've done to me?"

"I was just trying to help," he said. His whole body trembled as he bawled.

"I told you . . . I don't need your help, you little vulture!" I shouted. "I don't need anyone! Just leave me alone! You were going to leave me anyway, just like they all have. Just go now. Just go!"

Julian looked up at me one last time, pleading and sorrow in his wet eyes as his light began to fade. Seconds later I was standing in the corner of an empty, black room seething into the darkness.

"Are you happy now?" I screamed at the ceiling to a God who had turned His face from me. "You've taken everything from me once again!"

I struggled to breathe normally. My whole body quaked with the force of my despair. I collapsed, a pitiful heap, to the floor. *You're just like your father,* my mind whispered. Mutt's footsteps tinkered across the hardwood to where I lay. He plopped down on the floor beside me, his howls rising in pitch to match my own despairing cries.

Eight

I painted in only black and grey those last weeks before the show. The colors of regret and sorrow, those were the only colors my mind's eye could see now. For the second time in my life, the light had gone out.

Julian did not return, though I painted him day after day. I painted him more so into the night, a vain attempt to stave off the dreams that always came anyway. The first few days after I sent him away, I looked to the corner often, hoping to see Julian's brilliance there. There was only ever darkness.

The rage within me burned hotter than ever before, though I was no longer mad at Julian. I never really was, I realized with renewed self-loathing. I let the anguish of my past abandonment ruin what time we had left. *Why didn't I find a way for him to stay? Why didn't I fight to find the truth behind the fear in his eyes?*

The only way to deal with the questions was to realize the truth. Wherever Julian was, he was better off without me. He was safer away from me, where my darkness could not blot out his shining light. I found some solace in that.

Each time my phone notified me of an incoming email, I flinched. I checked it with trembling fingers, waiting to hear Logan's response to the rantings he was never meant to read. It was only ever Scott Bramble, informing me that he'd sold yet another of my paintings. I'd breathe, relieved only that Logan remained estranged and silent. Perhaps he had not received those emails, and that was for the best. He couldn't know me like this. No one could, ever again.

That is why I was adamant about not appearing at my own show, much to the dismay of Mr. Bramble. There was no way I could face a room full of people and pretend not to be the monster I'd become. In the end, Bramble respected my wishes to remain obscure. He said it would add a sense of mystery to my work. I had become an enigma.

The night of the show, I pressed an ear to my loft door and listened with feeble interest while Mutt grumbled in the corner. He didn't whine to be let down-stairs to greet our guests. He didn't even get up from his bed, only moped about as he had for weeks. He missed Julian too.

The gallery below teemed with the murmurs and movements of an enthusiastic crowd. The turnout was astonishing, though the joy of that fact was lost to me. Patrons lingered for hours, spurred on by the mystery of my muse and the champagne that fizzed in their clinking glasses. They wanted to know the story behind the boy in my portraits. I heard their questions from where I stood, wondering the same.

Bramble spun their curiosity into sales, marking the differences in each painting of the mysterious child. They also wanted to know more about me, about the elusive blind artist with an incredible ability. Some dared to climb a few steps toward my loft before being redirected by Bramble. I checked to make sure the lock was secured.

It was well past midnight when the last of the massive crowd shuffled out the door. Mr. Bramble's footsteps alone traversed the floor below as he tidied up. When he started up the steps, I backed away from the door. He knocked lightly and cleared his throat.

"You were a sensation," he said, his voice jubilant, "just as I said you would be. We nearly sold out. Only your latest portraits remain unsold. Perhaps use some color next time?"

Bramble waited at the door. I imagined his ear pressed against it, awaiting my response. When there was none, he cleared his throat again.

"I'll bring the money by in the next day or two when I come to collect the portraits. Even after my cut, you'll have a considerable sum," he finally said with a sigh. "You did it, Blake. You've made it. Art International is doing a piece on your work. The local newspaper ran an article just last week. This is only the beginning."

With that he made his way down the stairs. I listened to him walk out the front door as I stood stunned in the middle of my room. I'd made it, he'd said. I was the newest breakthrough artist, on my way to becoming famous. There was more money coming in these days than I knew what to do with. The box beneath my bed was nearly full of cash. My lifelong dream was coming true, but I was empty of joy. I felt nothing but remorse, saw nothing but darkness. None of it mattered without Julian.

Dejected, I opened the loft door to the lingering smell of fancy hors d'oeuvres and expensive perfumes. Mutt trotted along beside me as I descended the stairs and immediately turned to the corner. Only darkness lay before me. I felt like a ghost among the remnants of the living. My fingers slid along the displays in the center of the room. I imagined the scene only hours ago. The local art community had admired, studied and ultimately approved of what I'd created for months with Julian by my side. It felt like a farce, like a moment borrowed in time from someone else's life.

I doubted anything in my future would compare to those months painting with Julian. I knew that I should be thankful for the time I had with him, for his help in discovering a way to paint again. But that was impossible. Julian represented hope, and I could not be thankful for what I hated.

Across the room, Mutt chomped and slobbered. His back feet hopped between bites as his front paws floundered across a table.

"I see you've found the leftover food," I said. "Help yourself."

Mutt snorted in my direction and then went back to devouring whatever was left on the table. It smelled like caviar and soft cheeses. Running my hands along my grayscale reproductions of Julian's dirty face, I made my way to where Mutt pawed the table for remnants.

"Is there any champagne left?" I asked, feeling along the table until my fingers connected with polished crystal.

I lifted the glass to my lips and let the sparkling fluid run down my throat. Then I felt along the table until I located the bottle. Its heft told me that it was mostly full. Satisfied, I grabbed it and turned to go back upstairs.

"You know you're supposed to eat that slowly. You're supposed to savor it," I informed Mutt as I passed. "It's expensive stuff."

He answered with a belch. Then his paws scrambled off the table and onto the floor. He followed me up to the loft where he settled, content, into his bed in the corner. I sat at my table, committed to a night of blatant intoxication as I swigged from the bottle. Perhaps if I drank myself into a stupor, I could escape the dreams for just one night. Maybe if I drank enough, I could forget that I'd lost Julian.

I'd only finished a quarter of the bottle when the front door opened downstairs and deliberate footsteps sounded on the gallery floor. I'd forgotten to lock up.

"Julian?" I whispered, hurrying to the loft door. I cracked it, searching the darkness beyond for his light, but saw nothing. Shutting the door again, I rushed to lock it as footsteps took to the stairs. They rushed up them with no concern for noise or the hour. I backed away from the door as whoever it was banged against the other side.

"I know he's in there!" a female voice yelled, her voice frantic. "Open the door!"

My mind raced. Who was this woman, and what did she want? I didn't dare move, afraid that the creaking floorboards would give me away, but Mutt barked and charged for the door, ready to protect his territory and me. The voice on the other end was not deterred by his ferocious gnashing.

"I know you have him!" she yelled, still pounding. "I want my son!"

Her son? I thought of Julian, about all that he'd said about his mother. It couldn't be him she was looking for. It made no sense. This couldn't be his mother. She had abandoned him. She'd left him with not so much as a goodbye. It was obvious when I put together everything he'd said about her. Who, then, was this woman looking for?

"Open the door!" she shouted above Mutt's growls. Her pounding grew more intense.

I heard the creaking of the doorframe as it gave way little by little with each of her thrusts and Mutt's pounces. Flailing, I reached for Mutt's collar and pulled him away from the door. I silently bade him to back off, and he stepped aside with a defeated whine. The pounding ceased, and I knew the woman was listening. My heart pounded in my ears. I held my breath.

"I know you're in there," she said. "I know you have my son."

I didn't dare move as I held out a hand for Mutt to stand down. He took to a low growl beside me. The pounding started again, this time harder, more desperate than before.

"I'm not leaving until I have my son!" she shouted, and the intensity of her voice told me she was serious.

With each pound, I heard the door frame groan and splinter. She was going to break down the antiquated door. I raced to the closet and threw on a hooded sweat shirt and searched the table for my shades. Securing the hood over as much of my face as possible and adjusting the shades to hide my scarred eyes, I went to the door.

"Stop pounding before you break my door!" I yelled after taking a deep breath. "I'm opening it."

When the pounding stopped, I turned the lock on the door and cracked it open. She gasped on the other side at the sight of me. I expected as much and immediately resented her for it. The heat from her body seeped in through the crack. She smelled of sweat and lilac.

"I don't know who you think you are . . ." I began.

"I know you have my son in there," she said. Her calm tone was forced.

"I don't know what you're talking about," I said, my anger flaring. "There is no one here but me and my dog. This is a private residence. You need to leave."

"I'm not leaving without my son," she yelled and pushed against the door.

"There's no one here!" I yelled back, pushing against her frantic shoves.

"Julian!" she screamed. "Julian!"

The sound of his name hit me with the force greater than her shoves against the door. I staggered back, my head spinning. She pushed into the room, clawing her way across the door frame. Mutt charged forward and jumped at her, his jaws snapping. She backed off, but only for a moment, holding her ground just inside the door. I felt Mutt suddenly stiffen beside me as his snout caught her scent. He backed down, his tail wagging against my leg.

"I don't know where your son is," I protested, the truth tearing at me anew as I muscled her back.

"Mommy's here, Julian," she screamed again as Mutt whined and now took to scratching at the door. "I'm here!"

"I don't have your son," I yelled, my muscles weakening against the force of her. I panted for breath as I stood my ground. Below, the front door opened slowly and we both froze.

"It's just me. I left the receipt book . . ." Mr. Bramble yelled, his footsteps entering the gallery. He froze when he passed the stairs. "What's going on?"

"This man has my son," she said, turning toward Bramble but not letting go of her position.

"What in the world makes you think that?" he asked, walking to the foot of the stairs.

"His paintings," she said, her voice rising in pitch. "That's my son. He's been painting him."

"Oh," Mr. Bramble said. "I see what's going on. You claim to be the mother and suddenly you have a claim on the royalties. Is that it?"

"No!" she screamed, turning back to the door and shoving again. I couldn't hold her back much longer. "Julian!"

The woman shoved her head inside the door, I could feel her breath on my cheek.

"That's his painting!" she cried. "I know he painted that. Where is he? Where are you hiding him?"

My mind searched the room for what she'd seen. It dawned on me that Julian's cardinal painting still hung beside mine on the refrigerator door. They were in her direct line of sight from the entryway.

"That's Red!" she screamed, her voice frantic. "That's Red!"

"Ma'am, I am calling the police if you do not leave this instant!" Mr. Bramble said firmly from the bottom of the stairs.

The woman groaned and cried out in defeat. Her weight went limp against the door.

"I know he was here," she said to me. I felt the wetness of her tears against my arm. "You know where my boy is."

"This instant!" Bramble repeated, a shout now.

The woman slinked away from the door with a sob, and I shoved it closed. Securing the lock, I put my back to the door and slid to the floor, gasping for breath. Mutt whimpered and jumped at the door, but I patted his side and calmed him. He whined and sat beside me, scratching at the door. The woman's footsteps retreated slowly down the stairs. I heard the front door open and slam closed.

"Sorry about that. I know you don't want to be seen. I get it. She won't bother you anymore, Blake." he yelled up to me. "These things happen. She's just looking to exploit you for some money, I'm sure."

When I didn't answer, he continued.

"Blake, I've never asked you about the boy in your paintings. It's none of my business. But people are asking, and more people like her will claim to know him if you don't break your silence. Think about it," he said with a sigh. "Make sure you lock up behind me."

The front door opened and closed again, and then all was silent. Taking a moment to catch my breath, I rose onto my shaking legs and opened the loft door. I stumbled down the stairs, clinging to the railing.

Mutt charged ahead with his nose to the air in search of the woman. He sniffed along the front door but then whined and plopped down on his haunches when her scent ended there. At the bottom of the stairs, I turned to the corner as I always did, but was met again by only darkness. I locked the front door, feeling exposed by the unshielded windows. How I longed for the boards to be put back into place so I could once again shut myself off from the world.

It took me a while to climb the stairs again. My body was as heavy as my thoughts. As I called for Mutt at the door, my mind reeled with the possibilities. Bramble thought the woman was looking to make an easy dollar, to exploit my paintings by claiming to be my muse's mother, but she had called Julian by name. I searched my memory for an instance when I might have let Julian's name slip in one of my emails to Bramble, but I could recall none. There was no way he could have known, and therefore there was no way the public could have found out.

Walking to the refrigerator, I ran my fingers across Julian's painting, conjuring the image of his favorite bird into my mind's eye. I remembered how happy he'd been as his fingers spread the slimy red across the page, and I recalled my joy as he showed me how to feel colors.

"Red," I whispered, repeating what the woman had called the painting. *He's my friend*, Julian once said about Red. The woman knew what that meant.

I took the painting with me to the table and collapsed into my chair. Removing my shades, I clutched the paper close and was lost to my dark thoughts until morning.

Nine

I dozed fitfully in my chair until I was roused by the squawking seagulls and excited tourists outside. Mutt whined at the door to be let out for his morning romp. Unfolding myself from the table, I fixed my hood over my head and donned my shades. Then I floundered for the loft door. Mutt ran down the steps, and I followed, my legs stiff. I opened the door for Mutt and began to shut it when it pushed back against his body.

"Go on, boy," I said, trying to nudge him the rest of the way through. Then I heard his tongue whip out of his mouth with fevered excitement as he licked and whined at something just outside the door.

Again, my heart leapt at the possibility of being reunited with Julian. I pushed Mutt aside to investigate. Julian's light was nowhere to be found, but I stumbled against a mass of warmth on the sidewalk. I heard a slight moan as the soft scent of lilac met my nostrils.

The woman from the night before was lying unconscious just outside the door of the studio. Kneeling, I graced her frame with my fingertips, careful not to rouse her. As my fingers ran along denim and the soft cotton of her T-shirt, her image began to take shape in my mind. It surprised me how small she was in stature compared to what I'd witnessed of her strength outside my loft door.

I brushed my hand lightly over her expanse of wavy hair and saw in my mind her rounded nose and high cheekbones. There were fresh tears drying across each one. She hadn't been asleep long.

My fingertips found her arms and the stuffed animal that she cradled between them. I felt along the plush angles and found it to have a small beak. The woman was hugging a toy bird to her chest. I didn't need to see it to know that it was a cardinal. I was willing to bet that its name was Red.

With a sigh, I tried to figure out what I should do. Bramble thought the woman was looking for a quick buck, but I knew that wasn't the truth. I didn't know how or why, but this woman and I were both looking for the same thing. In our own ways, we were each searching for Julian.

"Miss," I said, shaking her gently to try and wake her. As much as I dreaded her reaction to my deformities in the daylight, she had answers to questions that had burned in me since the first time I laid eyes on Julian. When she didn't stir, I wondered how long she had been outside my door. The morning was brisk, the sun having not yet risen to where it could warm the ground below. The woman shivered with each gust of salty air coming off the river.

Taking a deep breath, I bent and lifted her into my arms. Mutt whimpered at my side and followed us into the studio where I laid her in the corner where Julian's absence seemed to darken the room the most. Then out of breath, I traversed the steps to retrieve a pillow and blanket from the loft. The woman stirred as I lifted her head to place the pillow beneath it, but she did not wake. Mutt paced the floor beside her before gently laying his body against hers as she mumbled in her sleep.

"Bring him back," she said, her anguish transcending consciousness.

With a whine, Mutt rested his head on the floor beside her, and I petted his ear and shushed him. We would get to the bottom of this, I promised him. This time I was determined to fight to find the truth behind the fear we all seemed to share.

Hours later, I heard the woman stir from where I sat in front of my easel. Her breathing quickened as I finished spreading the thick grey across the canvas, and I knew that she was conscious.

"No need to be alarmed," I said without turning. "You were asleep outside my door. I brought you in out of the cold."

There was a rustling as she sat up. Mutt jumped to his feet, his tongue lapping. His tail whipped through the air. I bade him to sit.

"Your dog is . . . friendly," she said. Her voice was hoarse but soft, disarmed perhaps by a wriggling Mutt who whined for her attention. "Is he yours? I feel like I've seen him somewhere before."

"He's mine, yes," I said. "I think you remind him of someone, too."

"Julian. You know where my son is," she said. It was more of a plea than a statement of truth.

With a sigh, I set down the palette and turned. I heard her breath catch in her throat, and I forced down the bile of resentment at her reaction to my appearance.

"I have no idea where your son is," I said, adjusting the shades over my eyes.

I heard her stand. In the silence of that tense moment, I could hear the quickening of her heartbeat, and I knew that she did not believe me. I imagined her searching the room for where I might have hidden her child. She took a step toward the stairs and then paused.

"You're free to search the loft upstairs. Look anywhere you want," I said, straining to keep the sternness from my voice. "You'll see that I don't have your son."

I listened as she took the stairs and heard her footsteps overhead as she traversed the loft. Mutt followed her, his nose to the floorboards also searching. More than anything I wished they would find Julian huddled in a corner, though it would mean trouble for me. I would be sent back to Central for child abduction for sure. None of that mattered at all.

When the woman walked back down, she paused at the foot of the stairs. I could feel her eyes burn into me.

"I told you he wasn't here," I said.

"You did something to him," she said, her voice shaking. "He was here, wasn't he? I know he painted this!"

I heard the crinkle of paper within her grasp and knew that she had Julian's painting in her hands.

"Yes and no," I said, getting impatient. "Look, we both have a lot of questions. Why don't you have a seat, and we can try to figure this whole thing out."

"Not until you take off those shades and that hood. I'm beginning to feel like I'm in a Victor Hugo novel," she ordered.

My heart began to pound at the thought of exposing my scarred flesh to this stranger.

"You don't want me to do that," I assured. "Quasimodo has nothing on me."

She held her ground. "I'd feel better."

"Trust me, you won't," I said, shaking my head.

"Then I'm calling the police," she threatened.

I chuckled, patting Mutt's head as he came to sit beside me. "You won't do that."

"What makes you think that?"

"Because you would have done it last night," I said. "Instead, you ran out of here when my associate threatened to call them. You don't want the police here anymore than I do."

With a huff she shifted her position on the bottom step, and I knew I was right.

"I'm not talking to you until you take off the shades," she said.

"I told you . . ." I snapped and then caught myself and took a deep breath. "It's not going to happen."

"I want to look you in the eyes while you tell me that you don't know where my son is," she said, her voice firm.

Rage bubbled up from my core, and I forced it back down with a cough. I reached my trembling fingers to my shades, a snarl curling my upper lip.

"You'll find that hard to do," I said, removing the shades from my scarred-over eyes.

Utterly exposed, I felt raw and vulnerable to this woman's perception. I awaited a gasp of horror to escape her throat, imagined her eyes growing wide in disgust. Instead she took a breath, exhaling slowly.

"So you really are blind," she whispered.

"Was there a doubt?" I asked, replacing my shades.

"Yes," she confessed. I heard her sit at the bottom of the stairs. "When I read about you in the paper, when I saw my son's face in your portraits, I thought the whole blind artist thing was a publicity stunt."

"And now?" I asked.

"Now I don't know what to think," she said. I could hear the helplessness in her voice. "How long have you been . . . this way?"

"It's been almost two years," I said. *Had it only been that long?*

"Did you see us? I mean, before you got like this. Did you see me with my son somewhere? Have you been following us?" she asked, no doubt trying to figure out how I'd been able to paint Julian's likeness.

"No," I answered.

"Then you can see through touch, right? You touched his face, and that's how you were able to paint all of these portraits," she reasoned.

"That's not how . . ." I began, but she cut me off.

"I know he was here. I know he painted this." The painting crinkled again as she took in a shallow breath. "He loves birds. Cardinals are . . ."

"His favorite," I finished for her. "I know."

She gasped, and then there was silence. I could no longer doubt that this woman was in fact Julian's mother. The only question left was what to do about it. Before I could think of what to say, Mutt rose and walked to the corner of the room. He paused and then walked back to me. He dropped the plush toy into my lap with a sad whine. I patted him on his head, reassuring him.

"Julian named this guy Red, didn't he?" I asked, holding up the stuffed animal.

"How could you know that?" she asked, her voice breaking with a sob as she rushed to snatch the toy away from me. "Please, just tell me that he was here, that you know where Julian is."

The sincerity and pain in her voice pulled at my sympathy, but I wasn't ready to tell her of my strange relationship with the child she'd so easily abandoned. I squared my shoulders, crossing my arms across my chest.

"First explain to me how a mother walks away from her child?" I spat. It was a question I had asked myself ever since my own mother walked out our front door. "He misses you. All he wanted was to go home. How could you leave him like that?"

The woman let out a cry that was strangled by her sobs.

"So you have seen him!" she cried, walking to me. "He thinks I left him? Did he say that? Did he say I left him?"

"He didn't have to," I said, no longer trying to keep the disgust from my voice. "It was obvious."

"It's a lie," she said, barely louder than a whisper. "He's lying to him."

"Who is?" I asked.

"My ex-husband," she said. "His father."

"Ha!" I spat back, standing to meet her face. "His father is the only one taking care of the kid."

The woman gasped again. I could feel her fear, a wave of tension and pure terror, at my mention of Julian's father.

"You know him?" she asked, stepping away. "Are you friends with Stephan?'

"With who?" I asked.

"Julian's father," she said, her voice full of contempt. "You obviously know him. Is that why he brought Julian here?"

"No," I said. "I don't know him. I only know what Julian told me. He said that you were gone and that his father told him that he was the only family he needed now."

"My God," she cried, her knees falling to the hardwood floor. I listened to her weep into her hands. The bitterness in my heart softened at the sound of her anguished cries. They echoed the cries of my own heart.

"You don't understand," she said. "I would never leave my baby. He was taken from me."

Though my legs ached with the effort, I crouched down in front of where her tears hit the oak slats. The sun streamed in through the window like a spotlight upon me. I felt its fleeting warmth through my hood. Again I wished the boards were still up, though I knew it was too late to lock the world out.

I hadn't realized it until that moment, but somehow Julian had become my world. My art and the things I thought were important now lingered in the shadows of the light he once cast. The light of the world had found me in my darkest days, I now realized with stinging remorse, and I had pushed it away. Now this woman was here, her heart burdened with the same crushing loss.

"What is your name?" I asked when her cries faded into an anguished moan. I could feel her eyes on my face and the wetness of her tears as they rolled to the floor. Her breathing slowed.

"Anna," she said. "My name is Anna."

"Anna," I repeated. "Tell me what happened. Tell me everything. Why can't you call the cops?"

"Are you going to tell me how you know my son?" she asked.

The desperation in her voice crushed any fear I had of telling her the truth. I would tell her exactly how it was that I came to know her son. Maybe, just maybe, she would believe me.

"I'll tell you all that I know," I agreed.

"When did you last see him?" she asked.

I sat back on my heels with a sigh. "It's been a little more than a month."

"A month?" she shrieked. "He could be anywhere by now. Why should I tell you anything?"

"Because I want him to be safe just as much as you do," I admitted, bowing my head. "He matters to me."

Anna was silent for a moment. I imagined her eyes looking me over, trying to decide whether or not to trust me. Finally, she took a deep breath and composed herself. I heard her swipe at the tears on her cheeks just as Julian had.

Though Anna's tears flowed more freely than his, I sensed that she possessed that same commanding strength. The fact that her emotions raged like the river outside spoke not of her inability to contain them, but rather to her weariness to continue trying. Mutt left my side to sit beside Anna. I heard his happy pants as she welcomed his company.

"My ex-husband is not what he seems to people who don't know him like Julian and I do."

"What do you mean?"

"When he wants to be, Stephan is charming and outgoing. He's a private defense attorney. It's his job to make monsters into kittens in the eyes of the people, and he's good at it. He knows how to play the role of a good man. I think he believes he is one. People meet him and assume he's this great guy, but that's only half the story. That's the part of him he lets the world see. It's the part of him I fell in love with six years ago." Anna sighed. "But as soon as we were married, he changed. Suddenly I was his possession. In his mind I was his to control."

Anna paused, perhaps gauging my reaction. She didn't realize just how well I understood.

"Go on," I prompted.

"I tried to make it work. I thought that maybe if we had a child, if we started a family, he would be happier. I thought he would treat me like a person again if I was the mother of his children."

"Did he hit you?" I asked between clenched teeth, her story all too familiar to me.

"No, he didn't have to. If you make someone feel worthless enough, if you break them down and strip them of their self-confidence . . ." Anna broke off. I heard her take in a shaky breath before she continued. "There are other ways to intimidate people into your control."

There was a moment of silence then, as she reflected on what she'd just revealed. Perhaps it was the first time she'd revealed it to herself.

"Things only got worse when Julian was born. Stephan became obsessed with him. He used him to control my every move. He threatened to take him away from me any time I failed to meet his approval. I was scared for my life, for my son's life. Stephan wasn't stable."

Anna leaned toward me. I felt her shallow breaths on my face.

"His past left him . . . broken," she said. "You don't know what a childhood like his can do to someone. I should have known . . ."

"I can imagine," I said, struggling to keep my own memories at bay. "I understand more than you know. Go on . . ."

Anna swallowed and continued. "When I suggested that Stephan see a therapist, he took Julian away from me for a week. I had no idea where my son was. I thought then that I had lost him. When Stephan returned a week later, I was a wreck. He told me to never speak to him that way again or he would take Julian for good."

I wrung my hands in my lap, my own childhood flashing in fleeting memory as she spoke. In my mind, my young face morphed into the look of terror I had seen on Julian's. I began to tremble with familiar rage but took a deep breath. Mutt licked my hand.

"I took my son and ran as soon as I could," Anna continued. "He was barely four years old at the time. We had nothing. I had no job. Stephan insisted that I stay home with Julian.

Stephan also saw to it that I had no friends in Charlotte where we lived.

"My mother took us in, but he came for us there. We stood our ground, calling the police when he showed up at the house demanding his son, but there was little they could do unless he physically threatened us. Stephan was too smart for that. When he realized that he would lose Julian if he resorted to violence, he took me to court. I had no money for an attorney, no home and no job. Stephan has charm, his money, and his friend on the bench. He was granted full custody."

Anna started to cry again. This time she fought back the tears.

"I tried to tell them that they were making a mistake. I tried to explain that Julian wasn't safe with him, but Stephan had never actually harmed Julian. How do you prove emotional abuse to someone who has never suffered it? The scars are invisible."

"So you took off with Julian?" I asked. She hesitated, then let out a shallow breath.

"Yes," she answered, "a year ago, during one of my visitations. I left everything I knew in Charlotte, gathered as much money as I could, and ran to Raleigh to stay with a friend from high school. It hasn't been easy, but we made a good life for ourselves in Raleigh. I found a job and started saving to move across the country and further away from Stephan. I really thought we could start over. I thought I could raise Julian without the fear I'd felt ever since I married Stephan. I only wanted to save him from that."

There was a pleading in her voice, a desperation for some kind of approval. I thought about my own childhood, about the nightmare of growing up in constant fear, and found that I felt grateful to Anna. She had somehow found the strength to flee with her child to seek out a better life. If only my own mother had possessed the same strength, how different my life might have been.

"That's why you can't call the police," I said, putting it all together. "You kidnapped your son."

"Yes," she said, barely a whisper.

"You did the right thing," I found myself saying.

Then I remembered the fear I'd seen in Julian's eyes each time he knew it was time to leave me. The mystery of what he was afraid of became clear at last.

"Did I?" Anna asked. "Because he found us anyway. He plucked Julian from his bed in the middle of the night. I didn't even know he was gone until I went to wake him for school. Stephan didn't know to take Red with him. It's Julian's favorite toy. What kind of a father doesn't know that kind of thing? Julian must be so scared and confused."

"Are you sure it was Stephan that took him?" I asked.

"Yes," she said, dejected. "He left me a voicemail . . . said I would never see Julian again. He said he would kill me if I tried to find them, but that won't stop me."

"Why didn't he just call the police on you?" I asked, confused. "If he had custody, then Julian would have been returned to him, and you would be in jail. Why take off like that?"

"I've wondered the same thing," she said, her voice breaking again. "I think he's trying to teach me a lesson."

"A lesson?" I asked. "What kind of lesson?"

"I'm afraid to know," she said, her voice bordering frantic. "I told you, he's not stable. His voicemail said that soon no one would be able to take Julian from him again. I don't know what he's planning. I just know that I need to find my son. I quit my job. I'm living out of my car. I've driven across the state and back searching. I have no help, no money, and until yesterday I thought I had no hope. Then I saw an article in the paper, and there it was, my son's face staring back at me through your art. I know that you know something. Why was my son here? Please, just tell me how you know Julian. Something tells me I'm running out of time."

I took a deep breath, processing this new information. If what Anna said was true, then Julian was in danger. That thought caused my blood to heat. I could feel my face flush. I remembered the way Julian looked each time he'd visited. His face had grown dirtier, his clothes shabbier each time he appeared in my studio. I remembered the way he huddled in the corner, clinging to the shadows. A picture of where he'd come from began to form in my mind.

"How long has Julian been missing?" I asked.

"It's been almost six months," Anna whispered, sniffing back a sob. My stomach lurched.

"Six months," I mumbled.

"What is it?" she asked, her breath catching in her throat.

"That's exactly how long it's been since the first time he visited me," I said.

Beside me, Anna rose to her feet with a gasp.

"The first time?" she asked, almost frantic. "He's been here more than once? Where is he now? You have to know. Where did he come to you from? Was his father with him? Tell me!"

"It's hard to explain," I said. "You're not going to believe me."

"Try me," she said.

So I started from the beginning, recounting every detail of my time with Julian. I told her how he had appeared that first night shivering and afraid in the corner of the studio. I described the joy he had brought me the night we painted those cardinals atop the loft table. I told her that Julian showed me how to see again.

Anna lowered herself to the floor beside me. She was silent as I recalled those months painting Julian, the months when our hearts had somehow melted together beneath his static touch. When I described the fear in Julian's eyes and the way he had pleaded to stay with me, Anna could no longer stave off her tears. The thought came to mind that I should reach out to her, to offer her some comfort. Mutt's whines told me that he was already on it. His tail thumped against me as he leaned into Anna. I imagined her throwing her arms around his strong canine body just as Julian had done, but I could not know for sure.

The only thing I did know was that she hadn't walked out, hadn't protested or called me crazy the entire time I wove together the story of how I had come to know her son. Morning turned to evening as she listened patiently to all of it. How I wished I could see the expression on her face or look into her eyes to know whether or not she believed me. I told her every last detail of my time with Julian. Everything but that last night. That night I kept locked inside to fuel my self-hatred.

When I was done, Anna took in a deep breath before she spoke. When she released it, her breath was shaky and shallow.

"You can see him?" she asked.

"I can see him," I confirmed. Julian's smiling face looked up at me from my memory. *I can see you.*

"And you can't see anything else?" I felt a sudden wind in my face. She was waving a hand in front of my eyes.

"No," I said.

"How many fingers am I holding up?" she asked.

"One," I said with a sigh. "Your middle finger."

Anna gasped. "Then you can see!"

"No, I can guess," I countered. "You saw for yourself. I'm blind as a bat. More so."

"Yet you can see my son?" she asked again.

"I don't know how it's possible, but I can see him more clearly than I've ever seen anything," I said, getting to my feet and pacing away. There was nothing in that moment I would not have done to see Julian's light again.

"I know what's going on here," Anna said, a sudden realization.

"You do?" I asked, turning to her, my heart quickening in my chest.

"You're insane," she said, jumping to her feet. "You must have seen us someplace, me and Julian. Then you obsessed over him just like my ex-husband. That's why you painted all of these pictures . . . made up that story. You actually believe it."

"No," I said. "I'm telling you the truth."

"I have to get out of here." Her footsteps stormed to the door. "I let you waste too much of my time. I have to find my son."

I lurched forward to stop her before she could leave. My mind raced with what I might say to make her stay. Then I remembered the picture that Julian took of himself and Mutt in front of the painting. I yanked my phone from my pocket.

"Wait," I cried. "I can prove that he was here. He took a selfie on my phone . . ."

The front door opened with a loud squeak and then stayed open a second before closing again. I knew from her heavy breaths that she was still inside. I knew I had her attention.

"Photos," I said into the phone after the beep. Then I flipped to what I hoped was the second to last photograph and handed it to her.

She plucked it from my hand, and I waited in silence for her reaction. Her breath left her in a disappointed rush.

"These are of your paintings and your dog," she said.

"No," I said, my heart now racing. "Scroll through. He took a selfie right here in this room. He's next to the dog . . ."

"I'll tell you like I told my ex-husband," she said, her voice full of disdain, "get some help."

"No . . ." I tried to protest, not understanding why she couldn't see Julian in the picture. Anna shoved the phone back at me, and my fingers failed to grasp it. It fell with a metallic thump to the floor. The front door opened again when my email ringtone sounded into the room. Anna froze at the sound of it.

"*This little light of mine,*" the tone sang. "*I'm going to let it shine.*"

The tone repeated those words once more, and then all was silent except for the sound of Anna's quickened breaths in front of me. I bent down to pick up my phone as the front door closed and Anna stepped toward me.

"Why do you have that song on your phone?" she asked, almost a whisper.

"It reminds me of him," I said with a shrug. "Julian used to sing it all the time. He said that you told him that it was good to sing because it makes you happy when you're scared . . . or something like that."

"I . . . I told him that the night he disappeared," she said, choking back fresh tears. "He just learned that song the day before at . . ."

"Church . . . I know," I interrupted. "He told me."

Anna's breath caught in her throat. I could feel her conflict. Taking a deep breath, I stepped closer to her, Mutt on my heels.

"I know what I've told you is crazy," I said as softly as I knew how, "but I'm telling you the truth. I never laid eyes on your son before the night he appeared to me in this very room six months ago. Somehow he was here. I saw him. With eyes that will never glimpse another soul or sunrise again, I saw him."

"This can't be happening," she said in a rush of breath as she turned from me. "Not again."

"Again?" I asked, confused.

"This has happened before, what people mistake for angels," she said, her voice barely louder than a whisper. "Guardians."

"You know about Guardians?"

For a moment Anna was silent. I could feel her eyes burning through the scars of mine, warring with some truth she had yet to believe. When she finally spoke, I heard the trembling in her voice.

"I believe that my son is in danger," she said. "And if what you say is true, if the stories are true . . . then that means somehow my son was able to come to you for help."

"For help?" I repeated, my mind reeling back to those months with Julian. Never once had he asked for help. He had only ever asked to stay.

"Perhaps . . . just maybe . . . something bigger brought us all together through your paintings. That's why Julian was sent to you," she said calmly. "So we could find him."

I let what she said penetrate my reality. Until that moment, I only half believed that Julian was sent as a lifeline to help me paint again, a cruel joke since without him I no longer cared. *But what if?* What if it was never about me at all? What if Julian did come to me for help somehow, and I had failed him? I wasn't sure which truth made me loathe myself more for sending him away.

"God should have picked someone else," I said. "I'm no hero."

"And yet you're the one to see my son," she said, her voice brightening. "God never makes mistakes. Your paintings drew me here. If this is all true, then when Julian appears to you again you can find out where he is. We can find him."

My soul burned as I thought about the night I sent Julian away. I remembered his huge, frightened eyes and my unrestrained anger. My legs trembled beneath me as I fought to remain standing, the anguish within threatening to scorch the remainder of my flesh.

"The only thing God has ever brought me is pain and suffering," I spat. "I'm sorry you and your son got caught up in my disaster of a life."

"What do you mean?" she asked, suddenly panicked.

"Julian isn't coming back," I said with a groan. "I sent him away a month ago. He hasn't been back since."

"You sent him away?" Anna repeated. "What do you mean, you sent him away?"

"I got mad at him one night. He sent some emails on my phone . . ." I seethed, my self-hatred never before burning so fierce. "I screamed at him to go and to never come to me again. He's gone."

Anna was silent, though I heard her breath quickening as my words slammed into her. The tension in the room was as thick as the humidity on a hot July night. She took in a ragged breath as Mutt whined beside me.

"My son is out there somewhere, trapped with a madman. He found a way to come to you for help," she said between clenched teeth. "And you sent him away?"

"Yes," I whispered, my soul lost in my guilt. *What have I done?*

"You used my son to make these paintings, to become rich and famous." I could hear her disgust. "You made money off of the visions you had of him. He came to you, to the only person who could help him . . . and you sent him away?"

"Yes," I repeated.

How could I possibly explain? In my time with Julian I had found my life again, never once considering that he might be in danger. In my mind it was only ever about me and my tragic life. All the while the real tragedy was right before my useless eyes.

Anna's anguished wail reverberated in the studio. Her footsteps staggered to the front door again and then out into the tepid night.

Ten

Mutt barked at me as I stood numb in the center of the studio. When I didn't respond, he grabbed hold of my sweatshirt with his teeth and tugged me toward the door.

"Just let her go," I said, yanking free of his grip. "Just let them both go. They're better off without me messing up their lives any worse."

Mutt growled at me, a sound I'd never heard before from him. He clamped down on my sweatshirt again, and this time when he pulled me toward the door, I couldn't help but to stagger forward. Then he jumped at the door and whined, begging for me to open it and go out. I knew he wanted me to bring Anna back, but how could I? Julian was in danger, and I was the only one who could have done something. Instead, I saw only my own anger and pain and took it out on the small child.

Mutt growled at me again, a deep, carnal snarl.

"Fine," I said, throwing my hands up.

Donning my shades and hood, I walked out the front door. Mutt ran off while I paused to take in the sounds around me. As the warmth of the late spring air caressed my face, I realized that this was the first time I'd left the studio in months.

An airplane passed overhead as tourists laughed and mumbled in the distance. They came in and out of the local shops and bars and waited in line for the next tour of the estuary. To my right a horse drawn carriage clomped down the old brick streets, its passengers excited to experience a piece of Wilmington's history.

Everywhere eyes were on me. I could feel their judgment as solidly as the breeze coming off the river. Ignoring them, I searched the sounds of bustling life around me for Anna. When I heard sobs in the distance as well as Mutt's panting, I knew I had found her.

I followed the sound of her over the brick street, across the gravel lot, to the Riverwalk on the other side. Clinging to the metal railing, I fought off the memories of the night when my sight was robbed from me at this very spot. When I turned toward where I knew there was a bench, Anna stopped crying. She'd seen me approach. Taking a deep breath, I thought carefully about my next words.

"I . . . I'm sorry," I forced the words out. They were black and bitter on my tongue and lingered in the space between us. When she remained silent, I dropped my shoulders and with them all pretension.

"I didn't know," I continued. "I was so caught up in what was happening to me that I didn't see what was happening to him. I thought he was some kind of . . . of . . ."

"Angel?" she asked, sniffling.

"Yes, actually," I said, lowering myself onto the bench beside her.

"That's a mistake," she said. "Not everyone sent from above is an angel. He can call on any of us, angel or human, at any time."

"How do you know all this?" I asked. "You talk like you've experienced that before."

Anna readjusted herself on the bench, perhaps to turn and face me. More likely to face away. "Something like that," was all she said.

"How did Julian do it?" I asked. "How did he visit me if he's really somewhere else? I don't understand."

Then I remembered Logan and his incredible story. Wasn't it the same for him? The woman he saw in the prison had visited him while she lay unconscious on her living room floor. Not an angel after all, but human. A Guardian. Was the same now happening to me?

I felt Anna lean over to pet Mutt's head as he whined beside her. A tuft of her soft hair tickled my face as it was lifted by the cool spring breeze. She huffed out a breath. When she spoke again, her tone was warmer. The anger in it had cooled, but the sorrow remained.

"It was his spirit that called out to you, that came to you for help," she said. "Whether you like it or not, you were chosen to see my son. It was for a purpose."

Chosen. That concept was harder to accept than Julian's very existence in my life. It couldn't be true. I was no hero. Surely the heavens knew better. I was nothing but a criminal, one who had lied, cheated, and stolen his way through life. I was a murderer.

There was a time when I was very young, Julian's age, when I believed that God would deliver me from the life He had given me. I thought that with God's help, I could somehow rise above my cruel circumstances. I prayed for it and begged for it. I waited for it. But the older I got, the worse things became, and the more belief dissolved into truth.

I was my father's son, destined to be just as evil. Destined to be without hope. God would never rescue me. He had done nothing but curse my very existence. God had turned His back on me. Anna was mistaken.

"You're wrong," I said, forcing down the anger that rose like pyre in my throat. False hope was all her words offered. "If the heavens are so gracious and kind, then why is your son not with you where he belongs? Why is he instead with a father that's unstable and dangerous? How does a loving God allow a child to be raised by a monster?"

"You sound like you've experienced that before," Anna threw back at me.

"Something like that," I countered. "If I was chosen, then where is God now that we need Him? There's no purpose for me, only torment, and I deserve it. You and your son got caught in the crossfire of God's wrath for me. That's all."

Seething, I shrugged back from my words, the bitterness in them too much for even my own ears. I wasn't sure if I even believed them, but the anger was too much, too heavy in my breast to allow for any other truth. In the distance, church bells began to chime the evening hour.

Anna scoffed, leaning in closer to me as she spoke. I could feel the heat of her breath against my cheek. "If you believe that," she said, "then you're blinder than you know."

With that, she stood and walked away from me, but not far. Her weary steps walked to the railing of the Riverwalk's edge. I imagined her leaning over the top rung to watch the reflection of the waning sun upon the rippling water.

Mutt wandered over to me and plopped beside me with a moan. He licked my hands, and I petted his head, the anger within me dissipating. I was doing it again, I realized. I was lashing out from the wounds of my past, hurting others with my words. Anna was scared for her child. She came to me looking for answers and found nothing but a dead end. As hard as it was to admit, I was scared too.

Julian was out there somewhere, homesick and frightened. He was in danger. Whether or not Anna and I agreed on why Julian appeared to me out of nowhere didn't matter. We had one thing in common. We both needed to find him.

"What can I do?" I asked, a desperate plea. "What can I do to bring him back?"

I heard a sob catch in Anna's throat.

"You can pray," she said. "That's all we can do. It's all I have left."

Pray. As if that would help. Again my thoughts flashed to Logan and to the hours he spent teaching me to pray again as we crouched in the back of my jail cell. A year I spent on my knees in that cell humbled before God, asking for deliverance. How many times had I prayed for my life to change, for a way out of my suffering? It was just when I thought my prayers had been answered, when I'd found this coastal city by the river, that my new life outside of Central Prison came crashing down around me. In the end my prayers brought only more anguish. What good could my prayers be when they were raised up only to be forsaken?

Yet despite the familiar anger in my mind, I felt my heart cry out. Desperation mingled with fear as I found myself petitioning on Julian's behalf. *Please*, my soul cried. My heart remembered that vulnerable stance of abandon that I'd learned in my prison cell. Only this time my prayers were not for myself. My prayers were only for Julian. *Please, God. Help me find him. I don't care if it's too late for me. Just let Julian live the life he deserves.* The words formed in my mind before I could contain them, desperation temporarily silencing my hatred.

As they did, I was overwhelmed by a flood of stark, vivid images. I saw a thousand things flash before me at once. The brightness of their light was blinding behind my flesh-covered eyes. My other senses paled in comparison to what I was seeing around me. The murmurs of tourists and the chiming of the church bells faded into the distance.

Disoriented, I stood and staggered backward, trying to make sense of what I was seeing. Colors and shapes that made no sense ran through my mind like a psychedelic projection reel. It was too much to grasp all at once.

"Are you okay?" I heard Anna ask, but I was reeling with the sudden flux of light and color. I felt her step forward and reach for me, but I shied from her touch as the jumble of images became brighter. With hands outstretched, I fumbled forward. Mutt was at my heels at once.

"No, don't touch me," I said, my feet finding the gravel lot across from the studio. "I . . . I don't know what's happening. I have to get back inside."

"What's going on?" Anna asked behind me. I barely heard her voice over the white hot static in my ears. "I'm going with you."

"No," I tried to protest, my arms flailing for the front door as I leaned against Mutt, but as I staggered to the door, Anna held it open for me.

"I'm not leaving. My son felt safe with you once. I have to believe he'll come back," she said. "I'm not leaving until he does. I've got nowhere else to go."

"Fine," I said when we were inside, too paralyzed by the images that continued to flash in front of me to argue. "Then find me a canvass."

"Are you going to tell me what's going on?" she asked.

"In the closet," I ordered, ignoring her question. "Grab the box to the right too. I need my paints. Hurry!"

Anna hesitated, then stomped to the closet. Within minutes she was shoving the box of painting supplies into my hands. Pulling my chair to the nearest easel, I tossed the portrait on display there aside and began to squirt paints onto the palette. Anna brought a stack of canvasses and dropped them at my feet. I grabbed one.

"You're going to paint while my son is still out there?" she asked, impatient.

"I'm seeing something . . . ," I tried to explain. "I have to get it down."

"Is it Julian?" she asked, her voice rising in pitch.

When the palette was ready, I began to smear my outline across the canvas with the thick white base. It was difficult to trap just one image and hold it still in my mind. I had to stop the others from coming until I could paint what I saw. It was like putting a finger to a flimsy fan to stop the blades from turning. It wasn't until Anna grabbed the brush from my hand that I heard her.

"Do you see Julian?" she asked again. "Are you seeing my son right now?"

"No," I said, snatching the brush back. "This is something else. I don't know what yet. I just know that I can see something, and I won't know what it means until I get it all out onto the canvas. I have to paint what I see before it's gone."

"What's going on?" she asked. "If you're not seeing Julian, then how . . .?"

"I don't know," I interrupted, agitated by the distraction. "I'm seeing images as clearly as if they were right in front of me. They could mean nothing. Or they could help us find Julian."

I painted feverishly, trying to capture what I saw. Anna was silent for a moment. She watched over my shoulder as Mutt plopped down beside me.

"It doesn't look like anything," she said with a huff.

"I'm not done," I said. "I'm just getting started."

"How long is this going to take?" she asked.

"Look, if you insist on staying, then I suggest you get comfortable," I said, wiping my forehead with the back of my hand. "I don't have much to eat, but take whatever you want. You can use the bed upstairs."

"Is this really going to take that long?" she asked. "Where are you going to sleep?"

"I won't be sleeping tonight," I said, using the inky black to add shadow detailing to the image taking shape before me.

Anna hesitated a moment, perhaps trying to figure out what she should do. I knew she didn't have a lot of options. She could get back in her car and drive away, hoping to stumble across a clue as to her son's whereabouts. Or, she could take her chances with me, the blind lunatic painting an influx of images his eyes couldn't see.

To stay would be a leap of faith, but I might just be her only hope. I almost laughed aloud at the thought. Me, the man cursed as hopeless was now someone's only hope. But as I completed one image and tossed it aside to grab another canvas, I began to realize that I too was clinging to hope once again.

"I'll be right back," Anna said. I vaguely registered her footsteps as they walked out the front door.

By the time she returned, I had outlined the newest image. She walked across the room and dropped something heavy in the corner. Her bag perhaps. She sat where the pillow and blanket still lay on the floor. Pages flipped, and I heard the squeak of a pencil across paper.

"What are you writing?" I asked, pausing to find my next color.

"You have your calling," she said, "and I have mine."

"You're a writer," I concluded.

"I'm trying to be," she said, still scribbling in her notebook.

"If you write," I said, searching out the brown with my fingertips, "then you're a writer."

"We'll see about that. Your name is Blake, right?" she asked. "Blake Roberts? That's what the article said. Is that your real name?"

I lowered the brush and turned to her.

"Are you writing about me?" I asked.

"I'm writing about this experience," she said. "I think I'm supposed to do something with it."

"Do something?"

She stopped writing and let out an impatient breath. "Look, it's a long story, and I'd rather not distract you from doing what you can to find my son. If what you're painting will lead us to him, then just get back to it. Please, pretend I'm not here."

With a sigh, I turned back to the painting and found where I'd left off.

"Blake is my real name," I said, focusing on the image I held in my mind's eye. It would be impossible to pretend that she wasn't there. Her sweet scent filled the room as she wore the lead of her pencil to its nub.

Not another word was spoken. I raced to capture each image as it flashed in front of me. Anna fetched another pencil from her bag and scribbled in her notebook late into the evening. The church bells outside chimed the midnight hour when she finally put the notebook away. I heard her adjust herself on the hardwood, heard Mutt circle and then plop on the floor beside her.

Anna fell asleep in the corner of the room where Julian had appeared to me so many times. I could hear her heavy breaths as I switched out canvasses for the fifth time. I understood why she didn't go upstairs to use the bed, why she chose to stay and wait by my side. Her faith was driving her to trust me and whatever it was I was seeing. It was all she had. Despite myself, I prayed that I would not let her down again.

I kept painting, though my arms grew as weary as my mind. The distant chime sounded twice. None of the images in my mind or on the canvas made sense to me. They were still a jumble of colors and edges. More than once, I doubted what I was doing, but I pushed on, spurred by the slightest hope that these paintings could somehow lead us to Julian.

When the last image finally settled before me, I captured it with weakened, trembling hands. Exhaustion seemed to weigh me down with ten times the force of gravity. I finished the last detail and dropped the brush and palette. I stumbled out of my chair to collect all twelve paintings. Running my fingertips over their surface, I tried to form some sort of pattern. I thought that perhaps they united like a sort of film reel, one image needing the next to come alive, but there was no direction, no logical beginning or end. I flipped the canvasses and swapped their placement, but nothing came together as a recognizable picture.

My weariness overwhelmed me, and I sank to the floor in a heap among my paintings. I had failed. Once again hope had let me down. I realized that the images that had flashed before me were nonsense. They were nothing but the memories of sight. Bitter disappointment took hold of me. The anger came, as did the hatred. My old familiar friends. They rode in on the wings of nightmares, clawing their way into my mind as I drifted to sleep slumped on the studio floor.

Again I fell helplessly into the past, to live out that fateful night when hope first died.

"Come back, Mommy!" my brother screamed as he ran to the door after our mother. "Come back!"

Catching him by the elbow, I swung him around and took him in my arms as he cried. I covered his mouth with my trembling hand, still numbed by the fact that our mother had left us with a monster.

"Sssshhhh!" I whispered as I stared with dread at the bedroom door. "You'll wake him up!"

It was too late. The bedroom door opened with a slow groan. My father stepped out into the hall. His clothes were matted. There were faint splatters of blood across his otherwise white tank top. I wondered briefly if the blood was my mother's or my own.

He stared us down with vacant eyes, his bruised fists balled at his sides. He looked drowsily around the house bejeweled with Christmas duplicity. The lights from the tree shone on us like a twinkling spotlight from where we stood pressed against the front door.

My father looked for my mother. Then his eyes widened with sudden realization. We froze as he stumbled back into his bedroom. We heard him throw open the closet and my mother's drawers. With a savage cry, he threw the emptied dresser to the floor as we watched on in terror.

When he stomped out of the room, his face was a mask of rage and hatred, his eyes blackened slats. He glared at us and raised a trembling finger to my brother.

"This is your fault," he screamed. "You did this!"

My brother shook his head, no. He backed into the front door, his sweaty palms leaving streak marks on its surface. My father stepped toward him, his fingers clenched at his sides. I raced to think of some way to escape, a way to get my brother to safety. When my father bent to pick up the discarded pistol from off the floor, dread froze my thoughts and pinned me to the stained carpet.

"She left because of you!" my father cried out, tears falling from his eyes.

He aimed the gun at my baby brother and pulled back the hammer. I couldn't react fast enough. My twelve-year-old mind could not fathom the horror in front of me. The darkness seemed to gather from the shadows. It oozed from every direction like the fluid from an open wound until I felt I would choke on it.

My brother's eyes grew wide with terror. A single tear rolled off his tiny cheek. When I could finally make my legs move, I dove at my father. A scream ripped from my throat as I threw myself at him. The gun went off just before I knocked him to the floor.

For a split second all was silent. The world around me was now drenched in black. I was afraid to open my eyes. My survival instincts kicked in as my mind surveyed my body for damage. My father writhed beneath me, and I jumped to my feet.

I turned to my brother in time to see his lifeless body collapse in a heap to the floor.

Eleven

"Blake!" a voice called to me from the abyss. "Wake up! It's just a dream."

As the nightmare dissolved into reality, I felt Mutt's tongue on my face. I sat up with a start, remembering that I had fallen asleep slumped on the gallery floor. Anna's voice spoke from beside me.

"Are you okay?" she asked. "You were calling out in your sleep."

"Yeah," I croaked, adjusting my shades and hood. "It's nothing. I'm fine."

"It didn't sound like nothing," she said. I could hear the sympathy in her voice.

"Happens," I said with a shrug.

"Yes, it does," she agreed.

I got to my feet. My limbs protested the movement. I felt the morning sun streaming in through the window but shivered in my perpetual darkness. When I stepped toward the door to let Mutt out, I tripped on one of the canvasses that still littered the floor. Kicking the useless art away, I opened the door to the sound of a boat engine as it traversed the river outside.

"What are they?" Anna asked, circling the floor around the paintings.

"Nothing," I said with a frustrated sigh. "They're nothing."

"They have to be something," she said. "They have to be."

"I tried all night to put them together in a row, or by twos," I said, putting my hands on my hips, "but no matter what I tried, they make no sense to me. I mean, you can see them. . . What do they look like?"

Anna was silent as she walked the gallery inspecting each painting.

"Separate, they don't look like anything," she said. "Just a bunch of shapes and colors."

I threw my hands up. "Exactly. It was a waste of time. I was just seeing things, useless things . . . not a gift from the heavens or whatever. I wasn't chosen to help you, Anna. I'm sorry I wasted your time."

Anna didn't answer, only shuffled across the floor as she moved the paintings around.

"You know what your problem is?" Anna asked, straining to get the canvasses into place. "You can't see the bigger picture."

I waited, listening to Anna rearrange them in front of me.

"What do you mean?" I asked, impatient. "Do you see something?"

"I don't know yet," she said, still shuffling. "You were right about one thing, though. These images don't go in rows or in pairs."

"I told you."

"They all fit together," she explained, excited. "It's one big painting, Blake."

"It is?" My breath caught in my throat, and my pulse quickened each time Anna moved a painting into place. Then she stopped and backed away with a gasp.

"What is it?" I asked. "What's it a picture of?"

"It's a room," she said, her voice lowering. "A bedroom."

"Describe it to me," I asked, my sanity hanging on her every word.

Anna took a deep, shaky breath. I could hear the tears she forced away. "It's a dark room, drenched in shadow. There's a mattress on the floor with a pillow and blanket. It looks like there might be a few toys on the floor too, I think. It's hard to tell. They're blurry."

"What else do you see?" I asked.

"There's a small window in the corner," she said.

"What else?"

"That's it." I heard her hands drop to her sides. "Just the mattress and the window."

"There has to be more," I whispered.

The dread that filled me now echoed the darkness of my dream. Anna didn't need to say it. We both already knew. This was a picture of the room where Julian was being held.

"Hold on a minute," Anna gasped, stepping closer to the paintings that formed a puzzle on the floor. "It looks like you painted a street sign outside of the window. It's blurry too, though."

"Can you read it?" I asked, trying to conjure the image of what I'd painted. I remembered using a crisp blue at the edges of several paintings. It was the same blue as the signs that I remembered marked each downtown street. I had detailed them with white, not knowing I was forming words.

"I think it says Grape, or Grade . . .," Anna said.

"Grace . . ." My knees weakened and threatened to buckle beneath me. I leaned on the wall for support. "It's Grace Street."

"Are you sure?" Anna asked, racing to my side. "Do you know where that is?"

"Yes," I said. "It's less than ten blocks away. Julian was right here in Wilmington this whole time."

Twelve

"Still don't believe that you were chosen?" Anna asked, her movements frantic as she collected her things in the corner. "You just painted our way to Julian."

I took in a shaky breath, trying to fathom the fact that Julian could have been only blocks away this whole time. The images that flashed into my vision had lead us to him after all. *Chosen*. I stood, dumbfounded, in the center of the room and tried to grasp the significance of it all until Anna yelled from the corner.

"Don't just stand there," she said. "Let's go get my son."

When I didn't respond, she walked to me and jingled her car keys in my face.

"Snap out of it," she said. "You did it. Your paintings showed us the way. Now let's go get Julian."

"I was chosen," I repeated.

"Guess you're not as hopeless as you thought," she said and then walked to the door. She held it open and waited for me. "I can't do this without you."

Mutt whined from beside me and pawed my leg. Snapping to, I bent down to him and petted his head.

"You need to be my eyes today, boy," I said as he licked my hand. "Let's find Julian."

I followed Mutt's excited panting out the front door. He stayed close. I could feel his warmth against my leg.

"My car is parked just across the street," Anna said as we met her on the sidewalk.

"Don't need it." I walked past her, bringing the image of the street to my mind. "It's easier to walk from here. Grace Street is the street before the Cotton Exchange. Just let me know when you see a huge hotel on the water. It's directly across from it."

"Okay . . ." she said, scrambling to catch up. "You should know it looks like it's going to rain."

"Then we should hurry," I said.

The morning air was crisp but carried a humid, salty breeze that smelled of fresh rain. A storm was on its way, but I didn't care. In the early morning, and with a storm approaching, the cobbled streets were quiet and clear as we walked with agitated steps. In the distance a boat horn signaled the departure of the first and perhaps last tour of the day. Cicadas announced the imminent arrival of summer. Despite the lack of people on the streets, I zipped my hood tighter and adjusted my shades as Mutt led the way.

"You really don't want people to see you, do you?" Anna observed as we stopped at a crosswalk.

"Can you blame me?" I asked. "I can feel their stares on me every time I come outside."

She paused, probably to look around. "No one is even looking at you."

"Yeah, right," I scoffed as the chimes from the stop walk sounded and we began to walk again.

"No, really," she continued. I could feel the stares of the people passing us on the street. "Okay, except for a little girl coming up on your right. She's staring. No one else is even looking at you, though."

I nudged Mutt with my knee as he began to veer toward the little girl, tongue at the ready.

"No time for that today," I said to him, and he got back on track.

"Hi," the little girl said as we passed. Her voice was soft and shy.

"Good morning," I said back, hunkering into my hoodie.

"That little girl was smiling at you," Anna said from behind when we were across the street. Even she sounded surprised. "Not quite the judgment you were expecting, was it?"

"No," I admitted with a shrug and kept moving. "No, it wasn't."

We walked two blocks, then three. My breath was shallow, and my legs felt heavy. I pressed on, following Mutt's warmth and listening to Anna's footfalls beside me. When the sunlight on my face turned cool, I knew that the storm clouds had rolled in.

"There's the hotel," Anna exclaimed as the first drops of rain tickled the tip of my nose.

When we stopped at the next crosswalk, I turned to Anna. "Do you still have Red?"

"Yes, why?" she asked, skeptical.

"This is one of the longest streets in the downtown area," I explained, holding out my hand. "If you want to find Julian, you'll have to trust me."

Anna hesitated. Then I heard her unzip her bag. She thrust the plush toy into my palm. Without hesitation, I bent down to Mutt and prayed he would understand.

"Take a good whiff, boy," I said, putting the toy in front of his nose. As Mutt sniffed it, I could feel the wind from his tail as it began to whip back and forth. "Good. Now we need you to find him. Find his scent. Find Julian. Can you do that?"

Mutt jumped up with an excited bark. He turned the corner, his nose sniffing the sidewalk as I quickened my pace to keep up. Anna stayed close behind us as we started the uphill trek into the heart of the downtown area.

"Does he know what he's doing?" Anna asked.

"I have no idea," I admitted. "But he's all we've got."

We followed Mutt past a multitude of restaurants and shops, filled with muffled music and cigarette smoke. When I followed him into a grassy area and stumbled into a fire hydrant, I nudged him and pressed Red against his snout again to remind him of his mission. We passed through the city blocks and continued into residential neighborhoods, the rain growing to a steady drizzle. We walked on. Frantic, endless minutes passed.

Then Mutt caught a scent that excited him. He wiggled beside me, agitated. Then with a bark, he took off at a jog down the street. I had to run, arms outstretched, to keep up with him. Anna ran beside me, her anxious breaths quickening.

"This way!" she led me with her voice as I staggered close behind.

Mutt paused abruptly, his nose searching the air for the scent. Then with a loud howl, he took off at a gallop across the street.

"Mutt!" I shouted, unable to follow.

"Do you need help?" Anna asked.

"No, I can do this," I said, shrugging away from her grasp.

"He's heading to that house on the corner. It could be the one," Anna said, breathless. "Cross now. Watch your step."

Stepping down into the road, I followed her footsteps. I stumbled on the curb, but caught myself as Mutt raced back to me with fevered excitement. He'd found something.

"This has to be the house!" Anna yelled through the rain in front of me.

"Is there a street sign?" I asked. "Like in the painting?"

"You're standing right beside it," she said, excited. "There's a window that faces it. I'm telling you, this is it!"

Anna was already pounding on the door and calling Julian's name when I followed Mutt up to the house. Three brick steps led up to a covered porch, which stopped the rain from continuing to soak my hood.

"Can you see in the windows?" I asked when there was no answer at the door.

"Barely," she said. The boards beneath her feet creaked as she traversed the porch. "The blinds are all shut. It's dark inside. I don't think anyone's home."

Arms out before me, I found the screen door and opened it with a metallic squeal. Then I felt along the door for the knob and twisted it.

"The door is locked," I said. When I yanked the knob, the whole door shook.

"There's a fence in the back," Anna said, coming to where I stood investigating the door. "I could climb it . . . see if the back door is open?"

"No need," I said. "I think I can force the door open. It's old. One good blow, and it will give."

"That would be breaking and entering," Anna said, hesitant. Mutt whined beside me and then jumped at the door himself. His insistence assured me of what I had to do.

"I've never had a better reason for breaking the law," I said, backing up.

"You've broken the law a lot, I take it?" Anna stepped away from the door.

"You could say that," I said, readying myself. "Is anyone looking?"

There was a pause as Anna looked around at the neighborhood I could not see.

"No," she said. "It's clear . . . unless the neighbors are watching from their windows."

"We'll know when we hear the sirens." I took a deep breath. "Mutt, move out of the way."

When I heard Mutt move away from the door, I ran as hard as I could and slammed my body against it. There was a loud splintering of wood and a pop before the door flew open and hit the wall inside with a violent thud. I fell to the floor, wheezing. The impact knocked the breath from my lungs.

"Are you okay?" Anna asked, running into the room with Mutt on her heels.

"I'm good," I panted. "Go . . . find him."

"Okay," she said, frantic. "There's a hallway to the right. It should lead to the bedrooms."

"I'm right behind you," I said, struggling to get to my feet. Mutt was at my side instantly, and I leaned my weight against him until I was upright. I showed him the plush toy that I'd stuffed into my pocket, but he was already following the scent along the thick carpet.

Mutt lunged forward, excited by what his senses picked up.

"He's got something," I yelled to Anna, whose footsteps came to a sudden stop.

I felt along the right wall as we followed Mutt's excited snorts to a door at the end of a long hallway. There, he began to bark and jump at the door. I heard Anna twist the knob with no luck.

"It's locked," she cried as she banged her fist against the door. "Julian! Julian, are you in there?"

We both held our breath, waiting for a response from the other side of the door. When there wasn't one, Anna tried the knob again, this time with frantic desperation.

Though I doubted I had the strength to break down another door, I pounded against the old wood and found it to be just as rickety as the last. I backed up as far against the adjacent wall as I could and took a deep breath.

"Julian!" Anna screamed as I got ready to charge.

Before I could stop her, she reared back and threw herself into the door. It opened with a crack, and I heard Anna stumble into the room. Mutt bounded after her, his nose to the ground.

"Are you okay?" I asked, following. The stale air inside smelled of musk and dust.

"My God," she said as she righted herself.

"What is it?" I asked, my heart pounding.

"This is the room," she said. "It's the room from the paintings."

"He's not here . . ." I said, knowing from her dejected tone that the room was empty, just like in the paintings. Mutt whined, a sad moan, in the corner.

Anna took a few steps forward. A sob escaped her throat as she picked up something from the floor. Pages crinkled in her grasp.

"He was," she said. "There are broken crayons on the floor and a few coloring books that have been colored in. There are no clothes, no other toys . . . only the crayons and a filthy bed."

I remembered how each time I'd seen Julian he had looked dirtier and shabbier. There were no clothes in the room because he didn't have any other clothes, I realized. He was abducted with the clothes on his back, and he'd stayed in them for six months. That thought sent me into a rage as I turned to the bedroom door and inspected the doorknob with my fingers. As I suspected, there was a locking mechanism on the outside only.

"Julian was locked in this room," I said between clenched teeth. "There aren't any clothes in here because he didn't have any . . . just the clothes you put him to bed in the night he was taken. They were the only clothes I ever saw him wear."

"Oh, my God," Anna cried into her hands. "Why? Why bring him here? Why lock my baby in this horrible room?"

"My guess is Stephan knew you'd find them. He knew you'd come," I said as thunder rolled outside. The rain battered the window now, sending the sound of a thousand pounding drums throughout the room.

The thought of Julian alone in this dank room with nothing but a few coloring pages and his thoughts to comfort him made me crazy inside. No wonder his spirit had reached out. His body was trapped. No wonder he was always scared and hiding in the shadows.

With an enraged cry, I kicked the door against the wall. The floor beneath me shook with the impact as it slammed against the drywall.

Anna dropped the coloring book and took a deep breath.

"Maybe they didn't go far. I have to search the house," she said walking out of the room. "Maybe I can figure out where they went. Maybe they're coming back."

Mutt followed Anna into the hall, but I lingered in the room that my mind's eye had painted. I pictured Julian, frightened and homesick, pacing the floor. As I felt my way to the mattress in the corner, I imagined him huddled in a ball as he had appeared to me so many times in the corner of my studio. Lowering myself onto the makeshift bed, I ran my hands along the matted sheets.

I don't want to go back. I want to stay with you.

I took the pillow into my arms and hugged it to my chest, regret tearing into my very being. All my life I'd wished to go back into my past and change things. I always thought that I would somehow bring my brother back, so I could protect him from our father. But as I sat alone in this room where Julian was held captive, I realized that my brother had been freed from a life of sorrow. He'd been freed from a lifetime of being trapped in darkness and fear. Julian was still trapped, but there was still hope for him . . . hope for a good life with a mother who loved him. In that moment I knew that if I could change just one thing, I would find a way to bring Julian back to his mother.

"I'm so sorry, kid," I whispered.

Leaning over to replace the pillow, I braced myself against the wall to stand. My fingertips stumbled upon a waxy, raised line on the paint where the mattress met the wall. I lowered myself back down and followed the line with my fingers until it joined with other lines. When I put my nose to the wall, it smelled of crayon. The lines were words.

My heart pounded in my ears as I felt for the beginning of the writing. The sentence wasn't very long, only a couple of sloppily written words. Words a child would scribble. I felt along the tacky-smooth wax until the words formed in my mind.

"See me", they said. I had no doubt the words were written in red.

Forcing back the sob that caught in my throat, I sank back down onto the mattress. I thought about all the times that Julian and I had laughed at the oddity of our relationship.

I can see you . . .

How I would have given anything to see him again, to be sure he was safe. Though my life had been consumed by misery and self-pity, the only thing I cared about now was getting Julian to safety. Nothing else mattered. In my desperation, I lifted my hands toward the heavens.

"Give me eyes to see," I prayed the words that I learned from Logan in a jail cell not much smaller than the dank room that surrounded me now. "If you chose me to see Julian, then I need your help. I know I let him down, but please, let me see him again . . ."

Before I could finish my sentence, light flashed before my eyes. It was blinding. I flinched away from it as images raced into my vision as before. I fought to contain them as I braced myself against the wall. Light contrasted with dark, angles with curves. My ears filled with muffled sounds and static. Overwhelmed, I tried to see everything at once, tried to make sense of what I was seeing.

It was hard to catch my breath. I knew what I was seeing was important, but I couldn't force it to gel into an image that I could understand. I thought of grabbing the crayons from the floor and trying to capture what I was seeing, but these images came too fast. They changed and flew by too rapidly. I cried out in frustration. Then, amid the chaos I heard a voice call to me.

"*Let go,*" it said to me as if in my own voice, though I knew it was not me. "*Just let go.*"

With a gasp, I followed the voice into the flashing brilliance. My instincts told me to turn from the light, to guard myself from what I didn't understand. I wanted to run back to the familiar darkness, but I knew that if I was going to find Julian, I had to trust the light that called to me. With a deep breath, I stilled my mind and let the images come. For the first time in my life, I stopped fighting . . . fighting the world, my circumstances, and myself. I let whatever was happening, just happen.

The light enveloped me, and I could suddenly see. All at once the images stilled and drifted into place. The lines combined and the angles found their position. Light illuminated the darkness, and what I saw suddenly made sense.

I was inside of a moving car. Trees and rooftops flew past the windows as the light from the cloudy sky reflected off the smooth, leather interior. Rain pelted the windows as I scanned the front seat for signs of Julian. The driver's dark hair blew with the wind coming in through the vents. His muscular hands gripped the steering wheel with white knuckles. I caught the glint of gold on his finger. He swayed to the beat of the classic rock song that played from the stereo. Julian was not beside him.

Inside the vision, I searched the back seat. It was empty. Light flickered from the floorboards, and I looked down to see it dance off the bottles of vodka that were hidden there, some empty, some full. At first I couldn't understand why I was seeing this vehicle. There were no signs of Julian. But when I searched my heart, I could feel the child there. So I looked deeper, reaching out into the dark edges of my vision.

The inside of the trunk was black and dank. It was nearly impossible to see a thing. Then I remembered something that Julian once said to me.

Eventually, you have to let the light in, he'd said. And so I did.

It took everything I had, but I sought out the light that had called to me. I beckoned to it to come with me, to help me illuminate the darkness. I trusted that it would. When the shadows scattered, I saw him.

Julian's tiny body laid huddled in a ball, his tousled curls bouncing with the movements of the car. When I looked into his dirty little face, his eyes opened, and their amber depths glared right at me.

"Blake?" he asked, his voice raspy but full of hope. "Am I dreaming again?"

Thirteen

"Stephan's clothes are still in his closet."

Anna's voice broke my concentration, and the vision vanished as she came back into the room.

"There are dishes in the sink. I think they're coming back . . ." she continued, but paused as I struggled to catch my breath. The shock of what I'd just seen jarred my other senses.

"What is it?" she asked as thunder rocked the small house.

"They're not coming back," I said. "They're in a car headed out of the city."

Anna was at my side in an instant. "How can you know that?"

"I saw them," I said, still trying to believe it myself. "A dark-haired man was driving. He had a gold class ring on his left ring finger. Blue stone."

"Stephan!" Anna gasped. "Did you see my baby? Did you see Julian?"

"Yes," I said, straining to keep the anguish from my voice. "Stephan has him in the trunk."

"What?" she shrieked. "Where are they? Where are they going?"

"I don't know," I said as helplessness gripped my heart and squeezed. "That's all I saw."

I tried to bring the vision back, to reach out to Julian and tell him that everything was going to be all right. Concentrating on what I'd seen, I fought to bring the light back, but all I saw was darkness.

"We have to find him!" Anna was frantic. "We have to find my baby boy!"

"We will. I promise you," I assured her, though I had no idea what to do next. "We should stay here until the storm passes, regroup. It's too dangerous out there to head back just yet. Julian is alive. He's not hurt."

With a sob, I felt the weight as Anna sunk into the mattress beside me. "For how long though?"

"We'll find him," I promised again. We had to.

Thunder raged in the rain-soaked sky as sheets of fat drops continued to pelt the single window in the corner. Mutt came into the room and plopped between us with a dejected moan. We all sat there amidst the shadows of what had been Julian's prison cell and wallowed in our shared fear.

In that moment I felt Julian's absence like the loss of my own eyes. I longed to bring back the light that would lead me to him. In my mind, I sought out its return. In my heart, I believed that it would.

"I told myself I would never let my son have the kind of childhood I had," Anna said, breaking the silence at last. "I failed him."

"He knows you love him," I said as memories from my own childhood surfaced once again. "You haven't failed him."

"Haven't I?" she asked, the anguish in her voice calling out to the deepest depths of my soul. "He's locked in the trunk of his father's car . . . dirty, scared, and all alone."

I didn't know what to say to comfort her. My own feelings of self-disgust were eating away at the pieces of my sanity. I was the one who had let them both down.

"I'm the one who failed, Anna. Not you," I whispered. "You're his mother, and you're fighting for him. That makes you a good mom in my book."

Anna took a deep, broken breath and then continued.

"No," she said, too numb to keep crying. "When I was a little girl, I was afraid of my father too, just like Julian must be so afraid. I swore I would never do that to my children. I swore I would marry a good, Christian man. I thought I had. I failed him."

"You didn't know who Stephan really was. All that matters is what you're doing now . . ." I tried to comfort, but she stopped me.

"No," she said, "I should have seen it. I should have seen the darkness in him. I'd lived with it all my life. I should have known."

"Maybe," I said, remembering the blackness that had clouded my own father's eyes. "Or maybe there's something in the dark that calls to people like us. Maybe a part of us finds comfort in the shadows, in the familiar, even if we don't realize it. Or maybe because we've seen what that darkness can do to people . . . to people we love, we long to understand it."

Anna was silent beside me, and I knew that I'd struck a nerve. I turned to her and wished I could see the soft features of her face. I wished I could see the tears I imagined filled her fearful eyes.

"Tell me about him," I asked, feeling a connection to our kindred pasts. "Tell me about your father."

I thought that perhaps hearing her story would somehow help me understand my own because I realized that she might have been right about everything. Maybe we were brought together for a reason. Somehow, she and Julian and I were connected to a plan greater than any of us. Inside, I surrendered to whatever that plan might be. The light that called me into the vision was calling me into the darkness once again, perhaps to illuminate the truth inside the shadows.

"Sometimes he was a great dad," Anna whispered. "He would make me and my sister laugh all the time. We have so many stories of those times . . . the good times."

"Yeah," I said, remembering the times when my own father was sober and the light in his eyes told a different story.

"But then it was like someone flipped a switch, and he would turn into someone else," she continued. "I would see the darkness wash over him, and I knew it was time to go somewhere else. Anywhere else. Those were the times I try to forget."

"Go on," I said, letting her know that I was listening and that she was not alone. I imagined my own father as she spoke.

"Saturday mornings were the worst," she said, her voice becoming distant as she traveled back to that time. Her words carried me with her.

"I remember that our favorite cartoons came on early Saturday mornings. That was the only time we could watch them back then. My sister and I would wake up early and go into the living room. My dad was the only other one awake that early on Saturdays. My mom never knew . . ."

Anna's voice trailed off. I scooted closer to her.

"Never knew what?" I asked, letting her know I was still with her.

"That's when it would happen," she said. "That's when the darkness had the strongest hold on him. I was too young to understand what was happening . . ."

"Did he . . . touch you?" I forced out between clenched teeth, my heart breaking for her.

"Yes," she said so softly I could barely hear. "He did."

"How old were you?"

"Five . . . maybe six when it started. My sister was a year older," she said. She could not keep the shame from her voice.

I tried to keep my hands from trembling, but imagining Anna as a young girl in the hands of the darkness ignited a storm of fury inside of me. We'd both been robbed of so much at such a young age. What should have been a childhood filled with carefree play and warm memories was instead a barren landscape of fear and insecurity. The men who were supposed to shape our identities and model for us what the love of a father looked like brought us nothing but darkness and death.

But Anna's father had stolen so much more from her than mine had. He'd taken her very innocence and replaced it with shame and abashment. That was a tragedy I couldn't fathom.

"Where was your mother? How could she not know?"

"She was young herself, as naive and trusting as we were. My sister and I vowed to never tell her," Anna said. "We were afraid of what would happen to us. We were scared that we'd be taken from her."

"Does she know now?" I asked, wringing my hands beside her.

"No," Anna said, sniffling back her tears. "She died after my sister got married and after I left for college. She never knew . . ."

I lowered my head and took a breath. "All my life I've asked myself how a father could willingly hurt his children."

"It took me all my life to realize that it wasn't my father that hurt me. Not truly," she said. "I realized as I got older that it was the darkness inside of him that changed him from who he was supposed to be. Does that make sense?"

"I know that darkness," I said. I knew it all too well. "I know how it captures you and lures you into the shadows. I've given myself over to it more times than I can count, but it was still my choice to do the things I've done. It was your father's choice to hurt you, the one man who was supposed to protect you from harm. Sometimes people make choices that trap them in the dark."

"It was his choice, yes," Anna said. "But we also have a choice to make, you know? With how we let the shadows affect us. I chose to forgive him."

"How can you forgive him?" I asked, wishing in my heart I could do the same. "After what he did to you? He was your father . . ."

"Because I know there's someone up there looking after me. I know I'm loved in ways my dad could never love me. It's the same for you, Blake," she answered. There was silence as her words sunk into the marrow of my bones.

"I admire your faith." I sighed.

Anna chuckled. "It's easy to have faith when you don't have much else."

"What happened to him?" I asked. "To your father?"

"He took off shortly after my mother died. I think his guilt was too much for him. I know that deep inside he knows what he did. I know he wishes he'd have made different choices," Anna said. I heard her wipe at her eyes. "I just wish he knew my choice. I pray every day that when I die, my dad will be on the other side waiting for me. I want to know my father the way he was meant to be . . . in the light."

When I imagined Anna in my mind's eye, I could see the light that smiled down on her. It cut through the shadows that surrounded us. I tried to imagine it shining on me with that same warm luminance, but when I did, all I could see was cold, dark shame.

"I envy your choice," I said. "I wish I had made the same one."

"It's not too late," she said.

"Yes, it is," I argued. "Far too late."

"Why? What happened to you, Blake?" she asked, her voice soft.

I'd never told anyone about the night that my brother died, as if not talking about it could somehow keep it from being real. After what Anna shared about her past abuse, I thought that, maybe, she might understand. I hoped the light would help her to understand.

Thunder erupted outside, and Mutt startled. I ran my hand over his broad shoulders, and he settled back down with a whine as I told Anna my story. I told her of the darkness that stalked me at night, the darkness that rode in on the fists of my father's addiction.

I told her about the night my mother left us. The dank room around me dissolved into the memory of when the shadows won in my life. Anna listened in silence as I told her how my father murdered my brother before my eyes. I could feel her tears as they fell to the floor between us.

"What did you do?" she asked, her voice a hoarse whisper. "How did you escape?"

"I didn't," I said, as the familiar anger and fear crept up from the black surrounding me. I forced them back. "I made a choice that day that changed my life forever."

"What happened?"

"When it was over, when the gun went off and my father realized what he had done, he dropped the gun and sank to his knees. I watched in horror as he crawled to where my little brother lay bleeding on the carpet. He took him up in his arms and cradled him back and forth."

A sob escaped Anna's throat as I went on.

"I remember not being afraid anymore. All I could feel was this . . . this rage. I was so filled with anger that I didn't notice that the darkness had left my father's eyes. I didn't see his anguish or his grief. I didn't see the self-loathing in my father's eyes until I was standing over him with the gun."

"No," I heard Anna gasp beside me.

"I will never forget that hatred that was in his eyes just before I pulled the trigger. For a long time I thought that hatred was for me, his murderer. But I understand now. What I saw in his eyes was his hatred for himself, for the darkness. When I pulled the trigger, I too, chose the darkness."

"I'm so sorry," Anna whispered. "I can't imagine . . ."

"I've made so many choices in my life because of that night," I said, turning away. "Choices that have trapped me in black."

"That's the beauty of the light, though. It calls you out of the dark. You don't have to live in the shadows anymore. You're not your father, Blake. You're not like him. You see the choices when all your father saw was darkness. It's never too late to choose the light."

A chuckle escaped my throat though I tried to contain it. I heard Anna adjust herself on the bed. I felt her wipe her tears away with the dirty sheets.

"Is that funny to you?" she asked, confused.

"Your son said something like that to me the last day we were together," I said, remembering those last good moments together while I blindly painted my portraits of him. "He said that some people are so lost in the darkness that they can't see the truth."

"What truth?" Anna asked, trying to keep the tears from conquering her again.

"That there's someone there in the darkness, and that he's handing you the light of the world," I said. "He told me that he learned that in church. He said you took him every Sunday."

Anna laughed a joyless laugh, her tears flowing again though she tried to restrain them. I heard Mutt lick her face and felt him lean into her.

"Julian loves church," she said with a sniff. "He would go every day if I let him."

"How did you do it?" I asked, turning to her.

"Do what?" she asked.

"Find the light in the darkness?"

"It found me," she said, wiping her tears with the filthy bedsheet. "Just like my son found you."

"Tell me," I said as the rain began to lighten and the battering at the window turned to a light patter. The thunder's growl lessened as it rolled away into the afternoon.

"It was the Saturday morning that I stopped going out into our living room," Anna explained. "I remember waking up as usual. My sister was already out there, so I was late. I wanted so badly to go watch our cartoons, but when I started to get up, I realized that someone was with me in the early light of my bedroom. I couldn't see him, but I knew he was there all the same."

"Someone was with you?"

"He was there, in the shadows. I wasn't frightened. He felt safe. He told me not to go out there. He told me to stay in bed until my mother was awake. His voice was so gentle and warm, I listened to him and fell back to sleep. When I look back on it now, I know that he saved me from whatever might have happened at the hands of my father those mornings. I only wish my sister had listened."

"She kept going out there . . ."

"Yes," Anna said. "She took the brunt of the abuse while I did my best to elude it altogether. I don't know why things were different for her. I only know that the voice saved me from that day on."

"I think I've heard that voice . . ." I said, remembering the way the light had called to me. The voice that led me to Julian in my vision.

"Throughout my childhood, that voice protected me and spoke truth to me," Anna continued. "He taught me that I didn't have to live as a victim of the darkness. That's not who I am. It's not who you are either."

I thought about the possibility of no longer thinking of myself as my father's punching bag, his victim. What a freeing notion, to no longer belong to the dark. Anna's words offered hope for something more. To know the light was to know who I was in the light. I never wanted to explore a thing more in my life.

"What else did the voice say to you?" I asked.

"It told me that one day I would write a book that would bring people out of the darkness," Anna said. "I never understood what that meant until recently. Now I think I know what I'm supposed to do."

"That's why you're a writer," I said, understanding.

"Yes," Anna said. "I was always meant to be one, and now I know why. There are people out there that have had encounters like mine . . . where the light has reached out to them in their darkest days and brought them into the light. I think I'm meant to write their stories and mine."

"Miracle stories?" I asked, trying to understand.

"More than that," she explained. "There are stories out there of incredible circumstances of God sending people to change one another's lives. Stories of Guardians. That's what brought me to Raleigh."

"I thought you went there to live with a friend?" I asked.

"I did, but that was only part of the reason," Anna said. "I read in the paper about this man there who has an incredible story. He was in prison when the light reached out to him. God sent someone to him from his past to help him stop a terrible tragedy. He escaped prison to save the lives of hundreds of runners in both Atlanta and Raleigh."

My heart began to pound in my chest at her words. I'd heard the story hundreds of times. In a large way it was a part of my own story. I stood and paced away to the window.

"I never got the chance to seek him out before Julian . . ." she continued.

"You wouldn't have found him in Raleigh," I interrupted as I listened to the rain slow to an intermittent sprinkle.

"You know the man I'm talking about?" Anna asked. "You know Logan Foster?"

I laughed and ran a hand over the scars beneath my hood.

"You could say that," I chuckled. "I tried to kill him a couple of times." I said.

Anna gasped. "You tried to kill him?"

"Yes," I said. "And in return, he saved my life."

Anna stood and came to where I leaned against the window frame. "Were you in jail with him, weren't you?"

"That's the first time the light reached out to me," I said, turning to her. "In that God-awful place, through Logan Foster."

"Can you get ahold of him?"

"Julian sent . . . there were emails," I struggled to explain. "I expected to hear from him, but it's been years."

"Maybe when this is all over we can all go to him," Anna said. I could hear the hope in her voice, but also the fear.

"We won't find him in Raleigh. He lives up in the mountains where there are other people with tremendous stories to tell."

"You're talking about Saluda," Anna repeated, brightening. "That's where Donovan and Alex Pritchard live. I read about their story too. They're on my list as well."

Shaking my head, I suddenly saw the pieces of my life fit together like the canvasses I'd painted of this very room. The bigger picture it created was more breathtakingly intricate than anything I'd ever seen.

And I was a part of it.

That truth filled me with a warmth I'd never felt before.

"Looks like the heavens brought more than just you, me and Julian together," I said. "It seems you and I are a part of a greater plan. I have to believe that Julian is part of that plan."

"We have to find him," Anna whispered.

"We will," I assured her. "I promise you. I will find your son."

"How?" She asked. I heard the doubt in her voice. "We don't even know where to look."

"Yes, we do," I said as Mutt stood and trotted over to us with a whine. I petted his head and smiled. "We have to look to the light."

Fourteen

The clouds lifted, taking with them the remnants of the storm. We rose to make our way back to the studio. As much as Anna wanted to jump in her car and search the highways, an indescribable conviction took hold of me as we started to leave the room. I couldn't shake the feeling that Julian was still close. Maybe he would appear to me as he always had, huddled in the corner of the studio. Maybe not. All I knew for certain was that I needed to get back home.

Anna took one last sweep of the house with Mutt on her heels. I lingered in the room one more minute, running my fingers along the crayoned words above the mattress. *See me*.

"I see you, kid," I whispered. "I see you."

When I finally turned to leave, Anna met me in the doorway.

"There's nothing in the house that gives a clue as to where they're headed. They left everything behind as if they were only going to be gone for a few hours. Something's not right. We need to hurry," she said, coming back into the room. "I just want to grab one thing . . ."

I heard the crinkle of paper as she bent down to pick up Julian's coloring book. She took a deep breath as she flipped through its pages, then turned to leave. As she did, my ears caught the subtle fluttering of a loosed page as it floated to the floor.

"A page fell out," I said, feeling for it along the carpet. When my fingers met the folded paper, I handed it to Anna.

"It's not a coloring page." Anna gasped as her fingers unfolded it. "It's a letter."

"A letter?"

"It's Stephan's handwriting . . ." she said.

"Who is it made out to?" I asked. "Whoever it is could help us find them."

"It's made out to me." Dread was thick in her voice.

She took a deep breath, and I stilled myself at her side as she read.

My Dearest Anna,

If you are reading this letter it means that you've found our little hide-out . . . just as I knew you would. You were always so smart, weren't you?

It also means that you are too late. Julian is mine forever now, Anna. Unlike everyone else in my life, he will never leave me. He and I will be united always.

You broke my heart, Anna. I gave you everything, and you left me with nothing. Now you will know what it feels like to have everything that you care about ripped away from you. You tried to take my son from me, but not even you can change our fate. He is my destiny. I can see it so clearly now.

Memorial Day . . . it couldn't be more perfect. Don't you see? The perfect day for Julian and I to leave the pain and misery of this world. I'm doing him the greatest favor, Anna – a favor I wish my parents had done for me. He won't have to grow up inside like I did.

He can fly with me from the house of light . . . We'll be united in eternity forever where no man, or woman, can tear us apart.

Goodbye, my lovely Anna.
-Stephan

"My God," I said, choking back the fear that gripped my throat. "He really is out of his mind."

"I don't understand . . ." Anna groped. "What does this mean?"

When I didn't answer, a great heaving cry escaped Anna as she sank against the door frame.

"He's going to kill him. He's going to hurt my baby, isn't he?" Anna asked.

"We don't know anything for sure," I tried to assure her, but the fear that gripped me knew the truth.

"You heard what he wrote. What else could it mean? He's going to kill himself and take my baby with him."

The desperation in her voice tore my heart from my chest, but I couldn't deny the implication in Stephan's words. I began to reach for her, but hesitated, letting my hand fall back to my side. With a whine, Mutt pressed his body between us. He licked Anna.

"I'm not going to let that happen," I said, praying for the strength to stop it.

"Stephan said that he was going to do whatever he has planned on Memorial Day," Anna cried. "That's tomorrow, Blake. We're running out of time."

"We're going to find him, Anna," I assured her. I felt the conviction of my words in the deepest parts of my soul.

"How can you be so sure?" Anna asked, an anguished whisper.

With a sigh, I adjusted the shades over my eyes. "Because Julian's story isn't over."

For a moment, Anna said nothing. Then I heard her take a deep, shaky breath as she folded the letter and put it in her pocket.

"You really think going back to the studio is what we're supposed to do?" she asked, finding her resolve.

"I do," I said. "I don't know why, but I need to get back there."

"Then let's go."

We walked in silence, our hurried steps pounding the pavement in unison as Mutt kept pace ahead of us. The late afternoon hum of passing tourists and ship horns were lost on us. The world felt strangely disconnected now. All that lay ahead of me was purpose, the rest of my life fading into the distance.

When we finally stepped inside the studio, Anna stiffened with a startled gasp.

"What is it?" I asked, my heart quickening.

"Your paintings are gone," she said, taking a cautious step forward. "The only ones left are the ones you painted in black and white."

I let out a long breath and walked into the studio.

"Mr. Bramble, my art dealer, must have come by to pick them up," I said, making my way up the stairs. "I'll be right back."

I felt along the floor in front of the loft door with my foot until my toes found the thick envelope. Picking up the cash, I went inside and tossed it into the box beneath my bed. The thought donned on me, as I patted down the full box in order to replace the lid, that I finally had all that I ever thought I'd wanted. There should be hundreds of thousands of dollars in the box by now. People had paid top dollar for my portraits of Julian. I had more money than I knew what to do with. And none of it meant a thing.

All that mattered, all I cared about, was finding Julian before it was too late. I would trade the whole box, the success, even the studio, for just one more conversation with the child who had opened my eyes to the light of the world. My muse.

Tossing the box back under the bed, I walked to the kitchen and clumsily threw together a couple of sandwiches. My body was exhausted. I felt a hundred years old, my limbs weak and my mind weary. How much worse must Anna feel, I thought? How much worse must her fear be? Anna's world was falling apart with every tick of the minute hand.

"Here, you need to eat something," I said, coming to where she stood in front of one of the remaining portraits.

When she spoke, I could hear the tears she sniffed back.

"How can I munch on PB&J while my son rides to his death in his father's trunk?" she asked.

"You're no good to Julian if you pass out from low blood sugar," I insisted, handing her the sandwich. "You have to take care of yourself, for him."

She hesitated, but took the sandwich from my hand with a disgruntled sigh. I heard her take an angry bite, her teeth making quick work of the meal.

"Why are we here?" she asked. I heard Mutt gladly devour the sandwich remnants she tossed to him. "We should be out there searching."

"I don't know," I admitted, taking a bite of my sandwich and deciding quickly that my nervous stomach couldn't handle it. I tossed it to a waiting Mutt, who caught it mid-air. "It's just a feeling I have . . ."

"A feeling?" Anna asked. I could hear her patience slipping.

"I don't know how to explain it," I said, turning from her to pace the studio. "It's like when I first learned to walk around in here after losing my sight. At first it was jarring, frightening even. I didn't know where I was in relation to the space around me. I had to learn to trust my steps. I had to remind myself that there was solid floor beneath me. When I took the stairs, I had to trust in that next step even though I couldn't see it. When we were in that room, I suddenly knew I needed to come here . . . . Just like I knew that those stairs would be under me. I'm sure this is the next step even though I can't see why."

The studio was silent as Anna processed what I'd said. When she finally spoke again, her voice had softened.

"There's a word for that kind of trust," she said.

"What is that?" I asked.

Anna walked to me. I could feel her glare hover on my covered face. I felt her reach for my shades and fought the instinct to flinch away from her touch. She lifted the black rims from my scarred-over eyes as my heart pounded in my chest. When she did not gasp or react, I lifted my hood and let it fall down my back. For the first time, I let someone gaze their fill of my wounds. And for the first time, I was not ashamed to share my pain.

"It's called blind faith," she said.

For a moment we faced each other in silence. Then Anna took a deep, cleansing breath.

"I have faith in you, Blake," she said. "I have faith in whatever it is you feel. I'll wait for the next step with you."

Before I could reply, the air grew thick like a haze of warm air. It raised the hairs on my neck. Something was coming. I was as sure of that as I was of my next breath. I couldn't tell what it was, only sense its approach. I stepped back, confused by the sensation as my breath came in shaky drags.

"Blake, what is it?" Anna asked.

When a loud knock sounded at the door, we both stiffened.

"It's the next step." I whispered, aghast. The knock came again, louder than before.

When I made no effort to answer, Anna's footsteps approached the door. Mutt raced ahead of her to greet the guest with a sloppy kiss. I stood, frozen by apprehension as Anna nudged him out of the way. The front door opened with a creak.

"You called the cops?" Anna's angry voice shrieked.

"No . . ." I started to answer, but was interrupted by the familiar voice on the other side of the doorway.

The man cleared his throat before he spoke.

"I'm not the cops," he said. "Sorry about the uniform. I came straight from the station back home. I actually came on personal business."

I didn't need to see him to know who had found his way to my door. A mixture of warmth and dread filled me as I stepped out from the shadows and came to the doorway. There I came face to face with my presumed foe, my would-be-savior, my mentor. My friend.

"Hello, Logan," I said.

"My God in heaven." He gasped, his shock causing his heavy feet to stagger backwards. "It's true."

"Yes," I said, "this is what I've become."

My first reaction was to cover back up, to yank up my hood and grab my glasses back from Anna. But I stood, secure in my resolve that I was becoming what I was meant to be . . . whatever that was.

"Boss . . ." he stammered, struggling with his words. "I don't know what to . . ."

"I know you got my emails," I interrupted. "Before you say anything, just know that I was wrong . . . everything I said was wrong. You were right all along, Logan. I can see that now."

Logan stood on the sidewalk in front of the studio as the gulls announced the approach of dusk. His shock was palpable. I could feel his gaze on my scar-shrouded eyes as he took in the horror of my appearance. His silence announced his stupor. Anna stepped into the door frame beside me.

"Logan?" she asked. "THE Logan Foster? . . . Who escaped Central Prison to stop that race in Raleigh? The Logan who sees Guardians?"

Before Logan could respond, I interjected.

"Logan, this is Anna," I said. "She is Julian's mother."

I felt Logan hesitate, then heard the swish of fabric as he extended his hand. Anna took it.

"Julian . . ." Logan repeated, turning back to me. "The child you can . . . see?"

"Yes," I affirmed. "I know it sounds crazy, but if anyone can understand, it's you, Logan."

"It's nice to meet you, Anna," Logan said. "It seems we all have a lot in common."

Logan's heavy footsteps followed Anna inside as Mutt greeted him with enthusiastic kisses. I heard Logan pat his head, but I could feel his eyes on me still. I tried to imagine how I must look to Logan, my old friend and foe. How different I must be to him, and not only because of my scars or the loss of my eyes. More than my features had changed, and I knew that he sensed it. I could FEEL that he sensed it. How wrong I had been back when I thought I was tough, when I thought I was important. I was the fearless leader of a gang of lost souls. The thought almost made me laugh. I could see the truth now. I could see what Logan had known all along. I'd never been fearless. In fact, I was consumed by fear. I led none, but was instead a willing slave to fear and hatred. To the darkness.

Everything was different now.

"Hey, there," Logan said as he finally bent to acknowledge Mutt's fevered excitement. "And who is this?

"That's Mutt," I said.

"He helps you?" Logan asked, standing. I heard Mutt's contented paws pace away, felt the swishing of his tail as he retreated to the corner.

"He does," I said. "He's been a good friend."

Suddenly Logan's breath caught in his throat. I knew his gaze had fallen on the black and white portraits of Julian that still adorned the studio.

"This is Julian?" he asked, stepping closer to examine the images. I knew he was putting the information from my emails together.

"Yes," Anna replied. "That's my baby boy."

"These portraits . . . they're incredible," Logan said. I could imagine him as he studied each one. "You painted these . . . after the accident, Boss?"

"That's right," I said. "Julian showed me how to see."

"Incredible . . . just incredible," he said.

"Why do you keep calling Blake, 'Boss'?" Anna asked.

"It was a name I used to use," I said, coming to stand beside Logan. "That name is dead now, Logan. Just like the man who wore it. Call me by my real name. I'm learning who the man behind it really is."

"It's nice to finally meet the real you, Blake," Logan said. I could imagine the proud smile that curved his thin lips as he spoke the words. "So where is he? Julian? I'm eager to meet this amazing little guy."

The grin fell from my lips as pleasantries were replaced by dread. "He's missing, Logan."

Anna took a tentative step toward us. "He was kidnapped by his father. He's in danger, and we don't even know where to look."

I heard the crinkling of paper as Anna dug Stephan's note from her pocket and unfolded it for Logan.

"We think he's going to hurt him." she said handing the note over.

There was silence as Logan scanned the letter. When he finished reading, he let out a deep sigh.

"Memorial Day is tomorrow," he said.

Fear gripped me anew. "I know."

"I think I understand now," he said turning to me. "Why you're seeing Julian, I mean. You have to save him, Boss - I mean, Blake. You have to find Julian and go to him before it's too late. You're the only one who can."

"Don't you think I've tried that?" I asked, throwing my hands up. "All I get are glimpses . . . pieces of a bigger picture."

"I don't understand. You're supposed to be the next step, Logan," Anna said, her voice desperate. "You are why we came back here instead of searching the highways, I know it. You are what we were waiting for. You've got to help us."

"I'm not the one . . ."

"You're a cop," Anna interrupted. "I don't have full custody of Julian, so the police here wouldn't help me if I asked. There has to be something you can do."

Logan paced away.

"I'm a deputy back in Saluda," he corrected. "I'm way out of my jurisdiction here. I'm not sure what I can do. Donovan . . . my father-in-law is the sheriff up there. He's got connections. Even if I called him, though, there's just not enough time."

"You're talking about Donovan Pritchard," Anna said, her shock causing her voice to rise in pitch. "He's your father-in-law?"

"You know him?" Logan asked.

"She knows about all of you . . . your stories," I interjected. "She's been looking for you."

"If you know the stories," Logan said, as I heard him run his hands through his thick blonde hair, "then you know that sometimes things aren't always as they seem. I don't think I'm here to save the day this time. This isn't my calling, Blake. It's yours."

Logan walked to me. When he spoke next, the urgency in his voice made it feel as though my heart had ceased to beat in my chest.

"You've been called to save this child, Blake," he said. "I'll help in any way I can, but you have to understand that if God charged you to save him, then He also gave you the tools, the ability to do it. It's all inside of you. You just have to find it and believe it."

"Like you believed that you could save those runners?" I asked.

"No," he said, coming close to speak directly into my face. "This is so much more than that, don't you understand? Saving Julian is why you are here. It's the reason you exist. Lay down all that has come before and the fear of what might still come. Make Julian all that you can see."

"Logan," I said, not bothering to hide the desperation from my voice. "He IS all I can see."

"Then see him, Blake," he whispered. "See him."

"Please," I pleaded. "Show me how."

Fifteen

"What do you see?" Logan asked, his voice hushed from where he knelt beside my chair.

Anna paced the expanse of the room behind me, whispering her prayers into the shadows of the studio. Day turned to dusk, leaving a chill in the air as the last of the evening light faded.

"Nothing," I said, frustration taking hold of me as I leaned back against the chair's wooden backing. "All I see is . . . black."

"Concentrate on Julian," Logan said into my ear. "Focus on only him. Think of nothing else."

I took a deep breath and again attempted to align my thoughts as I had when I'd seen the light that led me to Julian. I brought the image of the car and its dark-haired driver back into focus in my mind, but as hard as I tried to reach into the darkened depths of the trunk where I knew Julian was, my mind remained fixated on the driver.

In my vision the figure morphed, his dark hair thinning and lightening as he gripped the wheel with white knuckles. When the driver turned, it was my own father, not Stephan, who looked at me with desperate, black eyes.

"*Don't tell Mom*," he whispered, jarring me from the reverie.

I jumped up with a start.

"I can't!" I cried. "I don't know why, but I can't get out of my own head."

Frustrated, I shoved the chair back and walked to the window where the faint sound of a distant ship met my ears. Mutt trotted to where I stood, and I rested my hand upon his head.

"Maybe instead of worrying about what you're not seeing, you should just tell us what you are. When you go into your mind, what do you see?" Anna asked, coming to stand beside me.

I turned to her, momentarily soothed by her strength.

"I see my father," I whispered. "I see my past . . . my losses. Pain. I see my failures."

For a moment there was silence. Then Logan snapped to life behind me. I heard him push something along the hardwood floor.

"You got a blank one of these?" he asked.

"I know where," Anna said, rushing to join in whatever was going on.

The closet door opened with a squeak, and Anna's hurried footsteps met Logan's in the center of the room. It took a second, but I realized with curious anticipation that they had set up a new canvas and my paints.

"Come sit down," Logan called.

Hesitantly, I walked to him and took my chair again.

"We don't have time for this," I protested. "It's not going to help. I've painted a dozen times imagining, praying, that Julian would appear as he always had. It's no use, Logan. This isn't the way."

Logan knelt down beside me again, his resolve radiating from him in warm waves.

"This is different," he said. "This time you're not painting a portrait of someone else. You're not trying to capture who they are through color, or express what you see in them with your talent. You're not even going to try and capture what it is you see in your mind."

"Then what's the point?" I asked, my patience slipping. "What do you expect me to paint?"

"I want you to paint yourself, Blake," he said, his voice stern. "I want you to capture who you are, who you were created to be. I want you to paint yourself not as you see you, or how you think others see you . . . but how the light sees you."

"The light sees you as whole," Anna said from behind me, obviously seeing logic in this venture. "It sees you as perfect. Blameless."

"But I don't know . . ." I stammered.

"Let the past go . . . and the pain," Logan continued. "Forget the mistakes and the scars. Paint who you are in the light, Blake. Can you see it?"

With a sigh, I sat back as images of tear-stained eyes and bruised faces flashed into my mind in a wave of black shadow. I forced my way through them and searched deep within for the light on the other side.

Wading in the darkness of my mother's packed suitcase, and of blood-soaked carpets, I called out for the light to find me once again. Memories of my brother's motionless face and of my father's hatred clung to me like lost children. The fear screamed at me to quit this exercise and to shake the images from my mind. It was hard not to listen.

Then among the misery and death, regret and sorrow, I caught a glimmer of something. I heard a voice call my name.

"Flawless," it whispered.

Clawing through the muck, I fought the darkness back as it reached out its inky talons to claim me as it always had. Again, my nightmares arose, threatening to bury me in a prison of perpetual rage and death. I clung desperately to the light that called me forward, beckoning me to step out from the shadows once and for all.

"I can see it," I answered, taking up my paintbrush.

Vaguely, I heard Logan step back as I quickly loaded my palette. My fingers scarcely touched the colors, but I knew what each one was.

In my mind, the light grew brighter as I pulled myself from the darkness. With each step, the burden of pain and anguish lightened, and the chains that had bound me for so long fell to my ankles like a discarded robe. *Flawless.*

Then I burst through. The light overwhelmed me, welcomed me. A peace I'd never known enveloped me. I stood dazed, dumbfounded by the release. The fear, the hatred, and all the pain fell behind in the shadows. For the first time that I could remember, I felt secure. I was safe.

And I was not alone.

"*See,*" the voice whispered to me from the luminous expanse. It was the voice of a friend I had always known, yet only recently discovered. The voice of a father I always needed, but didn't know I had. It was the voice of love.

Turning, I saw a figure in the distance, surrounded by a luminous glow. As I walked toward it, I recognized my own face. Only it was not the face I'd grown to know. There were no burns, no scars, and no tattoos to memorialize my sin. There was no brokenness. Deep grey eyes held no sorrow or shame.

In the studio, I painted that figure with a fevered passion. The paint glided across the canvas with smooth precision as I reproduced my own likeness as I had never seen it before. I painted myself whole.

In my mind I could feel nothing but joy as I connected with that image and accepted it as my own. I laughed into the expanse, knowing that my cry had also rung out in the studio.

"He's doing it," I heard Logan whisper, but I was too caught up in my epiphany to take note.

As I began to feel as though I knew myself, as I was always meant to be, the image began to change.

"*See,*" the voice called to me again.

My image vanished before me, though not into thin air. I absorbed it, took it into myself and solidified it in truth. Then another image took its place as I stood secure in the warmth of a love I'd never fathomed.

The light around me dimmed, and the expanse closed in with walls of cracked sheetrock and worn wood paneling. The motel room was dim, lit only by the street light that shined through the curtained window. A small TV was perched on a rusting mini fridge. Brass wall lamps hung from the wall above two queen beds, their shades missing. One bed was empty. Its stained comforter remained tucked beneath a lumpy mattress. In the other bed lay a small figure, his face hidden by shadow.

I pushed into the vision and saw the child breathing fitfully in uneasy sleep. Tears blurred my perfected eyes. The love that I carried with me from the expanse of warm light overflowed in my chest as I took in his tattered clothes and smudged, cherub-like cheeks.

"Julian?" I called.

The boy mumbled and stirred.

Reaching out, I called to him again, and his eyelids fluttered and opened. He glared at me with glassy eyes, at first in confusion and then with sudden recognition.

"Blake?" he cried, sitting up. "Is that you?"

"It's me," I said, grabbing him up into my arms. "I'm here."

Warm static radiated from our bodies as Julian grabbed me and laid his head on my shoulder. A spasm of relief rocked his small body as he clutched me tight.

"You can see me," he whispered, his voice raspy.

I choked back the lump that formed in my throat and squeezed him tighter.

"I can see you," I answered. "I can see you."

For a moment we just held onto one another. I was too afraid to let him go. Yet in the back of my mind, warm assurance held my convictions firm. The studio fell away, as did all thoughts of painting. Even Logan and Anna ceased to matter. This was my new reality. Being with Julian was all that existed. His safety was the only thing I cared about.

"Where is he?" I asked, suddenly awake to the danger we faced. "Where's your dad?"

Julian pulled back from me and shrugged.

"I don't know," he said, fear making his voice tremble. "He said he had to go buy us clothes for tomorrow. He says we're finally going home and that we have to look nice for the trip. Blake . . . I don't want to go with him. I'm scared."

"I know you are, kid," I tried to soothe, "but I'm not going to let anything happen to you, okay?"

Julian nodded, but I saw the uncertainty in his wide eyes. My heart broke for his confusion. It was a turmoil I understood, not knowing who or even how to trust. I looked him squarely in the eyes.

"I'm sorry, Julian," I said, placing my hands on his shoulders. "I'm sorry I yelled at you. I was never mad at you. Can you possibly understand that? I was mad at myself."

"It's okay," he said as a grin parted his chapped lips. "You just weren't seeing right. It's hard to see in the dark."

"Yes, it is," I said. Tears filled my eyes again as I hugged him to me. "Yes, it is."

I pulled him away from me and brushed a wild curl from his face. His innocent doe eyes smiled up at me.

"Now, let's get you out of here," I said, pulling back the covers.

Julian's smile fell.

"I can't go," he said, bowing his head dejected.

It was then that I noticed that his right ankle was handcuffed to the archaic furnace beside the bed.

"No . . ."

I looked from his face, to the constraint around his ankle. Taking hold of the cuffs, I yanked as hard as I could against the furnace, knowing all the while it would be no use. Then I tried slipping the cuff from his ankle. I pushed it down his foot as far as it would go. When he flinched, I knew it was too tight to come off.

Desperate, I ran into the bathroom and grabbed the small bar of soap from the mildewed shower. Wetting it in the sink, I brought it to Julian and pulled up his pant leg. Once his ankle was fully lathered, I pushed the cuff down his foot again, this time gaining another inch, but it was no use. The cuff was too tight, and Julian cried out as it began to dig into his flesh.

I yelled my frustration into the smoky room and stomped over to the furnace. Taking a step back, I kicked it as hard as I could, hoping to break off the piece that held the other side of the cuffs. With every kick, the furnace shook, but refused to bend or even dent. By the time I gave up, I was weak and exhausted. My limbs felt heavy. I leaned against the bed to catch my breath.

"I can't go," Julian repeated.

I looked up at him, helpless but determined.

"We're going to figure this out," I promised.

Before I could formulate another plan, headlights shone into the window from behind the dingy curtain. A car door slammed, and brisk footsteps sounded on the walkway outside the room.

"He's back," Julian said, his eyes widening with alarm.

"I'm not going to let him hurt you," I said, hiding myself in the shadows beside Julian's bed. "Pretend to be asleep."

Julian lay back down, and I covered him with his blankets. Cloaked in the thick black in the corner, I watched as Stephan entered the room. He set his shopping bag on the floor and immediately walked to where Julian lay with his eyes closed. I sank back further into the shadows from where I was squeezed beside the bed and the furnace.

"Sleep peacefully, my son," he said, running his fingers along Julian's face. I could smell the stale scent of alcohol on his breath. "Soon all we'll know is peace."

Looking into Stephan's eyes from where I lurked in the corner, I saw only pain in their depths as he stared affectionately at Julian. I recognized the darkness in them, and a great sympathy welled up from my soul. A part of me wanted to reach out to him. To tell him of the light on the other side of the darkness.

"I'm taking you to a place where you'll never again feel scared or sad," Stephan whispered to Julian as he stroked his hair.

"A place where no one can take you away from me again. We'll be together always."

I longed to scream out from where I stood hidden by shadows, but filled with light. I longed to explain to him that the place he was looking for lived within him. That it had always been there.

Julian knew it. He felt it with the innocent abandon of a child. I would not let Julian lose that light to the darkness in his father's eyes. As much as I wanted to reach out to Stephan, I remained in the shadows standing guard over Julian.

His little body trembled. Stephan tucked the blankets around him, mistaking the trembling for cold. I knew the child trembled with fear. When Stephan turned his back to gather up his shopping bag, I reached beneath the covers and found Julian's tiny hand. He grasped mine and squeezed as Stephan walked into the bathroom with a dejected sigh.

"It's okay," I whispered.

"Blake?"

"I'm right here," I answered.

"I don't want to go with him." The desperation in his voice tugged at my heart. "He can't see."

I squeezed his hand beneath the covers.

"I'm not going to let him take you."

When Stephan came out of the bathroom, he was dressed in night clothes. A half-empty bottle of vodka dangled from his fingertips. He tipped the bottle to his lips as he gazed at Julian. Then finally, he set the bottle on the floor beside the end table and fumbled with the covers. With one last remorseful look at his son, he turned over in bed and closed his eyes.

I held onto Julian's hand as I watched Stephan fall into a restless sleep. When his snores sounded into the musty room, I uncurled myself from the corner. Letting go of Julian's hand, I walked around the bed to stare down at Stephan as he slept. Julian turned to watch me bend down to the man's head.

"It doesn't have to be this way," I whispered into his ear. "The light calls."

Stephan mumbled in his sleep and rolled away from me. I turned my attention back to Julian. He glared up at me, tears in his eyes.

"You need to get some sleep," I whispered, kneeling beside him.

"I want to go with you," he begged. "I don't want to be here anymore."

Running my hand through his tangled hair, I did my best to smile.

"I know you don't, kid," I said, "but it looks like we're stuck here for the night. We're going to have to wait until your dad unlocks your ankle to get you out of here. We'll figure something out, I promise."

Julian nodded, but a tear rolled onto his cheek. I grabbed his hand again and gave it a reassuring squeeze.

"You have to be brave for me, okay?" I said. "Be brave for your mom. She loves you very much."

Julian sat up with a start.

"My mom?" he asked in a panic. "You saw my mom? Don't tell her I was bad. She'll be mad at me. Dad said she'd be mad."

"Sssshhh," I whispered and bade him to lie back down. "Your mother isn't mad at you. She could never be mad at you. In fact, she's looking for you. The two of us are going to get you out of here and bring you home where you belong. Your mom loves you more than anything in the world."

Tears streamed from Julian's eyes as he struggled not to sob in the quiet room. "You saw her?"

"Yes," I answered, tucking him back in. "She's coming for you, Julian. We both are."

"Tell her where I am," he pleaded. "Tell her to come get me . . . please, Blake."

"I will. We're coming," I assured him, and the tension left Julian's eyes. He took a deep breath and relaxed into the covers. His face was a mask of fear and exhaustion.

"You have to rest now, okay?"

"Don't leave me," he whispered, squeezing my hand again.

"I'm not going anywhere," I promised, and Julian closed his eyes.

In the shadows of the dreary room, I waited for Julian to fall safely to sleep. In the darkness, I thanked the light for helping me to see Julian again. I thanked God for showing me the way and for helping me to see myself as I was meant to be. Then I asked for the light to show me what to do. I asked it to help me save Julian.

When Julian's breaths fell into the rhythm of deep sleep, I went inside myself again. Though I didn't want to leave Julian for even a second, I had to seek the warm brightness within. I knew it would guide me back to him. Following the vivid light back, I found my newly discovered place of utter peace and safety.

"*Now go*," the voice called to me from within the luminous glow. "*Go.*"

Assured in my task and the power behind me, I ran unhindered back through the darkness. Faith told me what I needed to do. I knew the next step.

Sixteen

The studio was quiet when I returned to myself. In the distance I could hear Logan's heavy breaths as he slept in the corner. Reorienting myself to the lack of sight, I shot up in my chair.

"I know where he is!" I gasped.

Logan woke with a start and was at my side within seconds. "You saw him," he said. "You did it!"

I turned to his voice. My heart pounded with new urgency. "I saw him, Logan," I cried. "I saw."

"It was incredible . . ." he stammered. "Your self-portrait . . . it's amazing. You painted most of the night."

"Where's Anna?" I asked. "I want her to hear this . . ."

"She's upstairs," Logan said. "She fought to stay awake for as long as she could. I finally convinced her to lie down. I've never seen a faith like hers, Blake. The clock is ticking, yet she believed that you would come through . . . and you did."

With a squeak the loft door opened, and Mutt galloped down the stairs to greet me with excited kisses as if I'd been away.

"You want me to hear what?" Anna called as she took the stairs by twos. "Do you know where Julian is?"

"Yes," I said. "No. Well, sort of."

"What do you mean, sort of?" she asked, coming to my side.

"They're in a cheap motel room somewhere," I explained. "Very rundown and dirty."

"A motel room? Where? Where are they?" Anna asked, almost frantic.

"It was dark in the room," I explained. "There were no fliers or anything lying around. I don't know where."

"Was he okay?" Anna asked. "Is my baby okay?"

"He's fine," I said. "For now. We need to find them. I promised Julian that we were coming for him."

I heard Anna throw up her hands as she stomped away to the window. "How are we supposed to do that if we don't know where this motel is? They could be anywhere!"

"No," I said, standing. "They couldn't have gotten too far. I saw them in the car this afternoon. It looks like they've been checked into the motel room for a while now, long enough for Stephan to go to the store for some clothes."

"Clothes?" Anna asked.

Mutt followed when I went to Anna. I heard him lick her hand, and felt her tension calm beside me.

"Stephan told Julian that they had to look nice for the trip home," I explained, keeping my voice steady.

"Home?" Anna said. "That means they're on the way back to Charlotte! Maybe Stephan came to his senses . . ."

"No, Anna," I said, my tone grave. "That's not what he meant."

For a moment there was silence as she processed what else "home" could mean. When it came to her, she cried out. I heard Logan grab the chair and bring it to her.

"Anna," I said, kneeling beside her. "There's a darkness in Stephan. I saw it in his eyes. He's blinded by fear and misery. Do you know where that comes from? What happened to him? Maybe we can reason with him somehow."

"I . . . I don't know much," she said, "but he's beyond reason, Blake. He's lost."

"Tell me what you know," I asked.

"He was raised by a single mother. His father left them when he was a baby. His mom took care of him until he was eight.

One day she left him at a foster home and promised to be back for him. He waited for years, but she never came back. He once said that was why he became a lawyer. He was so driven to make something of himself, to prove that he was worth coming back to."

"My God . . ." I whispered as memories of my own mother walking out on me flashed into my mind. I no longer felt the anger and rejection of those memories. All I felt now was sympathy and even warmth for Stephan. I knew his pain, and I knew there was a way out of it. If only he could see. So much about him made sense now.

"That would explain why he reacted so strongly to you leaving with Julian," Logan reasoned.

"He left me no choice," Anna said between clenched teeth. "We had to go."

"I know," I reassured her. "He was lost to the darkness long before you came along, Anna. It's been with him some time."

"Sometimes he would wake up in the night drenched in sweat. I know he had nightmares. I know they were about his time in foster care, but he refused to let me in. He would never talk about what happened to him in that home, but I know it must have been unthinkable," Anna continued. "That's how we grew so close in the beginning, I think. We bonded over our pasts, over our brokenness."

"That's natural," Logan said. "We gravitate toward what's familiar. None of this is your fault, Anna."

"No," she whispered, defeated. "I should have known that the past would come back to haunt me one way or another."

"You can't think like that," I protested. "You've overcome your past. Stephan can too. Don't let the darkness use the pains from your past to derail your future. We're going to find Julian."

"Well, listen to you . . ." Logan said into my ear, his voice brimming with pride.

For a minute, it was quiet. Mutt nuzzled my shoulder with a gentle whine. Then Anna took a deep, cleansing breath as she absorbed my words. I felt her resolve strengthen, and she sat up in the chair.

"What do we do, Blake?" she asked. "Where do we start looking?"

"Does Stephan have a cell phone?" I asked. "Logan, you could track his phone, couldn't you?"

My heart pumped with excitement and renewed hope with the thought. When Anna groaned, I knew those hopes were dashed.

"He left his phone in Charlotte," she said. "His apartment was the first place I looked when he took off with Julian. It was just sitting there on the kitchen counter. He was too smart to bring it with him."

"Think, Anna," Logan said. "Where would Stephan go? Why drive all the way here from Charlotte? There has to be some significance here?"

"I . . . I don't know," she said, thinking. "He used to talk about getting a beach house one day. He said he wanted to live beside the water, that the sound of the waves calmed him. I never took him seriously. I knew he would never leave his firm in Charlotte. He wouldn't even take a vacation."

"There are hundreds of miles of beach within a day's drive from here," I said, desperation tightening the walls of my chest. "Did he say which beach?"

"No," she said. "We never even went together. It's just something he would mention when . . ."

"When what?" Logan prodded.

"When he'd had too much to drink," Anna said.

"How often was that?" Logan asked.

Anna's voice turned tight, strained. "Often enough to make me kidnap my own child."

Logan sighed. I heard him lean against the doorframe as he thought.

"He's obviously not thinking clearly. Would Stephan rent a boat?" he asked, and though he kept his voice neutral, I caught the implication behind his question. Logan feared that Stephan might drown himself, and Julian with him. "We could call all the boat rental companies within a day's drive . . . ."

"No," Anna said, "Stephan would never actually go out on the water. That's another reason I didn't take him seriously. He can't swim. He's terrified of the water, even on a boat."

"Then we've got no leads," I sighed. "They could be anywhere on the coast. We're back to square one."

"Maybe not," Logan said, walking to where I squatted. "You could go back there. You could find something that leads us to them."

"I looked all over that room, Logan," I said, my heart sinking. "There was nothing."

"You said that Stephan went shopping?" he asked.

"Julian said he went out for clothes. Then in the vision, I saw Stephan come in with the bag," I said.

"What did it look like?" Logan asked.

"What did what look like?" I asked, confused.

"The bag," Logan said, his voice rising with hope.

"It was dark . . . I don't," I stammered.

"Think," he urged. "Try to put yourself back there again. What color was the bag? Did it have a store name or logo?"

"Please, Blake . . ." Anna pleaded. "Anything you can see, anything at all could help. You have to go back."

Taking a deep breath, I struggled to bring the image of the motel room back into focus. I could feel Anna's and Logan's stares, but I ignored them, digging deeper through the darkness into the light and beyond. This time the journey was easier because I knew what was on the other side. I knew the light was with me.

When the room came into focus, I heard the heavy breaths of both Stephan and Julian as they slept in fitful slumber. I glanced around the room for some hint of the motel's name or an address on a notepad or slip of paper. When I saw nothing, I made my way through the shadows to the bathroom where I'd seen Stephan take the plastic shopping bag. The bathroom was pitch black, the feeble light from outside was unable to penetrate the small corner room. In the vision, I closed my eyes and stretched out my fingertips. I made myself one with the dark I was so accustomed to.

When my fingers found the plastic bag, I attempted to lift it into my arms. The weight of the bag and the tinkling of glass made me stop abruptly. As I felt along and inside the bag, I discovered that it was packed with three more vodka bottles along with the new clothing. In order to get the bag into the light as quietly as possible, I had to remove the bottles one by one.

With my hand clasped around the neck of one, I slowly lifted it from the bag. It clanged against the other bottles. The sound reverberated into the next room. I froze, my heart thumping in my ears, as Stephan tossed in his bed, disrupted by the noise. When all fell silent, I again attempted to lift the bottle from the bag. Despite my best efforts, it clanged against the bottle beside it again. Stephan stirred.

Opening my eyes, I held my breath. My mind raced with silent prayers that he would go back to sleep. From the bathroom doorway, a light glow caught my attention. It dawned on me then that more than just the street light was beginning to illuminate the motel room from the outside. The sun was coming up.

That knowledge filled me with renewed urgency and panic. When Stephan settled once again, I lowered the bottle back into the bag. There was no time for this. Abandoning all hope of getting the bag into the light without waking Stephan to the new day, I closed my eyes again. My fingertips searched the surface of the bag. I felt along the smooth plastic until I came across raised edges. Hoping the raised portion would form words, I ran my fingers along them, trying to make sense of the curves and lines. The raised angles did not form words, but an image. I traced it with my fingers until a picture formed in my mind.

When I was sure I had it, I ducked back into the room where both Stephan and Julian lay sleeping. The sunlight from outside was beginning to penetrate the edges of the curtains. Soon the room would be illuminated by the dawn's light. Creeping to the window, I pulled the curtain back hoping to see a sign for either the motel or the street it was on. All I could see was a row of cars parked on a gravel lot and an aging oak tree that blocked the street light. Not a sign in sight.

Desperation propelled me forward. I went to the door and pulled back the deadbolt. A metallic click sounded in the otherwise silent room. I paused, my heart racing in my ears. When Stephan did not stir, I gave the door a tug. It opened without a sound. Relieved, I pulled the vision in my mind with me out onto the broken sidewalk. I looked left and right before deciding to go right in search of an address or street sign.

But with each step I took away from the room, away from Julian, the vision faded more and more. Within five steps, I was plunged back into total darkness. Whatever this vision was, whatever ability I had been granted, it had its limitations. I could interact with the surroundings here, but my sight was dependent upon my proximity to Julian.

"I'm only meant to see Julian," I whispered into the dawn's haze as I walked back to the room.

Closing the door behind me, I inched the deadbolt back into place. Then I went to where Julian slept, his little body momentarily at peace. I ran my fingers gently through his disheveled hair and prayed that he would cling to his sweet dreams and remember that we were coming for him.

Without warning, Stephan shot up in bed with a terror-filled cry. Panting, he wiped his brow and turned to me. I shut my eyes tight. In my mind, I ran through the light into the darkness on the other side.

When I came back to myself, anxiety threatened to consume me. I leaned against the wall to catch my breath as Mutt licked my hand reassuringly. This time coming back to my lack of sight was stifling.

"What is it?" Anna asked, panicked.

Logan came to where I stood. "What did you see??"

"We have to find him . . . now," I warned, still trying to catch my breath. "Stephan is awake."

"The sun is almost all the way up," Anna cried.

"Did you find anything that can help us?" Logan asked. "Did you see the bag?"

"It was too dark to see," I said. "Quick, hand me my brush."

Logan hesitated, but then I heard his heavy footsteps run to the other side of the studio to retrieve my paint brush. When he handed it to me, the tip was still damp with inky black. Turning to the wall, I began to trace the logo from the bag as I recalled it in my mind. I traced its edges and curves onto the wall's smooth surface even as the first of the sun's rays warmed my face through the window.

"This was on the bag . . ." I said as I worked.

Anna and Logan stood behind me, studying the picture as it took shape beneath my fingers.

"It looks like an anchor," Anna said.

"With rope wrapped around it," Logan said as I finished.

I turned to them, desperation mingling with hope.

"It has to be a logo, right?" I asked. "Do either of you recognize it?"

"I don't recognize it. That's all that was on the bag?" Anna asked. "No name or anything?"

"That's it," I said. "I tried to find a street sign or a sign for the motel, anything, but I could only see so much. This is all I could get."

"It's something," Logan said in an attempt to soothe Anna. "We can work with this."

"It's just a logo." Anna's voice held the same desperation I felt in my own soul.

"No," Logan countered. "It's the key to finding your son. I'll be right back."

Logan walked past us and out of the studio. Cool dawn air breezed by us when he opened the door. The beach combing birds were coming to life. Mutt whined at the door as he watched Logan leave. Anna came to stand close to me. The scent of her hair mingled with the scent of her salty tears.

"We're going to find him," I assured her. "Logan is the best man I know. He'll help us find Julian. I know it."

At first Anna was silent. Then she let out a heavy breath which I felt against my ear.

"You're the next step," she said to me at last. "It was always you, Blake."

I wanted to protest, to tell her that Logan was our best chance at finding Julian, but my heart could not deny the truth of her words. I felt it rise within me as I dwelled amongst the light on the other side of shadow. Julian's life was in my hands.

"I know," I said as fear rose up in me.

"I don't know how you do it, but I need you to stay with my son. If we don't find Julian in time . . ." Anna's voice broke, but she took a breath and continued. "I need you to stay with him. Do whatever it takes to keep him safe. Promise me."

"I don't know how . . ." I began when Logan's footsteps sounded on the sidewalk outside the door.

"Promise me," she said again, more urgent than before.

"I promise I'll do everything in my power to protect your son," I said. "On my life."

Anna seemed satisfied. She took a deep breath as Logan strode back in carrying something. My mind whirled with sudden doubt, though I tried to fight it. *What if I couldn't keep my promise? What could I even do?* Taking a deep breath, I remembered the light and the strength that filled me within. I struggled to keep that truth at the forefront of my mind.

"With any luck, there will be only one store within a day's drive with that logo," Logan said.

He sat on the chair, and I heard him open a duffle bag or briefcase and withdraw something. The laptop let out a series of digital chimes as he opened the screen and set it on his lap. I heard his rapid keystrokes as Logan typed his query into the search engine.

"There are dozens of shops with that logo!" Anna cried. "Or one like it."

Logan let out a sigh. "Let's see if we can narrow this down. Some of these are restaurants, some bars. Let's narrow this down to just clothing stores."

Logan's fingers flew across the keys.

"That brought up a little over a dozen shops," he said trying to sound positive, but I could hear in his voice an edge of uncertainty that made my blood run cold.

"We'll have to call each one and give them Stephan's description," Logan continued. "With any luck, we'll get a hit on his location."

"Most of these places don't open for a few more hours," Anna said. "We don't have that kind of time! What if the same workers aren't even there this morning?"

"We don't have a choice," Logan said, turning in his chair to us. "It's all we've got."

"Then let's get in the car and investigate them all for ourselves," Anna said, her voice frantic. "If we split up, there's a better chance of finding the motel room near one of the stores."

"That would take days," Logan said with a frustrated sigh. "These stores are all up and down the North Carolina coast. They spread into South Carolina as well. Best I can do is call the station back home and put more manpower into calling them up."

"Do it," Anna pleaded. "Please, call whoever will help us."

Logan stood and walked to the back of the studio. I heard him dial his cell phone and wait for a connection. Anna grabbed the chair and set it before me. I didn't need to see her face to know the desperation in her eyes.

"Go," she commanded. "Go to my son. If Stephan makes a move, you have to stop him. Find a way to keep my baby safe until we find him."

"I don't know what I can do . . ." I whispered, still wrestling with doubt.

"Yes, you do," she said, gently. "You can do all things . . ."

Her faith steadied me, and I lowered myself into the chair. I recalled the light on the other side of darkness. I remembered the voice that called to me there and reminded myself that I was not alone.

"I can do all things," I repeated, remembering the verse she quoted, knowing that I was not alone. Then I plunged back into the abyss to find the light again.

"I'm counting on you," I heard Anna say into my ear as I sought my way back through the darkness. "Julian is counting on you."

Seventeen

"*This little light of mine, I'm going to let it shine.*" Julian's voice rang through the darkness as I rushed to meet him on the other side of the light.

When the motel room came into focus again, he was sitting on the bed gazing out the window as the sunlight shone on his angelic features. For the first time since I'd known him, he was bathed and clean. His damp, auburn curls were swept into neatly brushed rows atop his head. He was dressed in fresh cargo shorts and a striped shirt. I glanced about the room, lit feebly now by the light of the new day. Memorial Day.

When I saw no sign of Stephan, I went to Julian. As I got closer, I could see that he was still handcuffed to the furnace.

"I knew you would come back," Julian said with a sad smile as he turned to me. "I knew you didn't leave me."

"I'm always with you, Julian," I assured. "I'm not going to leave you."

"I couldn't see you," he said.

"But I see you, Julian," I said. "I'm never losing sight of you again, okay?"

"Okay."

"Where's your dad?" I asked, looking around again.

"I don't know. He told me that he had to do something, but that he would be back and then it would be time to go."

"Go where?" I asked, praying that he would have some idea of Stephan's next move.

Julian only shrugged his trembling shoulders. His haunted eyes spoke volumes about the fear behind them. Though he put on a brave face, I knew that Julian understood the danger he was in.

"I want to go home," Julian whispered, wiping a tear from his cheek.

"I know you do," I said, going to him and wrapping him into my arms. "Your mother and a close friend of mine are coming to find you here. They're coming to get you and bring you home."

Julian perked up and pulled back from me with an excited smile.

"Your good friend?" he asked. "Is it Logan? The guy whose painting is on the wall? Is Logan coming?"

"Yes," I said, tucking an escaped curl behind his ear. "Logan is coming. He's the smartest guy I know."

"So when I sent him those emails," Julian asked, looking me in the eyes, "I did a good thing?"

Letting out a long sigh, I remembered the way I had screamed at him for sending those emails. It seemed a lifetime ago. The words, though from my lips, were from a different person. I hugged him to me again.

"You did a good thing," I agreed. "You did a very good thing."

Julian pulled away again and looked outside the window quizzically.

"When are they coming?" he asked, expectantly.

I stood and took a good look around the dusky room.

"Soon," I said as I searched, "but if we can find something that will help them find you faster . . ."

A small suitcase lay unzipped on a chipped dresser across the room. I went to it and flipped it open.

"Do you know where you are?" I asked as I rummaged through men's shirts and mismatched pants and socks. "I mean, do you know where this motel is? Did you see anything on the drive here? Any signs or landmarks?"

"No, I didn't see anything. My dad made me ride in the trunk. He said that bad people might be looking for me, that they wanted to take me away." Julian bowed his head. "He was talking about my mom, wasn't he? Is she the bad person looking for me?"

Giving up on the suitcase, I turned back to Julian. The sadness in his eyes when he looked into mine for an answer made my heart ache. I knew that look, the look that told me that he understood more than any child his age should know.

"To your dad, yes," I said gently. "It's just the way he sees things right now, though. She's not the bad guy, no matter what your dad believes. Do you understand?"

Julian nodded, and then with a sigh, he turned back to the window and let the sunlight warm his face.

"My dad's the bad guy," he said. "He's lost."

"It doesn't have to be that way," I tried to explain. "He doesn't have to be lost."

"He's in the dark," Julian said. When he looked at me, I knew he understood.

"Yes, he is," I said.

I turned back to the room and rummaged through the nightstand drawers. The only thing I found there was a worn, hardcover Bible. No cute notepad with the name of the motel, no local menus. There was no indication of where on the coast they were.

Then an idea hit me, and I ran into the bathroom to check the labels on the mini bars of soap and shampoo. I knew that sometimes the name of the motel was printed on the back. When I saw nothing on the counter, I pulled back the dingy shower curtain. A full-sized bar of soap lay smudged and frothy at the bottom of the tub. There was no wrapper.

With a frustrated groan, I flung the curtain back into place and turned. It was then that I remembered the shopping bag. Perhaps the name was on the front and I had failed to feel it in the dark. Maybe there was a receipt inside. But the bag was no longer on the counter.

"Where's the bag?" I asked, coming out of the bathroom. "The shopping bag your dad brought in last night. Where did it go?"

"He put our dirty clothes in it and took it with him," Julian said. "He had bottles in there too. He doesn't know that I saw them. He doesn't want me to know that he drinks that stuff, but I still know when he does. He smells different. His eyes look different. It scares me."

"I know exactly what you're talking about," I said, going back to him. "But you don't have to be afraid. I'm right here, and we're going to figure this out."

Suddenly it made sense why Stephan left Julian alone in the room. He was out drinking somewhere, and he didn't want the child to see. That meant two things: Stephan would be back any minute, and when he came back he would be intoxicated. It also meant that on some level, to some degree, Stephan cared about protecting Julian from his alcoholism. Somewhere among the desperation and brokenness, Stephan wanted to do the right thing by Julian.

I also knew the effects of liquor on a tormented soul. The darkness would take over, ushered in with every sip from the narrow bottle. He would feel reassured that taking Julian's life was doing the right thing. Any light inside of Stephan would once again be doused by numbing anguish. I knew from experience that when Stephan returned, he would be lost to the darkness, and Julian would pay the ultimate price of his pain.

I remembered my promise to Anna. I had to act now if I was going to keep Julian safe from his father's tragic plans. Wearily, I inspected the handcuffs that were again locked around Julian's ankle. If I could get him free, I could get him to safety until Anna and Logan could find him. That was our only hope.

"We have to get these off of you," I said, going to him and pulling at the cuff on his ankle.

Though it was looser than the night before, the cuff would not go below his ankle bone. I yanked at the end cuffed around the furnace, and again the whole thing wiggled but held fast against my repeated abuse.

"It's not going to come off," Julian said, and I heard the beginning of panic in his voice.

"Do you know where he keeps the key?" I asked.

"It's on his keychain," Julian said, solemnly. "It's with him."

With a sigh, I looked around the room. "Well, then, we'll just have to find another way to unlock it."

On the floor, a discarded paper clip lay rusting beneath the corner table. Grabbing it, I lengthened the straight edge and wiped the grime off on my pants.

"Is that going to work?" Julian asked, his body straightening.

"It's worked for me before," I said with a wink.

Julian smiled at me as I inserted the straightened paper clip into the handcuff lock. Concentrating all my soul into wiggling the end into place, I didn't notice the sound of Stephan's car pulling up out front.

"Hurry!" Julian cried.

When Stephan barged into the room, there was no time to react. I stood straight up and met him face to face. He looked right into me, and then to Julian, his eyebrows raised in suspicion. I held my stance, ready to fight with everything in me as he glanced back to me. The vodka on his breath burned my nostrils as he stepped closer. He stared at me a long moment as I met the darkness in his eyes. I could see my own reflection illuminated in their black depths.

As I waited there, hands balled into fists, I realized that Stephan was not looking at me, but through me. With a sigh, he turned his attention to Julian.

"Who were you talking to?" he asked Julian.

Julian looked at me. I raised a finger to my lips.

"He can't see me," I said, waiting for a reaction from Stephan. When there was none, I knew that he could not hear me either.

"Well?" Stephan asked, taking a step toward Julian.

"I . . . I was just singing," Julian said, his terrified eyes locked on mine.

"I said to cut that out," Stephan said, tossing his keys onto his bed and having a seat beside his son. "How many times have I told you? It's annoying, and you can't be making all that noise."

I watched the keys land with a jingle onto the thin mattress beside me. The small, silver cuff key was among them.

"I told you," Stephan continued. "There are bad people who want to take you away from me, away from our destiny. Soon they'll be too late though."

Stephan swayed as he wrapped his arm around his son. Julian's eyes darted from mine to the keys lying beside me. A single tear spilled onto his cheek.

"Soon we'll be together forever. Soon we'll be home where no one can hurt us," Stephan continued as he wiped the tear from Julian's cheek. "You'll see."

"Just do what I say," I whispered to Julian. "You have to distract him. Get him to look away."

Julian gave me a slight nod and took a shaky breath. I watched him collect himself as he looked into his father's drunken face with a somber smile. Getting onto his knees, he wrapped his arms around Stephan's neck. Julian pulled him close, even as the cuff on his ankle clanged against the furnace. His trembling body clutched at his father's shoulders as he wept.

"I love you, Daddy," he said into Stephan's ear as another tear fell from his eyes. "Please, see me."

Stephan was momentarily stunned. The blackness in his eyes flickered from the unexpected warmth of Julian's affection. All reluctance broke away as Stephan turned to his son and buried his face in the crook of Julian's tiny neck and hugged him tight. Unable to look away, I watched the light inside of Stephan fight against the darkness that held him captive in bitter despair.

The way Julian's small hands clutched the shoulders of the one who should be his protector, his rock, transfixed me. I found myself moving toward them with tears in my own eyes. Suddenly Stephan and Julian were gone, and it was my own hands that clasped my father to me.

I reached out to them, eager to draw my own father close. Wishing that it were possible, even if only in a dream within a dream. What would I say? If given the chance to face him again like this in a rare tender moment, what would I say? Would I tell him how deep the scars ran from the pain he inflicted? Would I look him in the eyes and make him understand what he'd done to me?

As I imagined him before me, neither of those rang true. Watching Julian embrace his father with a love beyond fathom, made me realize that I would have done the same. Since finding the light, I no longer feared the dark. I no longer yearned to bleed in hopes that my father would atone for my wounds. From where I wandered, drenched in the warmth of this new luminance, I no longer craved justice for his wrongdoings.

I felt only sadness. Sadness for what was lost forever to the darkness. I mourned my own inability to wrap my arms around my father, to cover him in the love that spilled over from where the light filled me and made me whole. My heart yearned only to show him the truth. If only it were possible . . .

Suddenly, Stephan cleared his throat, jarring me from my reverie. I stiffened and stepped back. When he drew away from Julian, I could see he was losing his battle against the darkness inside. His eyes darted from side to side as his mind reeled.

"Soon we'll be together forever, son," he repeated, more to himself than to Julian. "Soon we'll be home where there is no struggle or pain."

Stephan began to turn away from Julian. Frantic, I snatched up the keychain as silently as I could. I looked at Julian as the tears streamed freely now down his forlorn face.

"It's going to be okay," I said to him as Stephan rose from the bed.

Taking a deep breath, I closed the distance separating me from Stephan. Though I knew he could not see me, I spoke to him with the hopes that a part of him could hear me, the part that fought against the darkness.

"It doesn't have to be this way," I said to him as he stood dumbfounded. "You don't have to live and die in darkness. There's so much more out there for you. The light, it's calling to you, Stephan. I'm calling to you. Wake up!"

Stephan shook his head from side to side, his face contorted into a mask of confusion. His head snapped up, and he seemed to look directly into my face. The blackness in his eyes faded and ebbed as he looked into mine. For a moment I thought he saw me.

"Wake up," I repeated, almost a whisper.

Tears welled up in Stephan's eyes, his whole soul trapped in his glare.

"Who are you?" he whispered. Then faltering, he backed away.

In a blink, it was gone. The flicker in his eyes succumbed to the darkness, and I knew that he lost sight of me. The battle was lost. The black returned to his eyes on a sea of sorrow and guilt. He could not hear me. He shook his head from side to side and cried out in anguish. He started for the front door. I knew he was eager for more booze, eager to silence the war raging in his heart.

"I . . . I need to get something from the car," he stammered and then turned in desperation, remembering his keys.

He rushed to his bed to retrieve them. When he saw they were not there, he pulled at the sheets in frantic search. I went to Julian and wrapped him in my arms as Stephan growled and searched beneath the bed.

"Where are my keys?" he yelled, turning his fury on Julian. "What did you do with them?"

"I don't have them!" Julian protested.

Then without warning Stephan reeled back. He whipped his hand across Julian's face with so much force that he slammed into me with a cry. In shock, I clutched Julian to me as he held his cheek and sobbed into my chest.

"It's okay," I tried to assure him. "It's going to be okay."

"Where are they?" Stephan raged, stepping closer and grabbing hold of Julian's wrists. "I know you took them when you pretended to hug me. What did you do with them?"

"No, Daddy!" Julian cried. "I don't have them!"

When Stephan reeled back a second time, I mustered all the strength I had. I dove at him with a shriek. He hit the floor between the beds with a sickening thud. The breath rushed from his lungs in a mix of impact and confused shock. I floundered, my eyes darting around the room for something to use as a weapon.

When Stephan clutched at the nightstand to brace himself, I flung open the drawer. He staggered back with a gasp. With a scream, I grabbed the Bible inside and hit him in the face with as much force as I could muster. He fell backwards and flopped onto his side, clutching at his jaw. I shot up and clawed my way back to Julian, my legs weak and my breath gone.

"Hurry!" Julian cried.

With shaking hands, I fumbled with the keychain until I found the small, silver key. Julian clung to my shoulders and cried as I unlocked his ankle and dropped the keys to the floor. I took one last look at Stephan who writhed between the beds. The Bible lay beside him on the floor, the pages opened to Ephesians 5. Stephan choked on his screams behind us as I collected Julian into my arms and ran out into the warm sunlight.

Eighteen

"Here we go," I panted, running along the two-lane highway. "There's a dirt road up ahead."

Julian clung to me, his little legs bouncing with every step. I needed to get him out of sight before Stephan regained his bearings. Breathless, I veered off the main road and onto an overgrown gravel drive. With Julian with me, my vision was expanding. I chanced a look back. There was no sign of Stephan. The area surrounding us became clear. The motel sign loomed high above the towering pines.

"Pirate's Cove Motel," I said aloud, committing it to memory. Then I turned to carry Julian further down the road.

When my legs threatened to buckle and my heavy breaths became a steady wheeze, I stopped. Looking around frantically, I spotted a group of thick bushes among the trees on the side of the road.

"Here." I panted, setting Julian down. "Crawl inside, and don't move."

Julian was reluctant. He clung to me as I struggled to catch my breath.

"Stay with me," he pleaded.

I crouched down to him and took him in my arms again until his trembling subsided. Then I held him at arm's length and wiped back the hair that now clung to the sweat on his forehead. An angry lump was forming on his cheek, his eyes were wide with fear and panic.

"I have to go back to your mom now," I said, keeping my voice calm. "I have to tell her where you are so she can come and get you."

"No!" Julian cried. "Don't leave me!"

Taking a deep breath, I looked him in his wide, brown eyes and smiled at him.

"I will never leave you, Julian," I said. "You're just not going to see me for a little while. I have to go to them. I have to tell them where you are."

Julian cried out and grabbed me around the neck. All attempts at keeping a brave face shattered. I hugged him to me as I gathered all the strength I had left to him.

"You're going to be okay now," I promised. "You just have to wait right here. Don't move from this spot. We're coming for you. We're going to bring you home."

When Julian pulled away from me with panic still in his eyes, I knew I couldn't leave him here alone.

Then a thought came to me, and I reached into my pocket. To my amazement, my hand was met by soft plush. I withdrew Julian's small, stuffed toy. His eyes widened at the sight of it. I remembered Anna's last words to me, "*Anything is possible.*"

"Red!" he yelled with the beginnings of a smile.

"He's going to hide here with you," I said, handing him his long-lost friend. Julian hugged it to him, and I felt strength surge anew in his resolve. "I'm coming back for you both, Julian."

"I know," he said, wiping the tears from his eyes. "You can see me."

"I can see you."

I took him in my arms one last time and then positioned him deep into the thick of the brush beside the road. Then closing my eyes, I found my way back through the light, to the dark on the other side.

I returned to myself still wheezing and weak. Instinct had me rubbing my useless eyes in a futile attempt to see. The sounds of mumbled voices behind me made me turn in the chair and reach out. Mutt leapt up from where he lay at my side. He licked my hand as I tried to find my voice.

"Pirate . . . Pirate's Cove!" I stammered.

Anna was the first to respond. Her light footsteps rushed toward me.

"Thank you anyway," she said. I heard the soft beep of her phone as she hung up and knelt beside me. "What did you say? Is everything okay? Is Julian safe?"

"I know . . . where he is," I said, trying to steady my breaths. "Have to . . . hurry!"

"Logan!" Anna shouted.

Logan ended his phone call and rushed over.

"Tell me you have some good news," he said, desperation thick in his voice. "We've exhausted the list and have no leads."

I took a gulp of air as I turned in my seat to face him. "Pirate's Cove Motel . . . look up Pirate's Cove Motel. We have . . . we have to hurry, Logan."

Before I could finish my sentence, Logan had retrieved his laptop. He brought it to us as I struggled to sit up. His fingers flew across the keys as Anna leaned in over my shoulder.

"There are two motels with that name within a day's drive," he said. "One in the Outer Banks and one on Oak Island."

"Which one is it? Anna asked, frantic.

"I . . . I don't know," I said. "Can you pull up the satellite image?"

"On it," Logan said with a flick of the keys.

"Describe what you see," I said.

"The one at the Outer Banks looks to be a street away from the beach . . . surrounded by lots of palm trees and dunes. Is that it?" Logan asked.

"Look for a dirt road to the west of it," I said, my heart racing. "It should be half a mile or so down the highway. The motel's sign was blue and gold. It was tall . . . taller than the trees."

"That's not it," Anna said. "The sign is all wrong."

There was another flick of the keys and a pause as we all held our breaths.

"This is it!" Logan exclaimed. "The blue and gold sign, and there's what looks like an overgrown drive almost a mile down. Look at that store across the street. That's our logo!"

"We have to go," I pleaded. "Now!

The memory of Julian's panicked eyes prevented relief from penetrating my soul. I wouldn't feel better until his mother held him in her arms.

"Let's move," Anna said, jumping up. "The day is almost over. It says it takes almost an hour to get there. Was Julian okay? Did Stephan make a move?"

I staggered to my feet with a nod.

"He's safe," I said. "I hid him in the woods away from Stephan. Stephan was drunk, violent. We had to run. Julian's waiting for us on the side of that dirt road."

Then the meaning of Anna's words stopped me as I reached for the door. I turned back to her.

"What do you mean the day is almost over?" I asked. "It's still morning yet."

"No, Blake," Logan said as he packed up the laptop. "It's getting into the evening. You've been unresponsive for hours."

"Hours?" I shrieked as my mind reeled. "I was gone for twenty, maybe thirty minutes, tops."

Logan stopped suddenly and turned to me, his voice grave.

"To you it may have felt like minutes," he said, "but it's been hours. We've been on the phone all day . . . me, Anna, and the folks back home. We've all been searching for this store all day."

"This can't be . . ." I said, my heart dropping into my stomach as I thought about Julian waiting for his rescue on the side of that dirt road, scared and alone for hours.

"It was the same last night," Logan said. "You painted all night, but your mind was somewhere else. All night."

"Minutes," I croaked, fighting off the urge to despair. "It felt like only minutes."

My mind raced. How it could it be possible to lose that much time?

"Blake, I've seen a place that exists, a luminous place, where there is no time." Logan said. "I think you go to that place, Blake. I think that's where you find Julian."

I thought about the light I'd found on the other side of darkness. The place that called me to step out from the shadows. The luminous place.

"We have to go," Anna said through gritted teeth. "Now!"

Logan and I snapped to life and followed Anna out the door. Mutt stayed at my side, and I used his warmth to guide my steps.

"We'll take my car," Logan said. "We can ride with the siren blasting. With any luck, we can be there inside of thirty minutes."

It took everything I had not to go to Julian, to meet him on the other side of the light, but I was too afraid. I didn't dare lose any more time. Julian needed me in the here and now. Logan and Anna needed me to pinpoint where I'd hidden him among the brush. All I could do was pray that he was still there. We were coming for him.

No one spoke as we sped ninety miles an hour down the wooded, country highway toward Oak Island. The siren wailed, parting the traffic like the Red Sea and casting flashes of white and blue into the trees. Mutt whined as he rested his massive head on my lap. He could sense my doubt. I petted his head to reassure him that it would be okay. Perhaps to convince myself.

"He didn't tell me about this," Anna said, her tone grim as she finally broke the silence from the passenger seat in front of me. "He never said a word."

"What are you talking about?" I asked.

"My Guardian . . . the one that protected me from my father when I was a child," she said, numbly. "He never told me I would lose my son at the hands of a man just as sick. Where is he now?

Instead, he told me I would write a book. A damned book. As if any of that would matter to me now."

"You're not going to lose him," I said, my soul burning with the desire to force that truth. "You've been called upon to do something great. People need to hear about Donovan and Alex, about how the light brought them together. They need to hear about Logan's redemption . . . and they need to hear our story, Anna. Whatever the ending. The world needs to know there's light on the other side of darkness, because it's there, Anna. It's there."

I heard Anna's breath catch in her throat. The car swiveled slightly as Logan gave her hand a pat.

"Blake is right," he said. "Maybe your Guardian was putting you on the right path, like Donovan did for Alex in her darkest times. Or the way Hope fought for me. Either way, you have to use this experience to grow into who you were called to be."

Anna laughed, a sarcastic chide devoid of humor.

"Are you saying God let this happen to change me into what He wants me to be?" she asked, and my heart hurt for her. Her faith was waning, and for the life of me I couldn't blame her. If there was one thing I learned since meeting Julian, though, it's that it is in the darkest times that the light calls.

"No," Logan said. "This is a fallen world, Anna, filled with suffering and pain around every corner. No one knows that better perhaps than the people in this car, but the light can turn your worst days into something beautiful. The darkness is trying to keep you from your calling, Anna. Don't let that happen."

"And never give up hope," I added as it surged anew within me at Logan's words.

By the time we reached the bridge that joined the mainland to Oak Island, the sun was lowering in the sky. I could feel it warm the scars over my eyes as it hovered above the horizon. The late spring air cooled in its wake. Logan slowed the car. I felt the change in altitude as we passed over the Intracoastal Waterway.

"I can see the sign for the motel from here," Anna said. "Take this right."

The car shifted, and Logan extinguished the siren. Mutt struggled to stand in the swaying vehicle. My heart battered in my chest. I wanted to jump from the car and run to Julian as fast as my legs would take me. In the vision of him, I could. Trapped in my sightless body, I could not.

"Here," Anna said, her voice almost frantic. "The motel is down this small highway. Looks like the main street."

The car shifted again, and I dug my fingers into the upholstered back seat as I held my breath.

"There it is," Anna cried. "I don't see Stephan's car parked outside."

"There's a door on the first floor ajar," Logan pointed out. "Were they on the first floor?"

"Yes," I said, eager to help in any way I could. "I don't know the room number. It was near the middle, behind an oak tree."

"This could be it,' Logan said. "Better check it out."

I felt the car turn into the drive and slow. It took all I had to wait until the car came to a stop before I hopped outside. Mutt ran out behind me, ready at my heels.

"Stay in the car," I heard Logan say to Anna.

"Like hell I will," she argued, slamming her car door behind her with a metallic thud.

Logan led the way to the room with the open door. I groped at my surroundings, trying to make the vision line up with my impaired sensory projection. My fingers found the door, which swung wide as Logan entered. I heard him snap open the holster on his hip.

The dank smell of stale coffee and mold was familiar enough. I hung behind Logan until I felt his tension release. The room was empty.

"He's gone," Logan said.

Frantic, I felt along the wall until my fingers clasped the cool metal of the furnace. I followed the shape of the appliance until I came to the last rung and found what I was looking for. The handcuffs tinkered against the furnace as I held them up for Anna and Logan to see.

"This is the room," I said, dropping the cuffs to clatter against the wall.

Without a second thought, I took off running in the direction I had carried Julian in what felt to me like less than an hour ago. I only vaguely heard Anna shout for Logan to follow. Their footfalls were lost in my urgency. Mutt alone was able to keep up, and I welcomed his guidance as I ran with my arms outstretched.

Following the feel of gravel along the stretch of highway, I ran as fast as my once shattered legs would take me. By the time I felt the gravel shift to the right, I was dizzy from the lack of oxygen. I paused to catch my breath, but Mutt grabbed hold of my shirt and pulled me forward, pivoting me to the right.

"Find him," I cried between ragged breaths as I followed his lead.

Fumbling through the overgrowth on the side of the road, I followed Mutt's pants until he came to an abrupt stop and snorted at the air. My arms flailed out in desperate search of the thicket where I'd hidden Julian.

"Julian!" I yelled out, unable to restrain the panic. "Julian, it's me. Where are you?"

When I found the thicket, I thrust my hands inside, parting the branches in my search as they scraped at my flesh. Beside me Mutt let out a devastated howl and pawed at the ground. With a cry I dropped to my knees. I swept the dirt where Mutt indicated. My heart threatened to burst.

I expected to come into contact with Julian's small, unconscious body. What I felt instead was soft fluff and fuzz.

"No!" I yelled as I picked up the small toy, now dusty with gravel and debris.

Anna and Logan ran up to meet me. I could tell by the lack of pause in their steps that I had found all there was to find. With shaking hands, I held Red up to them. Anna snatched it to her and sank to her knees with a bitter cry.

Julian was gone.

Nineteen

"No!" Anna shrieked. Her helpless cries reached into my chest and tore at the remains of my shattered resolve. "We're too late."

I felt Logan kneel beside us and take Anna into his arms as she sobbed.

"We can't give up," Logan said. "This isn't over. We can still find him."

Logan leaned into me. His voice was a whisper, but his tone was stern, commanding.

"Where is he?" Logan asked me. I raised my head to meet his voice.

"I . . . I don't know," I said, the words bitter on my tongue. "Stephan must have found him."

Anna choked back her sobs long enough to turn to me.

"Go," she said. "Go to him. Find him! Stop Stephan if it's not too late."

As much as I ached to do just that, my mind raced with the possibilities. What if I went to Julian and it was too late? What would I face on the other side of the light? What if instead of light I was met by only darkness and death? What if I had failed?

I remembered my last words to Julian. I promised him that we were coming for him. I told him that I would never leave him. Going inside myself, I began to seek out the light, but then I stopped.

"I can't," I said. "Even if I find him, there's no guarantee I'll come back to myself in time to tell you. I can't stop Stephan on my own. We have to find him here and now. It can't be too late. It can't."

"We don't even know where to look," Anna cried. "They could be anywhere by now. The day is almost over!"

Logan stood. I could hear his heart racing as he shifted away from us.

"I'm going back to the room," he said. "Maybe Stephan left a note or a clue as to his next move."

Anna rose to follow as I lingered behind, unable to shake my devastation. Mutt nudged me in the arm, and I turned to him, helpless.

"We have to find him," I whispered to him. "We have to."

Mutt whined and nudged me again. Using his strength to pull myself up, I fought to catch up with Anna's frantic steps as we ran back down the dirt path. Clutching at Mutt, I struggled to catch my breath. My legs went numb beneath me.

As we reached the room, I heard Logan's heavy boots crossing the threshold. Leaning against the oak out front, I listened as he paused and looked around. Anna did not hesitate. She began tossing things aside in search of something, anything that could lead us to Julian. After a second, Logan joined her. I heard him throw the suitcase to the ground. As precious minutes passed without a discovery, I knew that they would find nothing. There was nothing to find.

I was exhausted. My body weighed me down as my thoughts turned dark. Anger bubbled up from a forgotten well within my gut. *Why?* Of all the questions on my mind, that one was at the forefront. I lifted my face to the heavens, my whole being caught up in that one question. *Why?* Why give me the ability to see Julian if I could not save him?

I didn't know what to do. More than anything, I longed for the voice from the glow to direct my next steps. I felt lost, longing for that luminous place. The light within me faded with each passing minute. What was I supposed to do? *Help me*, I prayed. *Please . . . . Help me. I need you. We all do.*

As the search within the room turned frantic, the sounds of mattresses toppling and drawers opening faded away. In their place came a different sound on the gentle breeze. A soft melody floated to my ears from somewhere in the distance.

This little light of mine . . .

With a gasp, I straightened and took a step toward the voice. Julian's song sailed to my ears on the gentle ocean wind, his tone urgent and strong.

"Do you hear that?" I asked.

Logan and Anna froze.

"Hear what?" Anna asked.

"I can hear him," I said, taking another step toward Julian's voice. "I can hear him singing."

Anna dropped whatever was in her hands. She stomped over the debris to stand in front of me. She stood still and silent, listening.

"I don't hear anything," she said. "Is it coming from another room?"

"No, he's not here," I said, straining to hear his voice again. "He's somewhere out there, but he's alive. He's calling to us."

Logan kicked a drawer aside and came to the door.

"What are you talking about, Blake?" he asked. "I don't hear anything either."

I'm going to let it shine . . .

With a gasp, I stumbled forward. The song was as clear to me as the call of the gulls above.

"There it was again," I said, ecstatic. "Can't you hear him? He's singing! He's singing!"

Full of renewed hope, I turned and ran in the direction of Julian's voice. Though it was far off and faint, I had to try and reach it. Julian was calling to me. My legs ached and felt like lead beneath me, but I didn't care. Mutt ran at my side, his excitement adding to my urgency as I traversed the gravel shoulder beside the road.

"Wait!" Logan called behind me. "Blake!"

I heard the jingle of his car keys, heard the engine of his cruiser turn over as Anna slammed the passenger door shut behind her.

By the time I made it back to the dirt road turn off, they were beside me.

"Get in the car," Logan ordered. "We'll find him together."

Without hesitation, I threw open the back door and ushered Mutt to get in. He whined as I climbed in beside him, as eager as he was to keep the momentum.

This little light of mine . . .

"He's that way," I said, pointing ahead toward Julian's song. "Keep going."

"Do you still hear him?" Anna asked, frantic as she turned in her seat to face me.

"Yes," I said. "It's like his voice is drifting to me on the wind. I can't tell exactly from where. I just know he's this way. Is there anything up ahead? Anything that stands out?"

Anna's hair tickled my nose as she whipped around to survey the area ahead.

"Just some restaurants and motels," she cried. "Do you think Stephan took Julian to another room? Maybe he knew we were coming somehow . . ."

I'm going to let it shine . . .

"No," I said with a sudden realization. "They're on the move. His voice drifts away as we get closer. Stephan's taking him somewhere. What else do you see?"

"Nothing," Anna said, her voice growing hysterical. "Just some houses and shops. I don't understand. Where are they? What's happening?"

"Wait, look!" Logan exclaimed, and the car slowed. "Look past those palm trees, at the horizon beyond those houses."

"I see it," Anna said. "Oh, my God!"

"See what?" I asked, my heart sinking. "What do you see?"

"Let me see Stephan's note again," Logan said, turning to Anna. "The one you found in the house."

"What do you see?" I repeated, frantic.

Anna dug the letter from her pocket as Logan pulled the cruiser off to the shoulder. Logan unfolded it as quickly as he could. There was deafening silence as he scanned it for what he was looking for.

"That's it!" he exclaimed. "It says it right here: '*He can fly with me from the house of light . . .*' That's where Stephan's taking him. That's where he's going to make his move."

The realization struck me with the force of a speeding train.

"A lighthouse," I muttered.

"He's going to jump," Anna cried. "God, help my baby. He's going to jump."

This little light of mine . . .

Julian's voice cut through Anna's sobs as panic rose up like bile from the pit of my stomach.

"Step on it!" I shouted.

Logan switched on the siren as he pulled the cruiser back onto the road and gunned the engine. Mutt and I were thrown against the back seat.

It took only minutes to cross Oak Island, but every second felt interminable. Logan dipped and dodged traffic like a soccer player through the field. Mutt whined beside me, his tail slapping my arm with nervous anticipation. No one said a word. We hardly breathed. I could feel the sun's rays warm my face from where it dipped into the horizon. Daylight was almost gone.

I'm going to let it shine . . .

Julian's words came more urgent than before, as if he were forcing them now. The anticipation became unbearable. Just as I thought I would shatter beneath the weight of my panic, an image flashed before my eyes and then vanished. It was there and gone like the flash of a camera's bulb. Gasping, I tried to make sense of what I'd seen. I sat up and held my breath with apprehension, waiting for the image to come again.

When the colors and angles flashed a second time, I fought to hold onto it, but it disappeared just as suddenly as it came. Only this time I was expecting it, and I knew what I saw.

Julian sat in the back seat of Stephan's car, tears staining his red cheeks as he sang out his song. Stephan kept one hand on the wheel while he turned to Julian. His eyes were inflamed with black rage as he shouted between gritted teeth for Julian to stop. In the seat beside him, Stephan gripped the handle of a revolver.

"He's got a gun!" I blurted out, breaking the tense silence. "Stephan . . . he's armed."

"What?" Anna shrieked.

"Did you see it?" Logan asked as he leaned on the gas. "Are you sure?"

"Yes," I said. "I'm sure. You've got to turn off the siren. He can't know we're coming. If we spook him, he may panic. He's lost to it, Logan. Stephan is gone."

Without question, Logan shut off the siren and eased off the gas pedal.

"Lost to what?" Anna asked.

"The darkness," Logan said, and I knew he understood.

"What about Julian? Did you see him?" Anna asked. "Is he all right?"

Before I could answer, another image burst into my mind like a bolt of lightning in the night sky. I jolted in my seat as the colors and shapes swept fleetingly through my mind.

"What is it?" Anna asked.

"The lighthouse," I stammered. "Is it striped . . . grey, white and black?"

"Yes, that's it," Anna confirmed. "What did you see?"

"They're pulling up to it now. It's got to be over one hundred feet tall," I said, not able to keep the dread from my voice. "How far are we?"

"Not far," Logan said. I felt the car tilt as he took a sudden turn to the left. "I'm going to try to get there from this side street. Maybe he won't see us coming."

"What?" Anna cried. "What are you doing? We're so close. We don't have time to get lost."

"Stephan has a weapon," I explained, remembering the life I'd lived on the other side of the law. "The element of surprise is our only play here. We can't risk him seeing a squad car pull up."

"Just hurry," she breathed.

We barreled down the road, slowing only to take a sharp turn to the right. Mutt fell into my lap with a yelp.

"Sorry, boy," Logan said.

"There!" Anna shouted. "I see Stephan's car. It's parked out front. Pull over here."

My heart raced as the cruiser slowed. I readied myself to hop out and go to Julian. This could all end now.

But before we came to a stop, another image flashed before my eyes. This time the image was accompanied by a loud and sudden blast. The shock took my breath away. Panic turned my blood to ice. Someone had been shot.

Within the cement walls of the lighthouse, the discharge echoed off the ship ladder staircase before everything went black again. My stomach heaved, and the darkness around me spun and contracted as soon as the image was gone.

"No!" I screamed, jumping from the car before Logan brought it to a complete stop.

Stumbling, I ran in the direction of the gunshot as Anna screamed for me to tell her what was wrong. Her pleas were lost to the trepidation that engulfed my entire body. I tripped over beach grass and plowed into sand dunes. My arms flailed out through the darkness in front of me in desperate search of the lighthouse's concrete walls. Each time I fell, it was harder to get up. Time slowed, ebbed, and strangled me as I pushed forward on leaden feet. Then Mutt was there. He nudged my arm, and I clutched his collar between my trembling fingers.

Together we made our way forward until the ground cleared beneath us, and I let go of him. Mutt charged ahead, as eager as I was to get to the entrance. I followed him onto a wooden boardwalk, adrenaline propelling me forward toward his excited pants. I heard his paws round the corner and charge up concrete steps. He halted abruptly, his claws scraping at the iron door as I found the railing below.

"Is this it?" I asked. "Is this the lighthouse?"

Mutt barked feverishly, jumping and scratching at the door above. Taking the steps by two, I hauled myself to the top. I patted Mutt on the head, and he moved aside with an anxious bark. With my arms outstretched, I felt along the double metal doors until I found the thick handle. It groaned in protest as I heaved one of the doors open and stepped inside. Mutt raced ahead before I could stop him, but he froze with a mournful wail only feet to my right. My stomach convulsed again, and fear gripped my shoulders as I staggered toward him. As I got closer, I slid on something slick beneath my shoes. When a pungent, copper-like smell filled my nostrils, I knew that it was blood.

"No," I whispered, crouching down to where Mutt whined incessantly.

Feeling along the floor, my fingertips came into contact with the warm, thick puddle. I could hear only my own shallow breath and Mutt's quickened pants. Whoever was bleeding out on the floor was not breathing.

My fingertips, in a frantic search, brushed against fabric and rubber. A shoe! As my mind raced with silent prayers, I ran my fingers along the length of it. A relieved cry escaped my throat when I realized it was too big to belong to a child.

"It's not him," I said, trying to breathe. "It's not Julian."

Logan charged up the steps with Anna close behind, then stopped abruptly. I heard his arms fly out to catch her before she could see inside, but it was too late. Her scream echoed inside the small concrete chamber.

"Who is it?" I asked. "Is it Stephan?"

"No," she cried, "No. It . . . it's a lighthouse worker. He's dead, isn't he? He's dead!"

Logan came to where I was crouched. I moved aside as he checked for a pulse.

"He's gone," he said as Mutt whined beside me.

"But where's . . . ." Anna began, but was interrupted by a cry from somewhere above.

Mutt barked, and I shot to my feet.

"That's him," I said. "How do we get up there?"

"There's a ladder that looks to lead to the main level. The staircase must start up there."

"Where is it?" I asked, already searching the wall.

When I clasped cold metal, I gripped the railing and readied to pull myself up.

"Wait!" Logan said, stopping me cold. "Let me go. I can reach them faster."

"What is Stephan going to do when he sees a cop coming for him?" I protested. "He's already killed once. We know he's desperate. We can't risk it."

"Let me go!" Anna cried. "I'm his mother!"

"You don't think Stephan will hesitate to kill you in front of Julian?" I asked. "I can't let that happen. It has to be me."

I climbed the ladder and was met by another iron door. Using all my strength, I raised it. My face was met by warm, acrid air that engulfed me in moist humidity. The sound of a child's cry mingled with that of boots scraping metal from high above. I could not tell how far.

Logan climbed the ladder below me and stuck his head in the opening.

"Describe it to me," I said to him, readying myself for the climb.

"It's steep." He sighed. "And it's high . . . extremely high. There's a series of ship ladders about sixteen steps up with a landing in between. I can't tell how many."

I nodded as he confirmed what I'd seen in my vision.

"Okay," I said. "I'm going up. Send Anna to get help. I don't want her to be here if something goes wrong. You wait right here, in case he brings Julian back down."

"Not happening," Logan protested. "I'll give you space, but I'll be behind you ready to back you up."

"No," I said, feeling along the wall by the door. "Stephan will see your uniform coming from a mile up."

"What's your plan for overtaking him?" Logan asked. "How are you going to do this alone?"

I took a deep breath and let the light within glow anew in my being.

"I'm not alone," I said, reassured. "And it's not my plan. I just know that this is my part of it."

"We can do this together," Logan insisted. "I'll stay to the shadows."

"It will be too dangerous for you," I said.

"Why?"

Once I found it, I flipped off the light switch. My body felt saturated by the sudden, oppressive darkness. Stephan's startled cry echoed off the tubular fortress followed by Julian's sobs.

"Because it's hard to see in the dark," I said, making my way to the first set of ladders. "I'll call to you when I'm coming back down."

Logan let out a disgruntled moan, but shut the hatch behind me, squelching the last bit of light that penetrated the concrete cave. Taking a deep breath, I grabbed onto the railing above and pushed myself up on wobbling legs. Remembering the first time I'd climbed the steps of the studio after the accident, I assured myself that the next step was there. The light inside me gave me strength to press on. Supported by blind faith, I ascended into the unknown, my ears searching for movement.

Stephan and Julian were motionless, no doubt rendered paralyzed by the overwhelming and sudden darkness. I came to the first landing and paused to catch my breath. Julian's voice reverberated off the staircase above.

"Please, Daddy," he pleaded. "I want to go back down."

"It's going to be okay," Stephan said, his voice flat and emotionless. "It's almost over."

I heard movement. The sound of fabric swishing against fabric alerted me that they were on the move again. Grasping the railing, I pulled myself up the next flight. With each new set of ladders, I grew more and more disoriented. The hollow space above and below distorted sound and space, making my environment impossible to gauge. I imagined a metal ladder suspended into infinite space, but quickly pushed the thought away, fighting back the panic it evoked.

"You're hurting me," Julian cried out. I was able to get a read on his location by the sound of his voice.

His feet kicked the railing above. The sound bounced off the walls in all directions. The metal under me vibrated, adding to the trembling in my legs. Stephan was dragging Julian further up the steep, inclined ladders.

"Julian!" I called out, chancing his father's reaction.

For a moment there was silence, save for the sounds of movement above.

"Blake?" Julian cried, his voice echoing down to me.

"Who's there?" Stephan raged. "Who are you talking to?"

"I'm right here," I said, ignoring Stephan. I fought to keep my voice calm. "I'm coming for you."

"Blake!" Julian yelled again, though his father shushed him. "I'm scared! It's so dark."

I took a deep breath to steady myself. My arms trembled from exertion.

"I know, kid. But you and I, we aren't scared of the dark, remember?" I said. "I need you to do something for me. I need you to sing, okay? Sing your song as loud as you can, and keep singing no matter what. Can you do that for me?"

He was silent again for a minute.

"He'll get mad," Julian cried. "I'm scared."

I listened as Stephan threatened him and bade him to be quiet.

"That's the best time to sing, when you're scared," I said. "Your mother taught you that, right? There's never been a better time."

I paused at the next landing and backed against the railing, panting. My voice echoed for what seemed like miles above and below. Pushing down the fear that crept up again from the pit of my stomach, I fought to catch my breath.

"You can do it, little cardinal," I assured. "Sing it out."

There was a moment then when even the air ceased to move. My heart slowed and my breathing stopped as I waited and listened. Then Julian's voice pierced through the darkness above. It quivered, but rang out like a homing signal.

"*This little light of mine . . .*" he sang. "*I'm going to let it shine.*"

"Good!" I yelled, getting a fix on his location above as I began to climb again.

"What did I tell you about that?" Stephan roared. "Stop that right now!"

"Don't listen to him!" I yelled. "Keep singing so I can hear you! I'm coming for you, Julian!"

Though my muscles were growing weak, I pulled myself up to the next landing. Julian's voice grew closer as I climbed. Stephan yelled and threatened, trying to make him stop, but Julian sang on. It was slowing Stephan down.

"*This little light of mine . . .*"

I clung to his song, forcing my body up step after step. With the next, my leg slipped between the rungs and dangled beneath me. As I scrambled to get a better hold of the railing, my glasses slid off my eyes. I heard them clank against the stairs before falling into the abyss below. Clutching the rail, I tried to steady my breathing. Then I pulled my leg back under me. My sweaty hands struggled to grip the metal. I wiped them on my pants and pressed on.

"I'm going to let it shine."

I followed Julian's voice, higher and higher. With each step, my stomach convulsed, and my legs quaked. In my mind we were transcending into the clouds, rising above the setting sun on the windswept landscape outside. No one could survive a fall of this magnitude. Thoughts of Julian's tiny body racing to meet the dirt below drove me to climb faster. I couldn't let that happen.

The lighthouse's mechanics buzzed around me. I was close to the top. I could hear Stephan's panting breaths as he dragged Julian up the flight of ladders just above me. Slowing my pace, I was careful to keep my steps silent as I approached. I pulled myself to the landing above and waited, contemplating my next move. Stephan staggered along the landing just ahead. He paused. I heard him struggle to catch his breath as Julian sang.

"This little light of mine,"

Stephan laughed, a feral growl. "Actually, that song is fitting. Can you see that glow above? Those are the lighthouse lights, ready to guide us home. We're almost there. Just one more ladder, and we'll be with the light forever, Julian. You'll never have to be scared again."

A sob caught in Julian's throat, and he stopped singing. I crept up the next rung and the next, desperate to reach them before they made it to the observation deck.

"No, Daddy," Julian said, barely more than a whisper. "There's nothing up there but darkness."

"You're wrong," Stephan seethed. "You should be happy . . . grateful that I'm giving this gift to you. But you'll see. You'll see."

Julian whimpered as Stephan hauled him onto what I was sure was the last set of ladders. I paused long enough to hear his heavy boots clunk against the metal above. Propelled by panic, I clawed my way up to the platform they'd just vacated and doubled over. Exhaustion vibrated in every muscle of my body. I felt weak, and trembled from excursion. They were only feet above me. I could hear Stephan's labored breaths over the machinery around us.

Hauling myself forward, I grabbed onto the railing above and pulled myself up to the next step, and then the next. I could feel the stir of the humid air from their movements just beyond my reach.

"Blake?" Julian cried out, and I wondered if he could see me, if there was enough light to give away my position. Or did he feel my presence. I put a finger to my lips. Keeping as low as I could, I pulled myself up another rung.

Stephan gasped, startled.

"That name again," he said between huffs. "Who . . . ?"

Before he could finish his question, my foot slipped again, and my hip slammed into the rungs in front of me. The sound reverberated up the railing, and Stephan froze.

"Who's there?" he yelled.

I didn't move, praying that the shadows would conceal me for just a little longer.

"Whoever you are, I know you're there," Stephan yelled again, his voice faltering. "But you're too late."

There was a clanging as Stephan dragged Julian up the remaining steps with a grunt. Then the sounds of a metallic whine echoed in the space between us. The cooling evening air caressed my face. Stephan had reached the door to the observation deck.

"No, I don't want to go!" Julian cried. "Blake!"

There were scuffs and the sound of rubber soles kicking against iron. I raced up the remaining steps as Julian struggled to get free of his father.

Light flashed in front of my eyes in a blur of shapes and movement. I froze and took it all in as I gasped for air. Silhouetted by the light of the open door, Stephan clasped Julian around the waist. Julian struggled and kicked and clawed at the doorway. His hand extended toward me. His eyes were filled with panic.

The image flashed, then quickly left me, and I was once again consumed by darkness. Holding the image in my memory, I raced forward and clasped Julian's hand. The familiar jolt of warm static assured me that I had him.

"Blake!" Julian cried with relief as I pulled with all my might until Stephan lost his grip on him.

When Julian's feet landed safely on the mesh floor beside me, I dove at Stephan. With a cry we flew forward, slamming into the railing of the observation deck and knocking the breath from our lungs. Stephan wheezed for air as I struggled to get to my feet. The wind off the ocean whipped across the platform, causing me to stagger. With arms flailing, I searched for the open doorway. Desperate to make it back to Julian before Stephan, I found the cool concrete of the lighthouse's exterior.

I felt my way across and found the doorway just as Julian screamed. The sound of Stephan pulling back the hammer of the revolver stopped me dead in my tracks. I turned to face him.

"Julian, get over here now!" he commanded. Stephan's voice was high pitched and trembling. He was barely in control.

"You don't have to do this," I said calmly to Stephan. "It doesn't have to be this way."

Behind me, Julian grasped my hand and stepped forward.

"No," I said. "Don't go to him."

"Come here, now! Don't make me come get you!" Stephan shouted.

The hysteria in his voice sent a cold shiver down my spine. It was the same tone my father used before he followed his threats with a hard fist. Julian took a shaky step forward before I could stop him. I reached for him, but Stephan snatched his hand from mine and dragged him away.

"Nothing is going to stop me," he said. "Do you hear me? We're going to be together forever. This is our destiny."

"No!" I cried, clutching for Julian. "No, please!"

"No, Daddy!" Julian screamed.

Frantic, I fumbled toward their voices, searching the darkness for Julian. Then another image flashed before me. The sun had dipped further below the horizon, casting an eerie crimson glow on the platform. Stephan tugged Julian up onto the railing where he stood facing the world below. We were more than one hundred and fifty feet up. With a sickening smile, Stephan held the gun to the boy's head and closed his eyes as Julian sobbed.

This time I didn't wait for the image to fade. With a scream, I bolted forward and thrust Stephan's arm into the air as the shot went off. The bullet rippled through the wind and off into the distance. As Stephan staggered from the shock, I kicked him in the gut. He doubled over and fell from the railing back onto the deck.

When he did, he let go of Julian.

Julian cried out as he lost his balance. His little body fell over the other side. From down below, I heard Anna's shrill screams rise in pitch to match the ones that ripped from my own throat. Then all went black again.

Twenty

Leaping forward, I clutched at where Julian's image had just been. Groping the railing, I searched with frenzied fingertips. *This wasn't happening. This couldn't be happening. Not again.* Images of my little brother's lifeless body sprang into my memory. I had been just as helpless to save him.

Fighting back the anguish and panic, I felt along the railing as prayers screamed through my mind. *Please God, no. Not again.* Then my fingers found the flesh of Julian's taut knuckles as he clung to the railing. He was dangling over the other side. With a relieved cry, I grabbed onto his wrists.

"I've got you," I assured him.

"Blake!" he cried.

I pulled him up inch by inch until I felt as though my arms would break. Reaching down, my fingers grasped the fabric of his shorts, but they began to slip through my fingers. I squeezed with all my might and pulled him back toward me. Julian clawed at my arms, trying to get hold. I let go of him long enough to grasp his hands. Then I yanked him back over the edge. I wrapped my arms around him and stepped away from the railing as the wind whipped around us.

"Thank you, God," I whispered as Julian cried into my shoulder. "I've got you. It's okay now. I've got you."

"Impossible!" Stephan's screams rose above the whipping of the wind. "You won't stop me!"

Julian flinched against me.

"Where is he?" I whispered to him. "Does he still have the gun?"

"Yes, he's waving it around," Julian shuddered. "He's standing in front of the door. He's looking for something."

"We have to get by him," I said.

Julian clutched me to him tighter, his small body trembling.

"Now he's pointing the gun at us," he shrieked.

"Get behind me," I said, moving in front of him. "No matter what happens, when I tell you to run, you go for the door as fast as you can. Get to the bottom. Help is waiting."

"I won't leave you," he protested.

"I'll be right behind you," I lied.

I braced myself for the bullet. I knew that as I went down, Julian could make a break for the door. Stephan stepped closer. In his hand, the gun rattled violently. He took a deep breath to steady himself.

"This is our destiny, our path," Stephan growled through gritted teeth. "It all ends here."

Shielding Julian from the blast, my thoughts drifted to my father. I wondered if I would see him among the light on the other side of this life. I was not afraid.

"Yes, it does!" shouted a familiar voice.

Logan stepped through the doorway. The authority in his voice let me know he had drawn his own gun. I turned and grabbed Julian and threw him to the floor as Stephan turned on Logan. I covered him with my body. There was a struggle. A shot went off. It ricocheted off the metal railing beside us. Someone's gun skid across the concrete platform and went over the side.

"Get downstairs, now!" Logan yelled, and then Stephan was upon him.

Flesh scraped against flesh, and bone crunched against bone.

"Go!" I yelled to Julian.

Wrapping my body around him, Julian led as we ran through the doorway into darkness.

"Get downstairs," I instructed him as Stephan and Logan continued to fight. "Find your mother, and get as far away from this place as you can."

"But it's pitch black down there," he protested. "I can't . . ."

"I have to help Logan," I said. "You can do it. I'm right behind you."

"Go now!" Logan screamed. "He's got the gun! Run, Blake! Go . . ."

Before Logan could finish his warning, there was a loud crunching sound as flesh met hard metal. Then Logan was silent.

Rage rose up within me. I ached to go to my friend, but Stephan's ragged breaths staggered toward us. I had to get Julian to safety.

"Go." I said to him, and we made our way to the first set of ladders.

"It's so far down!" Julian cried.

Though my legs wobbled, I bent down to him and flung him onto my back.

"Hang onto me," I instructed him. "Do not let go!"

"Okay," Julian said as he clung to my shoulders.

His static warmth surrounded me, and I was momentarily soothed. I felt along the railing until I knew where to take the first step. Then with Julian on my back, I started the climb down into the shadows. We made it to the first platform when Stephan's footsteps sounded on the rungs above.

"He's coming!" Julian cried.

I quickened my pace, careful to keep my sweaty grip on the railing. It was hard to catch my breath. My muscles felt drained of their strength. Julian clutched my hoodie and hugged me to him. When we made it to the second platform, I forced myself to the next ladder without stopping to rest.

"You can't run from destiny," Stephan spat as he traversed the ladders above. He was gaining on us.

"Hurry, Blake," Julian said, a desperate plea against my ear.

"He'll slow down once he loses the light," I assured him. "He'll be lost in the darkness."

"He already is," Julian whispered and then buried his head in the crook of my neck.

When we got half a dozen platforms down, Stephan's steps above us slowed. We were now drenched in shadow. I continued my pace though it felt as though my limbs would fall limp at any moment. I couldn't breathe. The black began to twirl and spin at the edge of consciousness.

Deeper and deeper into the black abyss we descended. I focused on each rung and the placement of my feet below me. I slipped once. Julian clung to me as my legs dangled.

"Grab the railing," I panted.

When his weight was off of me, I pulled myself back up. Then he clutched my shoulders again, and I continued down. Stephan's heavy breaths hung above us like an oncoming storm that would not relent.

When the echo of each step rang clearer, I knew we were near the bottom.

"I can see a light," Julian said, and I realized that Logan left the door to the main chamber open.

"How far?" I asked.

"Just a few more ladders," he said. "Hurry."

"Julian?" Anna called from the bottom.

"Mommy!" Julian cried, his voice filled with hope.

"Oh, thank you, God!" she cried. Below her, Mutt's bark echoed throughout the interior.

"Anna, back away!" I warned. "Stephan's right behind us . . . He's got a. . ."

A gunshot rang out with a deafening explosion that amplified within the concave walls. Anna screamed as the bullet scattered pieces of concrete near where she stood. Mutt yelped, and I heard his paws scatter to safety.

"Back into the chamber!" I yelled, all but sliding the rest of the way down.

When we found the bottom of the stairwell, I flung Julian off my back and he ran for the chamber door. I followed, listening as Stephan clamored down the steps faster and faster. When I knew that Julian was safely below, I stumbled down the last ladder into the chamber.

"Mom!" Julian yelled.

I heard him run to her. She threw her arms around him as they both sobbed. Mutt ran up to me and leapt to lick my face. Stephan's footsteps bounded above.

"Run!" I screamed to them. "Get as far away from here as you can. Mutt . . . keep them safe, you understand?"

I heard Anna's footsteps as she ran with her son from the building. Mutt hesitated as I listened to them traverse the concrete steps outside. He whined at me and pawed at my shirt.

"You have to go, boy," I said. "Take care of them."

As Stephan's steps bounded toward the chamber, I shoved Mutt out the front door. With a final whine, he ran.

Turning, I hauled the iron door closed just as Stephan came to it. I used every bit of energy I had left to hold the door shut against his frantic pushes for as long as I could. On the other side of the door, Stephan screamed and pounded and cursed. The darkness within him growled and threatened.

He heaved, and my footing slipped. With a grunt I shoved back against him. Digging in with my heels, I forced my muscles to hold, willing what was left of my strength to keep fighting. But I was fading fast.

My energy was drained like the juice from a battery. My legs, once broken and battered by a baseball bat, failed to hold the weight forced against them. With a savage cry, Stephan shoved against the door. I could no longer hold him. Taking a deep breath, I sprinted forward and let the door go.

On wobbling legs I followed the sound of Julian's and Anna's footsteps, stumbling across the wooden planks that formed a boardwalk beside the lighthouse. I staggered down the curb and across the street as Stephan's heavy footfalls followed.

The breath was knocked out of me when I slammed into a railing on the other side of the street. Fighting the urge to vomit, I coughed and rounded the wooden railing. Stephan's steps were closing in. The crashing of the surf rose over the sound of my pounding heartbeat. We were heading for the beach.

I ran on legs that could barely stand. Slamming into the railing each time the boardwalk zigged and zagged, I pressed on until my feet hit the soft sand and sank. Stephan's feet punished the boardwalk behind me. Ahead, all I could hear was the sound of the ocean as it flung itself across the shore.

Then in the distance I caught the faint sound of scattering sand, and I took off running to my right. Though my feet sank with each step, I raced through the grainy mounds.

"No, Stephan!" Anna's voice rang out from just ahead. "Just leave us alone!"

From the panic in her voice, I knew that Stephan was just behind me, but I couldn't see where. I could no longer hear his approach. The dense sand masked his heavy footfalls.

"Please, Daddy!" Julian cried, and I honed in on his panicked voice and ran toward it.

From somewhere next to me, Mutt growled a deep, primal snarl. His paws threw up sand as he charged past me in the opposite direction, toward Stephan.

"Mutt!" I yelled, reaching out to stop him. My arms grasped only air.

I heard Stephan cock the gun as Mutt barked and snarled at him.

"Mutt, no!" I yelled, but it was no use. I heard him slam into Stephan with enough force to knock him off his feet.

I started to go back, my panic turning to sheer terror. Julian screamed from just ahead, and I forced myself on. Unsure of how long Mutt could hold Stephan off, I knew I had to get to Julian.

Mutt was following my orders, I told myself. He was protecting Julian, just as I'd asked him to do. I had to do the same.

Behind me Mutt's growls grew more ferocious as he bore into Stephan. I heard his teeth rip into cloth and flesh. Stephan cried as he fought Mutt off. Then a shot pierced through the salt laden air. Mutt squealed. Then all was silent, save for the movement of the tide.

"No!" I cried, falling into the sand as my legs gave out from under me.

Though my own heartbeat thundered in my ears, I listened for Mutt's whine, a bark . . . anything. Instead I heard Stephan's heavy boots stagger through the sand. Julian's sobs came to me from down the beach.

"Mutt!" he cried.

"Julian!" Stephan screamed. "It wasn't supposed to be like this. You won't take him from me, Anna. You'll never take him from me again!"

The sound of metal clicking into place filled me with renewed terror as Stephan cocked his revolver again. Then he was running, running for Julian.

"Run, Julian!" I screamed. "Anna, get him out of here! Go!"

With renewed panic came a surge of adrenaline, and I bolted toward Julian, desperate to reach him before Stephan. As I ran, I longed for the light. I longed for the peace and the voice that belonged to that luminous place. Around me, all was black. It reminded me of that day, years ago, when the darkness had first become impenetrable.

Then suddenly a new vision took shape while I charged forward. I saw my father rear back his angry, bloodied fist. I saw myself as a boy, cowering from his blows. I saw the sadness in my wide eyes as I cried out for him to see me, to see his son. I saw my baby brother take the brunt of our father's blows as I lay helpless to stop them. I saw my brother's terror-filled face, his back against our front door. I saw my father raise the gun and aim it at his tiny head.

As I tore forward, I reached out to embrace the small child, to protect him as I should have all those years ago.

"Blake!" A small voice called to me as I wrapped my arms around him.

"Drop the gun!" I heard Logan yell suddenly as he charged over the sand behind us.

A surge of relief flooded my senses. *Logan was alive. He would stop Stephan.* But deep down, I knew Logan was already too late.

I covered Julian with my body as the shot rang out into the evening. The bullet hit my back with an explosion of white, hot pain. I felt it tear through my flesh. Somewhere in the distance Anna screamed, but her wail faded in my ears. Another shot exploded from behind me, and I hit the warm sand. I clung to the child wrapped in my arms as my consciousness faded into the blackness around me.

Twenty-One

"Julian!" Anna's scream pierced through the black. The desperation in her voice roused me from the dark. In the distance, sirens wailed.

The first thing I felt was the warmth of the setting sun. It penetrated my soul with its life-bringing fire. I could hear the ebb and flow of the waves, instantly lulling me with their unmistakable song. The cool water crept up the shore to greet me. It embraced my feet, making me momentarily one with the cooling sea.

My eyes tingled. The sensation confused me. The skin around them felt tight, encumbered by some foreign substance. With one hand, I reached up and wiped at the thick scars that covered them. When I did, the rough skin there broke apart like clumps of drying sand. With a gasp, they scattered in a gust of salty ocean wind.

And then they were gone.

With a shaky breath, I opened my eyes. I squinted against the brightness of the waning daylight. My eyes ached, as I imagine a newborn's would when using them for the first time. I didn't mind the sensation.

Blinking, I looked down into my arms at the warmth pressed against me. Julian raised his head from where it rested against my chest. His huge, amber eyes looked into mine as a tear escaped onto his cheek.

"Blake?" he whispered, a small smile parting his lips. "Can you see me?"

"I can see you," I said, tears coming to my fresh eyes. My mind reeled as my heart warmed.

"Julian!" Anna raced to where we lay in the sand. "Blake! Oh, God! Oh, God! Hold on, Blake. Help is coming."

I looked up and for the first time took in her delicate features. Her long, brown hair floated from her shoulders as she dropped to her knees in the sand at my side. Tears fell from her eyes, eyes the same shape and silken amber as her son's. Cradling Julian's tiny frame, I delivered him into his mother's arms unharmed. Just like I promised I would.

She clutched him to her and cried as she rocked him back and forth. Julian wrapped his arms around his mother's neck. When Anna wiped her tears away and looked into my face, she gasped.

"Your eyes!" she said. "How . . ."

The sirens grew louder. Anna watched the dunes as help approached. Numerous footsteps ran down the beach in our direction. I looked over to see paramedics racing toward us. Logan stood down the beach, waving them over. With two hands he held his gun steady, pointing down at a motionless Stephan who lay sprawled in a pool of red sand. When the paramedics rushed to help the fallen Stephan, Logan lowered his weapon and jogged toward us.

"Over here!" Anna yelled, desperate to get a paramedic's attention. "This man's been shot too!"

Anna let go of Julian and leaned over me. She took my hand. Warm static shot up my arm at her touch, and we both jumped. The paramedics ran up to us. Then they passed me by.

They bent down to examine Julian, a look of confusion on their faces as they turned to Anna.

"He's fine, ma'am. He hasn't been shot," they assured her. "Just a few bumps and bruises. We'd like to bring him to the hospital to make sure, though."

Anna's face contorted as she looked from them to me.

"Not my son," she said. "This man here. He's been shot. Right here!"

Anna motioned to where I lay. The paramedics looked at one another and then back to Anna.

"What's the matter with you?" Anna shouted. "He needs help!"

"Mommy . . ." Julian whispered as he tugged her free hand. "They can't see."

Logan came to stand beside us. He put his hand on Anna's shoulder.

"It's okay," he said to the paramedics. "She's just in shock. It's okay. I've got this. I'll drive them to the hospital myself."

The paramedics lingered a moment, watching Anna's shock and confusion. Then with a nod, they raced back to the others. Anna looked on in horror. My mind raced. I assessed myself. I felt no pain, only peaceful warmth. I looked into Julian's face. He smiled down on me from where he stood beside his mother.

"You can see now," he said. "You're not in the dark anymore."

With a deep breath I sat up. No pain. My muscles felt renewed and strengthened. Looking down, I saw no exit wound in my chest, though I'd felt the bullet tear through the flesh on my back. At least, I thought I had.

I looked to Logan. He smiled to me reassuringly as I got to my feet. I looked at him with my renewed sight.

"I can see," I said to him.

Logan nodded. "I knew you would, my friend, when the time was right."

Anna rose on shaking limbs, glaring at Logan then back at me. I looked into her face and smiled. She was even more beautiful than I'd imagined. She lifted Julian onto her hip as she stared at me.

"I don't understand," she stammered. "There's not a scratch on you. I saw you get shot! I saw the bullet hit you. How do you look . . . perfect?"

"The scars are gone, Logan," I said, reaching up to wipe my clear eyes.

Logan laughed, and smiled at me. He patted me on the back. Again, warm static emanated from his touch.

"They were never really there," he said. "You just weren't ready to see the truth."

My mind struggled to put it all together. *Never there? How was that possible?*

Closing my eyes, I thought back to that fateful night when I'd lost my sight. I remembered the fight with Smiley and his henchmen. I remembered my limbs being battered and broken at the end of the wooden baseball bat. I remembered the searing hot pain as the cigar's burning end was thrust into my eyes. I remembered lying there motionless, praying that someone would find me before I bled out.

Then my memories changed.

Suddenly a different truth presented itself to me. A truth I hadn't been able to see before. A truth I was only now ready to accept.

"You can see now," Julian repeated with a laugh.

I thought back to that night as memories played out like a memoir of someone else's life. As I lay bleeding on the Riverwalk, I remembered slipping into the void of my own self-inflicted purgatory. As the black memories had swirled and multiplied in my mind, I'd become one with their darkness. I'd failed to see the light coming for me, calling me out from the shadows. Now that I could see, I looked back on what happened with new understanding.

I watched myself being wheeled into the emergency room. I watched as I awoke to the sounds of hurried footsteps, frenzied movement and anxious voices. I now saw the crowded room and the people who flocked around me. I watched as the doctors worked feverishly to stop the bleeding from my broken body. I saw their grim faces as they shook their heads at one another.

I watched as the steady beeps of the heart rate monitor, my heart rate monitor, changed to a single, constant tone. I watched myself die and become one with the black around me, failing to accept the existence of the light. I remembered thinking that some lucky soul had died that night. What I didn't understand was that it was my own flesh that had passed away.

With my now opened eyes, I could see that the light was there all along, calling to me, reaching out with luminous warmth to accept me. I couldn't see it then. I was too lost to my own misery, too comfortable in my own wretchedness to accept the truth.

"The light of the world was there," I said, turning to Julian. "I just had to take it."

Anna looked from me to her son, then to Logan who grinned at me through misty eyes.

"I was at your funeral, Blake. I helped put you in the ground almost two years ago," he said. "I thought I'd lost my friend forever. Then I got your emails . . . I was so confused at first, but the more I read about your relationship with Julian, I just knew."

A tear slid onto his cheek. He wiped it with the back of his hand and smiled at me.

"The light is still here," Logan assured me. "It hasn't given up on you."

For the first time in years, tears fell from my eyes. I looked out into the fading light coming off the ocean and took a step toward it. I could hear it calling to me.

"I don't understand," Anna said, turning to Logan. "What's happening?"

Out of the corner of my eye, I saw Logan put his arm around her shoulders as they watched me walk into the coming tide.

"He's realizing what he is," Logan said.

Anna gasped. She choked back a sob as she clutched Julian tighter.

"A Guardian . . ." she whispered.

"A man," Logan emphasized. "A man charged by the heavens to save your son, and at the same time save himself. A man given a second chance to find the light."

I turned to them. Though my heart knew the truth, my mind still struggled to accept it. I'd been seen. I'd interacted with people since the accident, hadn't I? Then I remembered that I'd used email to communicate to even my art dealer. He'd never even seen my face.

But what about the others? I'd felt their stares.

"People saw me, people on the street. The bus driver . . . he saw me with Mutt all the time."

My heart sank in my chest as the memory of my fallen friend hit me anew.

"Mutt . . ." I whispered, remembering how he'd given everything to protect Julian . . . just as I'd asked him to.

Then in the distance, a soft whine sounded over the crashing of the tide. We all turned to see a grey and white pit bull limp down the beach, his right front paw tucked beneath him. There was a gash in his shoulder, but he looked otherwise unscathed. He paused and barked at us from the shore.

"Mutt!" Julian cried leaping down from his mother's arms.

With another bark, Mutt ran with his three good legs down the beach to greet him with a barrage of slobbery kisses. Julian giggled and hugged him around the neck. Beside me Anna gasped and put her hand to her mouth.

"I just remembered where I've seen that dog before!" she exclaimed. "He was on the news. He's that dog who rides the bus to and from the beach by himself."

She turned to me, tears falling onto her high cheekbones.

"Only, he wasn't by himself . . ." she said as Mutt ran up to me and licked my hand.

I squatted down and took in the sight of him for the first time. He was just as Julian described: grey with large, white patches across his torso. His big, dopey eyes looked into mine for the first time. I petted his head and ran my fingers down his bright red collar. His name tag twinkled in the waning evening light.

"It's nice to finally meet you, Michael," I said to him. He licked my face with slobbery abandon, and I hugged his face against mine. "You did good, boy. You did good."

"I guess not all seers are humans," Logan laughed.

"Seers?" Anna asked.

"Like me and you, Mommy," Julian said as Anna picked him back up. "And Logan and Blake. We can see real good, huh? Even in the dark."

I remembered the small girl who'd said hello to me in the crosswalk. *A seer.* With fresh eyes I could see that she'd grinned shyly at me and waved as we passed. She knew what I was.

Anna turned to me and smiled. I saw the pain from her past flash in her eyes. She was seeing through her darkness to the light on the other side. She hugged Julian to her as he giggled in her arms.

Just then a scream pierced the calm sway of the churning sea.

"This is our destiny!" Stephan yelled from where the paramedics fought to tend to his wound. "This isn't over!"

We all turned to see him shove them out of his way. He pointed to Julian as he sneered. Blood trickled out of the corner of his mouth as he struggled to sit up. Anna took a deep breath. Then she set Julian on his feet beside her.

"Stay here, baby," she said.

Then she walked to where Stephan struggled to sit up in the sand. Logan started after her, but I put my hand up, and he stopped. He went to Julian and put his arm around him and turned him away. Mutt stood, ready to charge.

"Stay, boy," I said, and he sat in the sand beside Julian. As I reached Anna, she bent down and lifted Stephan's gun from the frothy tide. "Anna . . ." I cautioned, but she ignored me.

When the paramedics saw that she was armed, they backed away cautiously. Someone radioed for the police. Anna pulled back the hammer and aimed it at Stephan as he writhed beneath her. He was bleeding from his lower abdomen where Logan had shot him. From where I stood behind Anna, I could see the black in his eyes go cold and still.

"Do it!" he yelled at her. Anna's hand shook as she squeezed the gun in her palm.

"You tried to kill our son," she said.

"Anna, no . . ." I called to her.

Anna did not flinch. She stared into Stephan's icy-cold eyes. He sneered up at her with seething hatred. It was the same look I'd seen on my father's face before I pulled the trigger a lifetime ago. I put my hands on Anna's shoulder.

"You don't want to do this," I said. "I know, remember? Don't let the darkness win, Anna. You're not like him."

Anna's tension eased. She took in a ragged breath.

"I forgive you, Stephan," Anna said, dropping the gun into the sand. The black in Stephan's eyes flickered and then faded. "I'm sorry for whatever happened to you that let all this darkness in. This isn't you, Stephan. You have to fight it. I hope you find peace one day. I pray that you find the light on the other side of darkness."

"It's calling to you, Stephan," I said, stepping beside Anna. "It's handing you the light of the world. You only have to take it."

Stephan's eyes grew wide as he stared at me. Then he shut them tight and sobbed. When he did, I watched in awe as the darkness drifted like a cloud from his body. It gathered in a putrid mist above him. As the paramedics gathered again and lifted him onto a gurney, the mist formed into an opaque figure, which lurked just beside the shore.

I turned to Anna. Her eyes were still on Stephan. She didn't see the mass that walked up to me with sickening, jerky movements. I stepped forward to meet it, unafraid.

When it reached me, I held fast to where I stood now confident as a child of the light. I stared it down as it bent to whisper in my ear.

"Go!" I commanded when I had heard enough. It dispersed with a wicked cry into the coming night. "We're not afraid of you anymore."

Anna turned to me with questions in her eyes. I smiled to reassure her as Stephan struggled to sit up in the gurney.

"It was you!" he said, pointing his finger at me. His eyes were clear and bright. The darkness was gone. He smiled at me as if I were the first thing he'd seen in years. Maybe I was.

"It was you who spoke to me those times. It was you, wasn't it? I heard you," he said putting it all together with fresh eyes. The paramedics turned and saw only Anna.

"Julian cried out for you. My God, what have I done? I . . . I couldn't see you. I couldn't see . . ." Stephan cried.

"It's hard to see in the dark," I yelled to him as they took him away. "But the light has found you."

We stood listening to his sobs until he was wheeled over the dunes. Then we turned, and Anna clasped my hand. We embraced the static warmth that emanated from our touch as we walked back to Julian and Logan. In the distance, I heard the light calling my name as I kneeled beside Julian.

"You have to go now, don't you?" he asked.

I patted him on the head and took him into my arms. Then I lifted him as I turned to look at the sun setting on the horizon.

"Not until dusk," I said. "I always stay for the sunset."

We gazed out at the ocean. The turquoise water spread out for miles and miles. Its foamy fingers painted the buff sand a dark, liquid brown. I saw the brilliance of the sun's reflection upon its glassy surface and laughed when I almost shielded my eyes from its luster.

The heat of the last of the day's light warmed my head and shoulders. This warmth I would feel forever, wrapped in the luminous glow that waited for me. I embraced it as I looked on at the vivid oranges and reds that streaked across the sky. The waves mimicked the scene on its fluid canvas. As the sun went down, darkening the sky in its wake, a new light shined in the distance. Its brilliance was unmatched by anything in this life.

It was time.

"We made a pretty good team, didn't we, cardinal bird?" I said, looking into Julian's smiling face.

"I'm a cardinal now?" he asked smiling from ear to ear. "I didn't like being a vulture. They poop on their legs."

"You're definitely a cardinal," I said with a laugh.

"But you said cardinals are resilient and beautiful and bring only joy."

Digging through my pocket, I found Julian's tiny stuffed animal. Julian grabbed it with a laugh and hugged it to him.

"You are the best cardinal that ever was," I said.

Julian smiled. I held him to me as Logan and Anna met us by the surf. We all looked out at the light extending toward us from the clouds. Logan patted me on the back.

"It's beautiful, isn't it?" he said.

"Even more beautiful than you described," I said.

"I've never seen anything like it," Anna whispered, staring at it in awe. "The luminous place . . ."

"You have to write about this," I said, turning to her. "You have to write about all of this, just like you were always meant to. There are so many others out there who are lost in the darkness. You have to write about Alex's redemption with Donovan. You have to write about Logan and the prison, and his message of hope . . . of his absolution. And you have to write our story, Anna. Write about your Julian and the light of the world. Write of my salvation. There are so many others who need to see."

"I . . . I don't know where to start," Anna said, her eyes growing wide. "We have to find a new home before I can think about any of that. We have nothing . . ."

"You have a home," Logan interrupted. "Up in Saluda with the rest of us. We're all family now. You can stay with Willow and me until you get on your feet. We would love to have you. How does that sound, little man?"

"We can come stay with you?" Julian asked, his eyes wide with excitement. "In the mountains?"

"In our little haven in the sky," Logan laughed, turning back to Anna. "Say you'll come."

Anna looked unsure, worried even. Her bright eyes glazed over with fresh tears. She wanted to say yes, but something stopped her. She looked at me as a tear rolled onto her cheek.

"Don't be sad about me," I said. "My life is just beginning."

Digging the studio keys from my pocket, I handed them to her.

"There's a box beneath my bed that I want you to have," I said. "I can never repay the both of you for what you've given me, but it can help you start a new life. There's enough there for you to live on, to not have to worry about anything. It's your time now, Anna. It's time to write that book."

Anna looked at the keys I offered and then back up into my eyes. Then with a sob she took them and opened her arms to me. I took her and Julian into my embrace one last time as the light around us grew brighter, the air warmer.

Somewhere in the distance, I heard someone call my name. It was the voice of a child.

"See?" Julian said, pulling away from me and pointing into the light. "You do have a home, Blake! It's where the people are you love the most. See?"

I looked up at his face as he smiled and waved at someone behind me. Slowly, I turned to face the light and the voice that called to me on the breeze.

There, silhouetted by the brilliance surrounding him, stood my baby brother. He was as perfect as I remembered him in my most cherished memories. He smiled to me and waved me over to him. The joy on his face was unmistakable.

I cried out in a mixture of joy and shock as fresh tears filled my eyes. I looked back to Anna and Julian with a smile.

"Thanks for being my Guardian," Julian said with a smile.

"No," I said as I patted his curly head. "Thanks for being mine."

I looked at Anna, who wiped the tears from her eyes. She nodded to me with a laugh.

"Go," Anna said. "We'll see you again someday."

"I'll be waiting," I said letting go of my hold on them.

I turned to Logan as he extended his hand to me. Taking it, I yanked him to me and threw my arm around his broad shoulders.

Mutt hobbled to me on his three good legs. I bent down and took his face in my hands. He slapped his tongue across my face, and I laughed.

"What would I have done without you, my own private angel? That's quite a scratch you took for our boy. I'm so proud of you," I said. "You have to take care of these two from now on, okay? They're going to get you patched up, and then I want you to look after them, you hear?"

I motioned to Anna and Julian. Julian squealed with delight.

"Can we keep him, Mommy?" he pleaded. "Can we, please?"

Anna smiled. "I wouldn't have it any other way."

Blake . . .

My brother called to me with a giggle. I turned to see him skipping away into the light. I looked back at my friends, at my piece of heaven on earth and laughed.

"Go home," Julian said, a smile lighting up his little face.

Turning from them, I ran off to meet my baby brother in the light. He turned to me and reached out his hand, and suddenly I was a boy again. The world full of pain and darkness faded as my friends waved to me from where the ocean met the coast. We ran on, children oblivious to anything but the light and the love surrounding us in the most luminous of places. As the brightness grew brighter and warmer, I looked back one last time.

"You were right about me, Logan," I yelled. "You were right."

As the darkness faded for good, I turned and embraced the light and the renewed life I would find within.

The End

Epilogue

You were right about everything, Logan. More than you even know. The light is everything. It's the home I never had. I've never experienced love like I know now. Life is here, covering you with acceptance and purpose. It's watching over all of us.

You need to know that.

He's here too, Logan, my father. He found the light in the darkness that night I pulled the trigger. For the first time, I've gotten to know him without the blackness, without the pain. Here, he is who he was always meant to be. We all are. The absence of the dark lets us be who we were created to be.

I wish words could explain . . .

I look in on you often. I've seen your struggles and your joys. I've seen your family grow. You're going to make a great father, though I know you have your doubts. If only you could see what I see . . . that the light shines so brightly within you.

It's contagious, Logan.

I've watched Alex take Anna under her wing. I've seen the way Willow has grown close to them both. Donovan, the anchor, keeps you all strong. Learn from him, Logan.

He is a true Guardian.

I've watched Julian settle and flourish among you all, among the seers. I've seen the house that Anna made a home for them both. My portrait hangs over their hearth, beside where Mutt sleeps peacefully at night. They don't mourn me. They know I'm looking over them.

They know we'll meet again.
Take care of them all, my friend.
Make sure they never lose sight of the light.

Now I have to warn you of what the darkness whispered to me on the beach. You have to know that hard times are on the way, times when you all will question if darkness is all there is. Hold fast to the light, Logan. Something is coming that will try to stop you all. You have to fight it.

Anna must write her book.

Something sinister has awakened, Logan.
Prepare yourselves. The darkness is coming.

To be continued . . .

The series continues with:

Death
Book Four

In Saluda, North Carolina, a group of seers has gathered. Their incredible testimonies of redemption, absolution, and salvation have the power to bring hope to the world. Anna Rayner is determined to bring the light of these stories to millions in the dark.

But the darkness has other plans.

When a pair of hooded strangers arrives in the quiet mountain town, unspeakable terrors follow. Temptation, hatred, and doubt are unleashed, and enemies thought long dead arise.

Donovan, Alex, Logan, Willow, Anna, and Julian will face their darkest moments yet, as Anna struggles to finish the books that will set millions free.

In the ultimate battle between
the darkness and the light, all will fight, some will rise, and others . . .

will fall.

A.L. Crouch

A.L. Crouch, author of the Guardian series, graduated with honors from North Carolina State University with a degree in English. She currently teaches high school creative writing in her hometown of Cary, North Carolina. She is a member of the NC Writers' Network and spends her summers off from teaching formulating tales of suspense and the supernatural. When she's not at work raising up young writers or keeping her readers jumping, she is spending time with her husband and two sons exploring the majestic mountains and coasts of North Carolina.

For more information and other titles by A.L. Crouch visit:
www.alcrouch.com

Made in the USA
Columbia, SC
11 August 2019